MEANT TO BE

MEANT TO BE

AN ANCHOR ISLAND NOVEL

Terri Osburn

Copyright © 2013 Terri Osburn

Published by Montlake Romance
PO Box 400818
Las Vegas, NV 89140

ISBN-13: 9781612183084
ISBN-10: 1612183085

For Isabelle. You will forever be my greatest achievement.

CHAPTER ONE

*W**hy did this godforsaken island have to be in the middle of the damn water?*

Even as the thought echoed inside her brain, Beth Chandler recognized the irrationality. But locked as she was in the grip of overpowering fear, rationality was not an option. Letting go of the steering wheel was also not an option. She swore she was sending the let-go signal to her hands, but her knuckles remained white, strangling the helpless circle of whatever hard plastic steering wheels were made of.

Maybe it was the kind of plastic that would float. When she and her car plunged to a watery grave, she could use the steering wheel as a flotation device. She'd thrown her car door open before coming to a full stop on the ferry. Just in case. (The idea of drowning in the car was more horrific than that of drowning outside the car.) By some stroke of luck she'd ended up in the farthest inside row, a railing and some kind of cabin to her left.

If the worst had happened and she'd been forced to park near the edge…This was not the time to ponder that scenario. The brief moment she'd looked out into the distance revealed nothing but water as far as she could see. A fact that only intensified the panic.

"I am not going to die. I knew this was coming. I can do this."

The affirmations she'd gotten from the *How to Defeat Your Fears* book were supposed to get her through this. She'd checked the book out of the library as soon as her fiancé, Lucas, mentioned meeting his parents would require riding a ferry to a tiny, remote island.

Technically, the first thing she'd done was panic and throw up. Twice. But then she went straight to the library. Now, bobbing along, surrounded by cars packed in like giant four-wheeled sardines, the book might as well have been about making the perfect soufflé.

Didn't these ferries have weight limits? What if they let on one car too many?

"There is nothing to be afraid of here. Nothing can hurt me."

Beth wondered if maybe she shouldn't have checked out another book. One on how to make your brain stop arguing with your affirmations. Because the rebuttal from her brain— *Floating on a giant barge covered in cars that could sink any minute is something to be afraid of!*—was anything but relaxing.

"We are not going to die. We are *not* going to die. Dear Lord, don't let me die."

This was Lucas's fault. He'd insisted she bring her own car in case he was called back to the office while they were gone, and then he'd been called to the office before they even left. Assuring he'd be on the road within an hour, two hours tops, he'd programmed her GPS and cajoled her to leave without him. Which was why he wasn't around to distract her now.

To be fair, she hadn't told him about her fear, so maybe it wasn't all his fault. And he had promised to make it up to her. Knowing Lucas, that would mean jewelry. Something she wouldn't mind if he'd ever let her pick out her own present.

The ferry lurched, dragging Beth back to the situation at hand. Eyes closed, she took several deep breaths. Another recommendation from the library book. Breathing in through her nose, she blew the air out through her mouth. Just then, hot breath fluttered over her left arm and an unpleasant smell filled her nostrils.

That could not be her breath.

Heavy panting invaded the silence of the car and Beth opened one eye to find the source. Big brown eyes surrounded by rust-colored fur stared back. One ear flopped forward while a black tongue lolled to the side. The animal tilted his head and lifted a large paw, propping it on her thigh.

She might have flinched had she not been frozen in fear.

"What'd you find, Dozer?" asked a voice from somewhere behind the intruder.

Looking past the mutt, she saw a man draw up behind him. Bright blue eyes and a stubble-covered chin were all she registered before shifting her focus back to her hands. Defending herself against a madman on a barge was probably going to be difficult without the use of her hands.

"Hi there," he said, giving the dog a pat on the head. Then he mumbled, "Good boy." Presumably to the dog.

The stranger's voice, low and sensual, vibrated down her spine. Her hands relaxed enough to allow blood flow back into her knuckles. The book hadn't suggested finding a sexy guy to talk her down. She should have looked harder until she found one written by a woman.

"Hi," she said, her brain now as uncooperative as her hands. She ventured another glance in the dog owner's direction and her entire body sighed.

The man was, as her Granny would say, built for sin. Full lips, strong jaw, and one deep dimple finished off a face gifted with the bluest eyes she'd ever seen. Wide shoulders filled out a navy-blue T-shirt that tapered down to a narrow waist and low-slung jeans. She couldn't see his feet behind the dog, but would bet her best business suit he sported work boots.

Talk about answered prayers. This was a flotation device she wouldn't mind going down with.

A sound that could only be called a *meep* escaped her lips. Engaged women were not supposed to have lustful thoughts about men who were not their fiancé. Being engaged for a mere two weeks was no excuse.

"Are you okay?" he asked, clearly recognizing insanity when he saw it.

"I'm fine," she yelled, panic raising her voice several decibels. Though she wasn't sure if the panic was still over imminent death or her heightened hormone levels. "No problem here. Move along, please."

The dog set his other paw on her leg and nearly climbed onto her lap, his head popping up between her arms. "What's he doing?" she asked.

The man chuckled and Beth shivered. "Saying hello."

A dark tongue dangled dangerously close to her nose. "Do you feed him black licorice or something?" The dog's entire tongue was black.

4

"That's the chow in him. Also what gives him that big head. You should hear him bark."

Right on cue, the dog did just that, making her ears ring. If she hadn't been staring into the face of a dog, Beth would swear a grizzly had climbed into her car. "You need a breath mint. Bad."

"You've scared her enough, Doze. Get off the pretty lady." As the dog backed out of the car, Beth tried to ignore the compliment, but felt a blush heat her cheeks. "This crossing takes a while," he said. "You could come out and walk around. Most people do."

"People are walking around?" Fear momentarily trumped by amazement, Beth turned toward the stranger as far as the seat belt and her grip on the wheel would allow. "How can people be taking a leisurely stroll as if we aren't all about to perish in the sea?"

"Just trusting, I guess." The man smiled as he took a step back. Her libido tried to take a step forward. Seat belts really were lifesaving devices. "Not a fan of the ferry ride, huh?"

Beth shook her head, embracing her right to remain silent.

"If it makes you feel better, I've ridden this ferry a thousand times with no problem."

"I'm sure you have. I feel better now," she lied. The man needed to go away. She needed him to go away.

"Right. We'll leave you alone then." He turned to leave and Beth felt as if a lifeline were slipping away.

"Wait!"

Bright blue eyes turned back. "I'm still here." Bending down, he leaned an arm along the top of the car. "You're really not okay, are you?"

Beth sucked in a breath, squeezed her eyes tight, then nodded once. "This is going to sound really strange, but could you sit with me? Just until we reach the other side."

Heart racing, she watched the stranger purse his lips, then glance up and down the ferry. His eyes darted to her backseat. "If you mean for me to sit in your car, Dozer will have to sit in the back."

Since the idea was to distract her from the imminent death bobbing beneath her, adding a dog to the mix sounded perfect. "Not a problem."

Seconds later a muscle-bound dog the color of autumn leaves filled her backseat, blowing hot air across the back of her neck. The black tongue hung over his bottom jaw, but he didn't drool. Much. He was cute, in a mutt sort of way. He could use a Tic Tac and a bath, but he was cute.

His owner filled her passenger seat in much the same way his canine filled her backseat. The word "Evinrude" sprawled the expanse of a wide chest that could double as a brick wall. He adjusted the seat to accommodate his long legs, which looked firm and well muscled beneath the worn denim.

She'd been right about the work boots, which sported dark grease stains. Her human tranquilizer could have stepped straight out of a blue-collar beefcake calendar, though he'd likely take insult at the word *beefcake*.

He settled into the seat, his knee leaning close to hers. Beth's mouth watered.

You're here to meet your future in-laws. Showing up to dinner with a date is not a good idea.

An awkward silence, broken by the shrill of seagulls and steady rhythm of canine panting, settled in the vehicle.

"I guess—"

"So you—"

They both spoke at once.

"I'm sorry, you first," she said, playing hostess as if this were a dinner party.

"No, it's your car. Go ahead."

"Right." Beth cleared her throat, stalling. "You've probably figured out I'm not comfortable with water. And boats."

"I got that. Though this is a ferry, not a boat," he said with a grin. His face held a dark tan around the shadow of whiskers, and small creases were etched at the edges of his eyes. Clearly no stranger to the sun.

"If you could just distract me from thinking about where we are and what I'm floating on"—her voice hitched on the last two words—"then I should be able to make it to the other side."

"You want me to distract you?" His voice showed a little more enthusiasm than it had when he first climbed in. Her body turned traitor, growing enthusiastic about his enthusiasm.

"Talking," she squeaked. "Talk to me as a distraction."

"Right," he said, with noticeably less enthusiasm. "Afraid talking's not my thing."

"We'll muddle through." Telling him his stellar body made sparkling conversation unnecessary didn't seem like a good idea. Though the thought sent heat crawling up her cheeks. "I'm sorry. I'm not usually like this."

"What are you usually like?" he asked, leaning against the door. His voice calm. Soothing. He was already better at this than he knew.

What was she usually like? She had to think about that one. "More sane. Usually. Rational. Practical."

"I see," he said. "Then it must be your practical side that has you holding on to that wheel. Since there's no need to steer right now, maybe you could let go. Sit back. Enjoy the ride."

"Right. Sure." By some miracle, her hands cooperated. Blue-collar guy had serious skills. He'd be excellent in divorce negotiations. Lowering the windows, she nodded toward the dog. "He won't jump out, will he?"

"Dozer won't go anywhere."

"What kind of a name is Dozer?"

"A dog's name." She raised a brow and he caught the hint. "When I got him he was either plowing dirt or sleeping, so I named him Dozer." The stranger shrugged, and even that was sexy. "It fit."

Another glance at the dog and Beth could see the rationale. The size of a small bulldozer, the fur ball covering her backseat looked to be on the brink of snoring. "Yes. That makes sense." Turning back to his owner, she asked, "You said you've ridden this ferry thousands of times?"

"Yeah. I live on Anchor."

Maybe he could fill in some island facts she hadn't been able to find on the Internet. "I hear there aren't many natives who live here year-round."

"We do all right."

Vague answer. This guy would be a pain to cross-examine. "Is the island really as small as the web makes it sound?"

"Depends on your idea of small. The first twelve miles down are a landing strip, but the village isn't bad. Couple miles across."

"Landing strip?" She gulped. "A wide landing strip?"

"Wide enough. Are you afraid of all boats?" The ferry bobbed, and she grabbed the wheel again. "I guess you are."

"Not afraid of boats exactly. It's not as if I see a picture of one and break out in a cold sweat." She tucked a wayward curl behind her ear, though efforts to control the stubborn curls were useless against the strong, salty breeze. Who knew the Outer Banks would be so windy? "It's being *on* a boat that bothers me. Houseboat incident from my childhood."

"Houseboat incident?" He chuckled then sobered when she glared. "Sorry. What was the houseboat incident?"

"You don't want to hear that story." Why had she even brought it up? She'd learned not to tell anyone the houseboat incident.

"Why not?" he asked. "Must be a big deal if you're this scared."

She huffed. "Because you're going to tell me I'm stupid for letting something so insignificant feed my fear all these years later."

Silence reigned. Even Dozer seemed to stop breathing. Beth kept her eyes on the steering wheel.

Mr. Evinrude cleared his throat. "I'm no shrink, but I'm guessing someone's made fun of this fear before?"

"Maybe." She picked at the wheel with her nail. "I'm not crazy. I know it's irrational." Turning to face him, she waved her hands in the air. "And I'm normally a very rational person."

"Right. You mentioned that." Turning his body toward hers, he stretched an arm across the seats, resting his hand inches from her shoulder. Beth fought the urge to lean back. "Tell me about it."

"About what?" The proximity of that hand was shorting out her brain.

"What happened on the houseboat?"

Now she'd done it. Since talking had been her idea, she couldn't refuse to talk herself. He was doing as she'd asked, after all. For her, a stranger. If he laughed, she could always shove him out of the car.

"I was young," she began, summoning the painful memories. "My grandparents' best friends had a houseboat out on Tappan Lake. We'd go several times throughout the summer, and I always looked forward to the trips."

Children's laughter filled her ears. A splash followed by a squeal of delight.

"One Father's Day weekend we were pretty far out, away from the beach and swimming area." She looked around to the other cars. *Stay in the present, Beth.* "A speedboat shot by too close, and the wake made the houseboat list hard to one side. My best friend, Lily, and I were playing near the back." Beth stared at the steering wheel and blurted, "Lily managed to hold on, but I didn't."

"You fell in?"

"Yes. Lily tried to reach me, but I kept sinking." An ache started in her lungs and Beth rubbed her chest. "I don't know how many times I went under, but at some point my legs got tired. I couldn't kick anymore."

Beth didn't realize she'd been holding her breath until the ferry horn blew. She looked to the man on her right as if he'd just appeared out of nowhere.

"Relax. You're okay." His voice lacked the derision she expected. "Who pulled you out?" he asked, brows drawn.

"Grandpa. He heard Lily's screams and came to check on us. Yanked me out by the scruff of my shirt as if I were some brainless puppy who'd jumped in without knowing any better." She blew out a breath and dropped her shoulders, feeling lighter. "After that I wouldn't get back on a boat. Ever. They yelled and pushed and told me I couldn't let some silly fear keep me from doing things." Eyes locked on the letter *H* in the center of the wheel, she said, "I couldn't do it, and they never understood. No one ever does."

Beth went quiet, waiting for the lecture about life being full of risks and not letting fear win.

"Screw 'em," he said.

"What?" Beth shook her head, confused. "Screw who?"

"Whoever gives you a hard time. Doesn't matter what anyone else thinks."

She couldn't have heard him right. Didn't matter what other people thought? Crazy talk. "Of course it matters."

"No, it doesn't." Dozer stuck his head between the seats as if sensing an argument. His owner scratched behind his ear, never taking his eyes from hers.

Beth's brain couldn't compute the concept of ignoring what others thought, so she switched to deflect mode. "Anyway. If I could stop the panic attacks, I would. Instead, I avoid boats."

"Until now." He grinned, teasing with the hint of a dimple.

"Until now what?" That dimple could fell a stronger woman than she.

"You're on a boat now." He shook his head. "Now you have me doing it. You're on a ferry. Something important must be waiting on Anchor Island."

"Very important." She debated how much to tell. What if he knew the Dempsey family? What if he told them he met her on the ferry and she was a nutjob? She bit her bottom lip and glanced his way. His full lips curled and she bit harder.

Better to learn more about him before confiding her mission. "You said you live on the island. Does your family live there, too?"

"My parents do."

"Siblings?"

"No. My brother lives in Richmond." Beth's radar went up. "He'll be here this weekend though. Bringing his newest collectible to meet the family."

"Excuse me?"

"His fiancée. He's bringing her home to meet the parents." His face pinched as if a skunk had passed by the car. "That's who I was looking for when Dozer found you."

"You were looking for your brother?"

"No, his fiancée."

Sweet baby peas. "Is she supposed to be on this ferry?"

He shrugged, looking out his window. "Hell if I know, but I figure if I see a hard-edged, high-maintenance blonde bimbo driving a fancy car, that'll be her."

Beth sat up straighter. "You haven't met her before?"

"No. But if I know Lucas, the description will fit."

"Lucas?" This could not be happening.

"Yeah, my little brother."

Oh boy.

CHAPTER TWO

Beth summed up the situation in her mind with the hope of forming some kind of plan. Her future brother-in-law, whom she'd been lusting over for several minutes, resided in her passenger seat spewing less-than-positive opinions about his brother's fiancée. A woman he had yet to meet, though unbeknownst to him sat an arm's length away.

No matter how she twisted this scenario in her mind, one thing was clear. Nothing positive could come from revealing herself now. A glimpse out the windshield revealed what she assumed was the ferry landing ahead.

"Looks like we're close to the other side," she said, pretending the sight of land wasn't the greatest relief ever. "Guess you should head back to your car."

"You sure you're okay?" he asked, the concerned, kind-hearted citizen returning.

"Yes, thank you. I think I can make it from here." Her heart rate kicked up a notch at the idea of driving off the ferry alone. Then she imagined revealing her identity and the panic attack didn't feel half as scary.

"You never told me what's so important on Anchor Island to get you on this ferry." The dimple made another appearance, sending butterflies flitting around her stomach.

If they used that dimple on tourist ads, thousands of women would make this crossing every day.

"Just a visit," she said. Knowing her inability to lie, she kept her eyes averted.

"I could show you around while you're here," he offered.

"Thanks, but I won't be alone." Not a lie, but the guilt continued to mount. Maybe she could campaign on her own behalf. "So you don't think you'll like this fiancée? Doesn't seem fair when you haven't met her yet."

"She might not be so bad," he conceded. "The chick is a lawyer at Lucas's firm, so the bimbo thing might not fit." He rubbed a line across his forehead. "I just know my brother. To him life is a game."

"A game?"

"Yeah. I call it He Who Dies with the Most Shit Wins."

Beth pictured the brand-new golf clubs Lucas had purchased the weekend before. The ones sitting between the never-used scuba gear and a box of discarded cell phones. None of which he'd used for more than a few months.

The description had merit, but Beth preferred to think of Lucas as active and tech savvy. Not shallow and materialistic.

"You don't see life that way?" Beth asked.

"I don't need anything but my island, my boat, and my dog."

His words echoed a simplicity she admired. Longed for, even. "Sounds like a nice life."

Blue eyes went wide. "Not many people agree with you."

"Like you said. Screw 'em." His reaction to that statement bordered on comical. A horn sounded above them, forcing Beth to cover her ears. "What the heck is that?" she asked.

"Means land ho. We're pulling into Anchor." Lucas's brother climbed from the vehicle, then leaned through the passenger window. "I'm Joe, by the way. Dempsey. Offer still stands to show you around. Bring your friend along, too."

"I don't—"

"Think about it," he interrupted. "If you change your mind, ask around. Someone will know where to find me."

The horn sounded again. "Thank you for sitting with me," she said, hoping if she left him thinking of her as friendly and grateful he might not be too upset when they officially met. Again.

"My pleasure," he said, flashing his pearly whites, brighter thanks to his deep tan.

Beth wondered how two brothers could be so different, then remembered the two weren't actually blood related. Lucas's mother had married Joe's father when the boys were young.

"Okay then." Beth started the car and Dozer hopped up in the backseat. "Nice to meet you, Dozer."

The dog panted in her ear for a few seconds, then licked the right side of her face.

"That's enough, Doze," Joe said, opening the door for the mutt. "Might not seem like it, but that's a compliment. He doesn't like a lot of people."

Using her sleeve to mop up the slobber, Beth tried to smile but knew she failed. "Great. I'd hate to see what he does to people he doesn't like."

"If he doesn't like them, they don't get close enough to find out." Joe closed the door once the dog made his exit. Beth pulled a tissue from her purse to wipe the slobber out of her ear. "I didn't get your name."

She debated whether to lie. Surely he knew his brother's fiancée's name. "Beth," she said, going for a shortened version of the truth. Maybe he wouldn't make the connection.

"Beth. That suits you." The dimple shone full force, knocking the wind out of her. "I'm sure we'll see each other again." Oh, he had no idea how soon. With a wave he walked off, an orange tail trailing behind him.

Watching him fade into the crowd of vehicles, Beth couldn't help but compare the brothers. Lucas was slender but muscled with a runner's body, while Joe looked more like the UFC fighters who worked out at the gym near her apartment.

Joe's clothes were well-worn, his jeans tattered at the bottom. Lucas would max out his credit card before he'd wear anything remotely approaching tattered.

"So much for making a good first impression." She sighed and went for positivity. "Maybe we'll laugh about this." Something told her the sun would set in the east before Joe Dempsey laughed about feeling like a fool.

She'd just have to work twice as hard to win him over. No matter what, before Beth left Anchor Island, Joe Dempsey would have a much better opinion of his brother's fiancée.

~

Three hours after driving off the ferry, wild curls and jade-green eyes continued to haunt Joe's mind. Scanning the cars for Lucas's bimbo, he'd never have spotted the brunette in the blue Civic if Dozer hadn't climbed in with her. When she invited Joe in, he'd been feeling pretty good about his chances.

But then she wanted to talk. Not his strong suit.

If she'd really wanted a distraction, Joe could think of a dozen more distracting activities. Not that he'd have tried any of them on the ferry. Or on a total stranger. But he hoped his ferry girl wouldn't stay a stranger for long.

He should have gotten her last name. The name Beth wasn't exactly uncommon. But that was one good thing about the close quarters on Anchor Island. They were bound to run into each other at some point.

Though another meet-up might have been more definite had he not brought up his family shit. What the hell was his problem?

That was an easy one. His little brother was his problem. Ever since Patty announced Lucas was bringing home a fiancée, he'd been dreading the day she'd show up. Joe didn't always agree with his brother—hell, he never agreed with his brother—but he still wanted Lucas to be happy.

If Lucas picked his fiancée the way he picked everything else, he'd shoot for expensive, sleek, and high maintenance. The type of woman who'd chew him up and leave with half his shit. If he was lucky.

Joe's stomach growled, a reminder he was late for supper. Patty would have his ass since the big introductions were tonight. Moments when he was running late for something were the only times Joe wished cell phones worked on the island.

Parking his truck in the gravel patch between his parents' place and his own, Joe decided to leave Dozer in the Jeep while he ran in to let Patty know he was there before heading home for a quick shower. He and Sid had made the valve lash adjustment, but they were both covered in grease for the effort. The stench of diesel was so strong on his clothes, even Joe could barely stand it.

He took the steps two at a time and followed the porch around to the kitchen. "I know I'm late," he said as he opened the door, "but I need to take a quick shower and I'll be back."

The last word trailed off as he hovered in stunned disbelief. What the—

"You certainly do need a shower." His stepmom waved a tea towel in the air in front of her. "Were you working on the boat or rolling around in a puddle of diesel fuel?"

Green eyes, pale skin, and caramel-colored curls were all Joe could see. His ferry chick loitered at the edge of the kitchen island, paring knife in hand, cutting board on the countertop before her. She had the nerve to look innocent.

Son of a bitch.

"Covered in grease is no way to meet your future sister-in-law, but I guess it's too late for first impressions now." Patty had no idea how late. "Joe, this is Lucas's fiancée, Elizabeth Chandler. Elizabeth, this is Lucas's older brother, Joe."

"Elizabeth?" Would she admit they'd already met?

Beth crossed the space between them. "Hi, Joe. Nice to meet you."

Fine, she wanted to play it that way. He took her pale fingers in his grease-stained hand. "Nice to meet you, too."

As her hand slid from his, he knew she longed to wipe it off, but then it would be a shame to ruin her fancy outfit. How could he have missed the uptight Ivy League getup before?

Because you were imagining her out of the clothes, not in them, dumb shit.

"Lucas has told me a lot about you," she said.

"Funny, we haven't heard anything about you. Somehow, I thought you'd be blonder."

"Nice, Joe. Way to welcome her to the family." Patty moved up next to Beth. "Why don't you finish slicing the tomatoes, and we'll leave them in the fridge while the burgers are grilling."

Beth did as ordered, giving Joe a parting smile.

Keep smiling, darling. This isn't over by a long shot.

"Go take that shower and try to find a little charm while you're at it. And send Dozer in. I might as well feed him while you clean up."

"Fine, I'll be back in ten minutes." Pissed, Joe slammed the kitchen door harder than he should have, which meant Patty would have his ass for one more thing when she got him alone.

Lucas's fiancée was worse than Joe expected. He'd take a bimbo over a liar any day.

∾

If it hadn't been for Joe's cold welcome, Beth would have felt immediately at home in the Dempsey house. The open floor plan, with the dining room and living room occupying the same space, reflected both the Dempsey parents. Sturdy built-in bookshelves lined the back wall, standing tall like the patriarch of the family, Tom. But the decor was all Patty: warm and inviting, full of color, and oozing charm.

When they sat down for dinner, Beth occupied the chair next to Lucas, which put her directly across from Joe. When her fiancé's brother wasn't pretending she didn't exist, he was staring at her as if trying to brand a scarlet letter across her forehead.

"Lucas says you work at the law firm, Elizabeth," Patty said. "What kind of cases do you handle?"

"I don't—" Beth started, but Lucas cut her off.

"Elizabeth works in research and is terrific at her job." He threw an arm around her shoulders, pulling her toward him. "But I'm working on convincing her to step out and start working directly with clients."

"What does doing research involve?" Tom asked. "Is that where you do all the work and the other lawyers take credit for it in court?"

Lucas had described his dad as a big guy, an apt description if by *big* he meant roughly the size of a city bus. Tom towered over Beth by at least a foot, which put him around six foot five. His eyes were a lighter shade of blue than Joe's, but the strong jaw and thick, wavy hair were the same. She had no problem seeing why Lucas's mom had fallen for the sweet-natured giant. He winked and Beth assumed that meant he was joking, but she answered anyway.

"I don't mind not getting the credit. It's all for the good of the firm."

"That explains it," Joe said, contributing to the conversation for the first time since they'd sat down. "This is that opposites attract thing." He kept his eyes on his plate as if talking to his knife and fork.

"Funny, Joe," Lucas said, but no one was laughing. "Elizabeth and I have a lot in common."

Joe leaned back and finished chewing the bite he'd taken before speaking again. Beth felt a cloud of tension stretch thinly over the gathering. "Like what?"

No one had ever asked that before. At least not to Beth's knowledge. Lucas looked at her, his mouth moving but nothing coming out. She longed to help him but nothing came to her mind either.

How could that be? Of course they had things in common.

"The law," Lucas answered finally. "And the law firm. And Elizabeth likes the same music I do." She didn't really, but never wanted to hurt his feelings and admit the fact. "And we both prefer white wine."

Beth preferred red. Another little fact she'd never admitted. Lucas always ordered her drinks on the rare occasions they went out. His hours didn't provide much opportunity for date nights.

But to be fair, Lucas had never asked her preference on either topic. He'd just assumed. And she let him. Because that's what she did. Letting him believe these things seemed like a harmless way to make him happy.

"There's our love of the city," he added. That one was up in the air. She didn't want to return to her hole-in-the-wall small town, but Richmond was busy, loud, and anonymous. She didn't have many friends there outside of Lucas and a few other coworkers. Though they were more acquaintances. She'd never been good at making girlfriends, and always felt like the one on the fringe who couldn't quite make it in the circle.

"And best of all, we want the same things." Lucas flashed Beth the charming smile that always made her feel so special. Of course they wanted the same things. Lucas wanted to be a successful lawyer and make partner, and Beth wanted Lucas to be happy. Which meant she wanted those things, too.

"I see," Joe said, returning attention to his dinner. "You're made for each other." The sarcasm was lost on no one. Lucas looked ready to argue but Beth quieted him with a hand on his arm. The meal proceeded in silence, animosity hanging in the air like the smell of saltwater that permeated the island.

Lucas had mentioned Joe could be difficult, and though he'd phrased it as "Joe's an asshole," Beth assumed he was exaggerating. Siblings were always harsh on each other, or so she'd heard; being an only child meant she had no personal experience to go on. But it turned out Lucas wasn't exaggerating in the least.

Joe really was an asshole. Nothing like the nice guy she'd met on the ferry. Beth blamed the pheromones and her traitorous libido for missing the obvious. Too bad she hadn't introduced herself as the gold-digging, blonde bimbo and put him in his place.

Not that she'd ever put anyone in their place before, but Joe made her long to do so.

For the rest of the meal, Patty and Tom directed their questions to Lucas, ignoring Joe and seemingly choosing not to return Beth to the line of fire. Which she appreciated, but it didn't keep Mr. Cranky Pants from shooting her the occasional dirty look.

She'd thought they might laugh about the whole ferry deba-
cle someday, but based on her limited time with him so far, Beth
now believed Joe Dempsey never laughed about anything.

~

"You can't let Joe bother you," Patty said a short time later
while she and Beth did the dishes.

"Excuse me?"

Patty rinsed another plate. "He'll come around eventually."

Patty Dempsey was close to Beth in size, but that didn't
seem to matter when it came to ruling the men in her
family. With short auburn hair and coffee-colored eyes,
she was as quick to deliver a set-down as she was to offer
a hug. The latter she'd offered to Beth upon arrival; then
two hours later she greeted Lucas with a whack to the back
of the head for allowing his fiancée to make the long drive
alone.

"He and Lucas are so…different." Beth added the dry
plate to the stack in the cupboard and picked up the next
one. "It's hard to believe they're brothers."

"Lucas has told you how this family came together,
hasn't he?"

Beth blushed. "Yes. I'm sorry. I didn't mean—"

"No apology necessary. I just wanted to make sure my
boy wasn't keeping you in the dark about anything." Patty
leaned a hip against the counter. "Lucas was three when his
father died in action. Five when I married Tom. That child
settled into a new family like a duck strolls into a pond."

Lucas had a knack for adapting to his surroundings, whether blending in with the wealthy and powerful or entertaining the locals at the corner bar. Not surprising he'd been born with such confidence. "Lucas talks about Tom a lot. I know he loves him."

"I got lucky when I found Tom." Patty stared out the window over the sink. "Thought I was crazy for going out with another sailor after losing Steven. But I knew by the end of that first date I'd marry Tom Dempsey." She smiled, revealing a resemblance between mother and son. "Within a month, he proposed."

"That fast?"

"When it's right, it's right."

"And Tom had Joe?"

Patty sighed. "Joe was ten, still mourning his mother, and resentful of anyone who tried to get close. Needless to say, he was not happy about a new stepmother."

Beth's heart went out to the little boy missing his mother. She knew the feeling.

"But he came around." The older woman went back to washing dishes. "The boys may not have the same blood, but they were as close as any blood brothers could be."

"What happened? I mean, Lucas doesn't talk about Joe much, at least not in positive terms, and the feeling seems to be mutual." Though most of Joe's contempt had been aimed in her direction that evening. "If I'm prying just tell me to mind my own business."

"You're going to be part of this family. You can ask anything you want." Patty passed over another wet plate. "The boys made different choices. Sometimes it's hard to understand how something so important to you isn't just as important to someone else. Does that make sense?"

Beth had always done what was important to everyone else, so the concept of deciding what *she* wanted felt completely foreign. Then again, she could imagine how hurt her grandparents would have been had she not followed their dreams for her.

"I think I understand." Sliding the last plate into the cupboard, Beth looked around for something else to do. "Do you have a garbage can outside? I can take this bag out for you."

"Sure, thanks. It's off the porch, around the side of the house. Large black can."

"Okay, I'll be right back." Beth closed the kitchen door and let her eyes adjust to the dusk so she could see her way off the porch without falling on her face. She'd created enough of a mess already, the last thing she needed was a trip to the emergency room. Did they even have a hospital on this island?

"Hello, Elizabeth," said a voice from the darkness. Beth tensed. Time for the moment of truth.

CHAPTER THREE

How Joe managed to make her name sound like an insult, Beth didn't know, but she didn't like it. Following the sound of his voice, she found him several feet away to her left, lounging in an Adirondack chair, legs stretched before him, ankles crossed, beer in hand. Dozer filled the chair next to him, looking happier than his master to see her.

"Hello, Joe." *Be nice, Beth. He's going to be family soon.* "I don't suppose you'll let me explain about this afternoon?"

"You mean let you explain why you let me look like an idiot? Or why you lied about who you are?"

"I didn't lie," Beth argued, counted to ten. Fighting would get her nowhere. She needed him to see her side. "I just didn't tell you I was the blonde bimbo you were looking for. Embarrassing you the first time we met didn't seem like the best way to start off."

Joe snorted. "Right. So are you Beth or Elizabeth? Are you my brother's faithful fiancée or a woman who invites strange men into her car?"

How dare he.

"I was Beth when I was younger, but I've gone by Elizabeth since college. I'm going to pretend I didn't hear your other question." Stepping over Joe's feet, she stomped down the steps in search of the garbage can. Too bad she couldn't throw Joe in the can along with the trash.

She'd crossed back over the porch and reached the door before Joe spoke again. "Which one do you like better?"

"Excuse me?"

Joe leaned forward, balancing his elbows on his knees. "Which name do you like better? Beth or Elizabeth?"

She considered her answer. The name Beth conjured images of a young, barefoot girl with wild hair and simple dreams. A girl she hardly recognized but suddenly missed.

"Beth. I like Beth better."

"Good. So do I. Makes you sound like less of a tight-ass."

The thin string holding her temper frayed. "Am I supposed to take that as a compliment?"

"Take it however you want." He waved his beer bottle in her direction. "Where's the ring?"

Beth glanced down to her bare ring finger. "Being sized. It was too big."

"Isn't that convenient."

She'd had enough. "I'd thought Lucas was exaggerating when he told me about you. But he was right. You *are* an asshole."

With that parting shot, Beth stormed into the house, certain she'd never disliked anyone half as much as she disliked Joe Dempsey.

~

Joe had to hand it to Lucas. He'd finally found something they could agree on. And that something was Beth Chandler. Why couldn't she have been the blonde, materialistic bitch Joe expected? Instead of the sexy she-cat with mouthwatering curves who'd just called him an asshole.

No woman had called him an asshole in at least two years. He couldn't help but smile. Not that Joe had any desire to try his hand at another engagement, but if he did...

Fuck.

This night was going to require several more beers, which Joe preferred to drink alone. He'd say his good-byes, whisper an apology to Patty for being such a prick, then head across the yard to his own place.

"Do you really have to go?" he heard Beth say as he walked through the front door.

"The DA filed new evidence and the judge moved the hearing up a week," Lucas said. "You know I don't want to go, but I have to." Lucas pulled Beth against his body. "This is why we brought two cars, remember? We knew this might happen."

"But we just got here and—"

"You'll be fine. My parents already love you like I knew they would. It's a vacation at the beach and I'll be back as soon as I can. Promise."

Beth backed up a step. "But this is *our* vacation, not just mine. Our chance to spend some time together. You've been working nonstop since we got engaged."

All valid arguments, Joe thought. What kind of man left his fiancée for his job?

Lucas pulled Beth forward again, locking his arms around the small of her back. "We'll have plenty of time together once this case is over. I'll make it up to you. We'll go to that steak house you love. I'll make the reservations as soon as I get home."

A fancy meal to replace an entire vacation? Talk about getting the short end of the stick.

"Now let me see that smile," Lucas cajoled. "Don't make me feel guilty about this."

Beth smiled, but even from his vantage point Joe could see her heart wasn't in it. Not that he blamed her. Lucas's priorities were clearly out of whack, and he was lucky his fiancée wasn't stomping her foot and making demands like some women would.

Joe knew they hadn't spotted him yet, and disliked feeling like a creepy Peeping Tom, so he coughed as Lucas moved in for a kiss. "What's going on?"

The pair looked his way. "I got a call from the firm," Lucas said. "Turns out they've been trying to reach me on my cell and had to get Mom's number from my secretary. I can't believe there's still no cell service on this island. Is there any talk of putting in a tower?"

"No," Joe said. Lucas never did get the concept of being disconnected from the rest of the world. Heaven forbid he miss something.

Lucas sighed. "A case I've been working is about to blow up, so I'll be heading back first thing in the morning." He approached Joe. "Elizabeth is going to stay here. And she's going to have a good time, right?"

A challenge from little brother. This was new. Joe shrugged. "She'll be fine. Patty'll take care of her."

"She's here to get to know the whole family, not just Patty. I'd like her to still want to marry me when this visit is over, understand?"

Joe lowered his voice. "If she changes her mind about marrying you, it won't be because of me." With those parting words, Joe headed for the kitchen.

Patty and his dad were hovering near the sink and Joe knew they'd heard the conversation from the living room. All but his parting words. They stopped talking when he entered.

"I'm going home. Burgers were great, Dad, as usual."

"Can't say as much for the company."

Tension rolled through Joe's shoulders. "I've gotten the look enough from Patty tonight, I don't need shit from you, too. I was an ass. I apologize." Joe dropped his empty longneck in the recycle bin. When he looked up, the two most important people in his life were staring at him as if he'd grown a new eyeball in the middle of his forehead. "What?"

"Who are you and what have you done with Joe?" his stepmom asked. He'd have been pissed if she hadn't said it with a smile.

"Funny."

"Patty," his dad said. "I think our boy is growing up."

"You two ought to take this act on the road," Joe said, closing the kitchen door behind him.

~

The next morning, Beth followed Lucas to his car, pretending his imminent departure didn't bother her. "It's a shame you have to drive back after just getting here."

"I'm not looking forward to it, but you know I don't have a choice," Lucas replied, pulling her against him. Maybe he didn't have a choice. These cases were important to his career. "I'll do what I can to get back, but if this evidence is as damning as it sounds, this could take a week to straighten out."

"Are you sure no one else on the team can handle it? What about Miller? Or Bainbridge? They've been with the firm longer than you have."

Lucas kissed the top of her head. "I'm the bulldog on this team, and this evidence is going to take all the bite I've got." A gentle finger lifted her chin until their eyes met. "If I'm going to make partner, I have to win these big cases. We talked about the sacrifice that would take, right?"

They'd talked. And Beth had nodded at all of Lucas's valid points. Making partner was his dream and she needed to be supportive. At least she got to see him every day in the office. A few weeknight dinners alone wouldn't kill her.

"I'm sorry. I shouldn't give you a hard time." It wasn't as if he was choosing the job over her. She would be fine. "Be careful, and call me when you get there so I know you made it safe."

"You're cute when you're being all motherly." He smiled down at her, and Beth thought it a shame Lucas didn't have Joe's dimple.

Where did that come from?

"I need to go." A quick peck on the lips, and Lucas climbed into the car. "I'll hit traffic before Williamsburg, but should still make it to the office before two. Don't let Joe bully you. He's probably going to be a jerk for a while, but I know you'll win him over. If he's still being an ass in a few days, let me know and I'll sic Mom on him."

31

As if mentioning his mom had conjured her into being, Patty appeared on Beth's right. "Don't worry about Elizabeth, we'll take care of her. You be careful and call us when you get there."

Lucas gave Beth a smile that said, "See? Mothering." She stepped back with Patty so he could close the door, and seconds later, his BMW faded into the distance. She was alone, with her future in-laws on a tiny island surrounded by water and boats. The only element missing from her childhood nightmares was the boogeyman.

"There you are," Joe said, coming up behind them.

On second thought, all nightmare elements present and accounted for.

"I'm meeting Sid to test the boat and I don't know when we'll be back. Can Dozer stay with you today?"

Patty feigned irritation with the dog leaning against her side, but the bond between woman and mutt was obvious. "I wish I could help, but I need to be at the restaurant to set up for lunch. The crowds are picking up, and Daisy is still up in Norfolk visiting her grandmother."

"Never mind then."

"I can watch him," Beth said. She may not like Joe, but she still needed to win him over. Winning over his dog might be a good place to start. She hadn't had a dog in more than ten years, and never one the size of the small horse leaning on Patty. But how hard could it be?

"You'll watch Dozer?"

Beth shrugged. "You said he likes me."

Patty looked over in surprise. "Dozer likes you? When did this happen?"

Joe tilted his head to the side, letting her handle the mess she'd just made. Shoot. She couldn't lie to her future mother-in-law, could she?

"Um…last night when I took out the garbage. Joe and Dozer were out here on the porch, and we got to know each other a bit." At Joe's raised brow she added, "Dozer and I. Dozer and I got to know each other."

Patty looked from Beth to Joe as if seeking confirmation. Joe dropped the subject. "I've got to go, Sid's waiting." Turning to Beth he said, "I've already fed him, so he's good until dinnertime. Did you plan on taking him anywhere?"

It was Beth's turn to look confused. "Where would I go? I don't know my way around here."

"I have a map," Patty said. "We keep them in the house for the tourists. The village spans two miles of sand. Tough to get lost in a place that small." Then she turned to Joe. "With Lucas gone and business picking up at the restaurant, you need to show Elizabeth around. She shouldn't have to be on her own the whole time she's here."

"I run a business, too, you know."

Beth felt like the new girl in the neighborhood trying to get the boy next door to play with her. Well, she didn't want to play with him either. "Really, it's okay. I don't mind wandering around on my own."

"Maybe you could take her out on the boat," Patty said, as if neither of them had spoken.

"No!" The word came out much louder than Beth intended. "I mean, I don't want to put anyone out. And, uh, I don't like boats. Much."

"Joe's isn't a small one, if that's what you're worried about." This conversation needed to end. Especially considering the look that comment put on Joe's face.

"How about we take it one day at a time. I'm sure Lucas will be back before we know it, and then he'll show me around." Beth headed for the front door.

"Ahem," Joe coughed. "Aren't you forgetting something?"

Beth turned, looking around. "I don't think so."

Joe glanced at Dozer.

"Oh, right." She called over her shoulder, "Come on, Dozer. Let's find that map and plan our day."

～

"Well? What's she like?"

"Who?" Joe asked, playing dumb and avoiding eye contact while untying the dock lines.

"Betty White, jackass. You know who."

Joe shrugged. "She's not what I expected."

Sid dropped onto the side of the boat, boots resting on the bench. "Not a blonde or not a bimbo?"

"Neither." He envied Dozer for the third time since leaving him with Beth. Not that he wanted to spend the day with the pain in the ass. She didn't even like boats. Who the hell didn't like boats?

And there was that little detail about her calling him an asshole.

"I usually appreciate your strong, silent-type personality, but you're starting to piss me off." Sid crossed her arms under her breasts, eyebrows raised.

"What do you want me to say? She's a brunette. She dresses fancy and is afraid of boats. And water. I'll be surprised if she lasts the week."

"You think she'll leave him?" A note of enthusiasm entered Sid's voice, but Joe ignored it. He knew Sid had a thing for Lucas, but he sure as hell wasn't going to talk about it.

"He already left."

"What?" Sid came off the side of the boat in one motion. "He's gone? But he just got here."

Joe moved to the next dock line. "He got a call, said he had to head back for a case. I didn't ask a lot of questions."

Sid followed him toward the bow. "So she's still here? He left her here alone?"

Joe stopped and Sid slammed into his back. "Could we get on with this? She's here. He's not. End of story."

"Fine," Sid said, bristling at his attitude. "So Patty's stuck with her all day?"

"No, Patty had to work. Beth is on her own. She's watching Dozer for me."

Sid let go of the line she'd just picked up. "She's watching Dozer?"

He'd barely had breakfast and Joe already had a headache. "Yes, she's watching Dozer. What is wrong with you?"

"What is wrong with *you*? It took you a year before you'd let your mother watch Dozer. This chick strolls onto the island and suddenly she's your trusted pet sitter? There must be something about her you're not telling me."

"Sid." Joe crossed his arms to prevent himself from throwing his boat mechanic overboard. "I needed someone to watch the dog. She volunteered. He seems to like her, and I don't figure she's going to kill him, so it's fine. Now, can we please just test this fucking engine?"

Sid narrowed her eyes but didn't fire off any more questions. Thank God.

"Whatever you say, Captain. Let's fire up the fucking engine."

CHAPTER FOUR

Beth spent an hour studying the map of the island along with a few tourist-attraction flyers. For a tiny speck of sand, Anchor offered a wide variety of shops and businesses to explore. There were the usual suspects selling T-shirts and souvenirs, including coconut bikini tops and endless beach-themed water globes, but the number of niche stores was surprising.

"What do you recommend, Dozer?" At hearing his name, the dog turned, splattering drool across the top flyer. "Okay, we'll skip the Blackbeard museum for now." She slid the wet pamphlet into the garbage. "I'll just look through these up on the counter, where you can't drip."

The third flyer down caught her attention. A small, bright-blue cabin nestled between low-hanging trees burst from the page. Soft-pink and fuchsia flowers hugged a welcoming porch, while varying-sized flowerpots lined the porch rail like birds crowding on a power line. The sign read ISLAND ARTS & CRAFTS.

"I've found our first destination."

Thankfully, Patty had circled the location for the Dempsey home on the map, so according to Beth's calculations, one left and two rights should get her to the art shop. Based on the key, the distance would be just under a mile. She debated taking the bicycle Patty had offered, but opted to walk with Dozer instead. Her future mother-in-law had assured her the canine did not need a leash. Fingers crossed the dog didn't make a liar out of her and run off to parts unknown.

All she needed was to lose Joe's dog in the first hour. He'd likely throw her off the island. Or feed her to the sharks. He did run a fishing boat. The man was sure to know where to find some sharks.

New sandals on her feet, mutt by her side, and map in hand, Beth headed off in search of British Cemetery Road. She'd tied a light jacket over her shorts, but the cool breeze had her slipping it on before they'd traveled a full block. If this was a typical late-spring day, she looked forward to the next two weeks.

Beth was used to battling other pedestrians on a daily basis, so walking along a narrow road with no one but a dog for company felt wholly unfamiliar. The absence of vehicles left the sound of birds echoing above, flitting from treetop to treetop, caws and tweets making up their secret language. Dozer stuck his nose in a bush, forcing three birds to seek refuge at a higher level. Beth understood their skittishness.

She wouldn't want her world invaded that way either.

But this place was nothing like her world. Even the cedar trees looked casual and laid-back, branches bending low as if their cloak of bright-green needles was more than they could bear. A man in hip waders and a floppy hat covered in hooks used the fishing rod in his hand to wave a hello. A young couple, the mother pushing a stroller while the father steadied a toddler on a two-wheeler, called out a greeting as they passed.

Maybe there was something in the water that made everyone so nice on this island.

Each tiny business she passed, from the coffee shop, appropriately named Hava Java, to the log cabin with a porch covered in every kind of wind chime she could imagine, looked welcoming and homey. Definitely something in the water. And the air. Her exhaust-choked commute felt a million miles away.

This was the way to live.

She walked on, Dozer by her side, enjoying the serenity and charm of Anchor Island until her day took an uncomfortable turn somewhere near the bookstore.

A blister.

"Stupid sandals," she said to no one in particular. "This is what I get for buying new shoes and not breaking them in." Determined to reach her destination, Beth ignored the blister and kept moving. By the time the little blue building came into sight, she was limping enough to rub a matching blister onto the opposite foot.

Unable to hobble another step, Beth dropped onto the stone wall in front of the art store. Pink, yellow, red, and white flowers of varying heights and widths crowded around her like preschool children clamoring for a spot near the new teacher. The scent from the blooms reminded her of the perfume her grandmother used to wear to church. Closing her eyes, she breathed deep, seeing Granny dabbing the perfume stopper behind her ear while assuring Beth that one day she could wear the pretty scent, too.

"You're a long way from home, Dozer. How did you get all the way up here?"

The voice jarred Beth back to reality. She leapt to her feet, which protested immediately, making her plop back onto the wall.

"I didn't even see you there amongst my flowers, honey. Is Dozer with you?"

An island had to be really small when even the pets knew everyone else. "Yes, ma'am, he's with me."

The waiflike black woman floated down the porch steps, gnarled hands skimming the rail, and her magnolia-covered skirt dancing on the breeze. Beth half expected the woman to sprout wings and send glitter into the air.

"You're the poor thing I saw out my window. You were limping something fierce. Are you hurt bad?" The wrinkles around the elderly woman's eyes deepened, and Beth rushed to relieve her worry.

"Oh no, I'm fine. I didn't mean to sit on your wall like this." Beth pushed to her feet but pain sent her down again. "Oh, sweet peaches and cream, this hurts."

"Child, what have you done to your foot?"

Beth glanced down to see blood dripping from the side of her sandal. "Crap."

"Honey, that's blood. That calls for a *shit* or a *damn* or something stronger than *crap*."

A giggle escaped upon hearing profanity from the elderly woman. Whoever this creature turned out to be, Beth already liked her immensely. "It's my fault. I bought these new sandals right before coming down here. They would have been fine to wear in the city, but not so much for walking around this island. Which is bigger than it looks on this map," she said, waving the paper in the air.

As Beth lifted her foot to examine the damage, the sweet woman wrapped a gentle hand around her ankle. "First thing we need to do is get this shoe off." Full lips pinched together as the woman looked to Beth for permission. "You ready? It's probably going to hurt."

Beth took a deep breath, blew it out, then nodded. The sandal slid off quickly but not without sending a tearing pain all the way to her knee. "Shit, that hurts."

"That's more like it. How bad is the other one?"

A quick survey of Beth's left foot revealed the blister to be less severe. "Might as well take that one off, too. Then we can burn them," Beth said.

"Sounds like a good plan to me." A quick tug and the left shoe joined the right in the sand. "Come inside and we'll fix you right up. Aunty Claudine's ointment will take the sting out, but you're going to need some new shoes." She tapped her chin twice, then her brown eyes lit up. "I know. You must try these Heaven-Sent slippers I just got in the mail. You'll think you've stepped into a cloud."

"I don't want to put you out," Beth said, rising to her feet with less pain than before. Sand shifted between her toes. "I feel better already."

"Don't be silly, child. If you came with that mutt, you're too far from home to walk back barefooted." Dozer chose that moment to pounce on one of the discarded shoes, thrashing it from side to side. "Looks like he's going to kill the sandals before we can set fire to 'em."

"Let him have them. They'd probably stink to high heaven if we burned them anyway." The two women laughed together, as Beth hobbled beside her new friend. "My name is Beth, by the way. I hope I didn't take you away from anything important."

A small hand waved her words away. "This early in the season it gets lonely around here. I'm happy to have some company."

"Do you own this store?"

"That I do." With a bow from the top step, the woman made her introduction. "Miss Lola LeBlanc at your service. I run this little burst of color year-round. There aren't many of us who stay throughout the year, so I like to think that makes me a rare bird."

"Miss LeBlanc, I get the feeling you'd be a rare bird no matter where you lived."

With a mischievous wink, Lola said, "I think you're right. Come inside and let's get you those slippers."

"But what about Dozer?" Beth asked. She hadn't thought far enough ahead to know what she'd do with the canine once they'd reached a destination.

"We'll get you off your feet, then I'll bring him out a bowl of water and a nice ham bone I've been saving for just such an occasion."

As if understanding the words "ham bone," Dozer took a seat beside the door and licked his lips. "Looks like Dozer approves of that plan."

Lola chuckled. "I'm sure he does. Never met a male yet didn't go on his best behavior at the promise of a fine-tasting treat."

Beth blushed at the innuendo in her new friend's words as she hobbled into the store and smiled at the sight before her.

~

"She's running like a dream," Sid said, clearly proud that she'd figured out the problem before Joe did.

"I've admitted you were right three times now. Forget about hearing it again." Joe threw a dock line hard enough to knock the smirk off Sid's face. "And stop smiling like that. It's creepy."

Joe turned to throw the second dock line but noticed Sid was no longer looking in his direction. She wasn't smiling either. He followed her gaze to see what had taken her from smug to pissed.

"Son of a bitch," he muttered, jumping over the side and tying the dock line himself. Unfortunately, pretending the leggy blonde wasn't there didn't make her go away.

"Aren't you going to say hello, Joe?" purred a familiar voice. "I know you saw me coming up the pier."

A man would have to be dead not to notice the swing in Cassie's hips. And Joe was definitely not dead. Though the woman made him wish he were once upon a time.

Bracing himself for the blow, Joe's jaw tightened as he turned. The slim curves and perfect face didn't invoke the lust they once had. Some relief there. But seeing her again stirred the memory of what a fool he'd been, igniting the anger he'd never managed to get past.

To reveal the anger to Cassie would mean revealing a weakness. That he wouldn't do.

"Hello, Cassie. What are you doing here?"

"So much for a friendly greeting. Couldn't you at least ask how I am first? It's been a long time since we've seen each other."

Two and a half years didn't qualify as "a long time" in Joe's book, but he wasn't going to argue the point.

"How are you, Cassie?" Without waiting for an answer, he added, "You remember Sid."

His mechanic walked up beside him. "No one told me the bitch was back in town."

Cassie narrowed her eyes. "I see some creatures never change. Once a grease monkey, always a grease monkey."

Sid charged, but Joe grabbed her before she could throw the first punch. Cassie was smart enough to take a step back. "What do you want, Cassie? I doubt you were just in the neighborhood," Joe said.

His ex kept her eye on Sid for an extra second before answering. Then she turned to Joe and flashed him a thousand-dollar smile. "Let's just say I'm on a working vacation. I was having dinner when I saw you pull up."

"A working vacation?" Joe held firm to Sid. She should know better than to let Cassie get to her.

"Maybe we could grab a drink while I'm here. Talk about old times." The woman had the nerve to flutter her eyelashes. "Take a walk down memory lane."

There wasn't enough liquor in the world to make him take that trip. "I'll pass."

The doe eyes turned sharp again. "I'll be around for another week or two. Think it over, and when you change your mind, give me a call." She slid a business card into the pocket of his flannel, then swung her ass back up the pier.

"Why didn't you let me hit her?" Sid asked. "One good punch, for old times' sake."

Joe exhaled. "She's not worth it, Sid. She's not worth it."

∼

One afternoon with Lola LeBlanc, and Beth was convinced the woman had been sent from heaven. The slippers were better than walking on clouds. They were like walking on air, if air actually molded to your foot, lifted you off the ground, and levitated you through your day. Though she'd offered to pay for them, Lola insisted she take the slippers as a welcome-to-the-island gift.

Island Arts & Crafts exceeded Beth's expectations. The building stretched back beyond what was visible from the front, affording ample space for artwork of all kinds. The walls were covered in prints, oils, watercolors, and sketches, all reflecting the island feel. Sunsets over dunes. Charming cottages in blues, greens, and yellows. Boats of all shapes and sizes bobbing in a harbor that looked so real Beth could almost see the waves rolling against the hulls.

Other areas held everything from small sculptures to homemade porch signs and delicate glass creations. After a short negotiation, Lola agreed to let Beth pay for a deep purple vase in what looked to be a swirl of glass and light, but she still refused to accept payment for the slippers.

No sooner had Lola finished wrapping the vase than the chimes hanging from the front door signaled the arrival of a new customer.

"Looks like we have a fancy one here." Lola patted Beth's knee. "Go ahead and pour your tea. This could take a while if he's looking for something for a lady love."

Beth nodded but kept her attention on the new stranger. He smiled, but in an "I'm here to sell you something" sort of way. Half the lawyers in her office used that smile.

"Can I help you, sir?" Lola asked.

The fake smile grew wider, revealing teeth white enough to blind. "I'm looking for Ms. LeBlanc. Is she in today?"

Lola's smile slipped. "I'm Lola LeBlanc. Did someone send you to see me?"

"As a matter of fact, someone did." The man pulled a card from his coat pocket. "I'm Derek Paige. I work for Tad Wheeler of Wheeler Development. I believe we've contacted you previously."

Lola's smile disappeared. "I'm not interested in what Mr. Wheeler has to offer. I'm sorry you wasted your time coming all the way down here in person, Mr. Paige, but perhaps you'd like to purchase something to remember your trip?"

Though she was being extremely courteous, there was no missing the derision in Lola's voice. Beth couldn't help but wonder what Wheeler Development would want from a small-island art shop owner. The construction development company owned by Tad Wheeler happened to be a client of her law firm, and though she didn't work on the account, she knew Wheeler usually aimed for larger prey.

"Mr. Wheeler is willing to negotiate the terms of the deal. I assure you, Ms. LeBlanc, it would be well worth your time to sit down and discuss the matter further. We are highly motivated in this endeavor." Though he slipped his hands into his pants pockets, there was nothing relaxed about Mr. Paige. Beth imagined his boss would not be happy if his representative failed in his mission. Whatever that mission might be.

As if shifting personalities, Lola threw one hand on her hip and waved the other in front of the unwelcome visitor's nose. "I told your people on the phone, and I'll tell you again. I'm not selling my store. Mr. Big-Shot Developer Man will just have to find another island upon which to stick his hoity-toity sandbox."

Selling? Wheeler wanted to buy the art store?

Mr. Paige maintained his pasted smile in the face of Lola's temper. "Now, Ms. LeBlanc, don't make any hasty decisions. Your neighbors have received similar offers. I'm sure you wouldn't want to ruin this chance for everyone else."

The frail-looking woman moved around the counter with impressive speed. "No one on this island is going to take what Mr. Wheeler is offering. I don't care how many zeroes he puts behind the number." She'd actually backed the man to the door without touching him. Though Beth hoped she'd poke him in the chest. He deserved a poke for that sleazy smile.

"Now unless you intend to buy a souvenir, get out of my store."

The man had the good sense to do as ordered, but threw a parting shot before making his exit. "At some point,

Ms. LeBlanc, you're not going to have the option to negotiate. The sooner you get on board with this, the better your chances will be. If you wait too long, the terms will be much less generous than they are now."

The lawyer in Beth came alive, and she stood. "Ms. LeBlanc has obviously given Mr. Wheeler her answer. Any further contact will be deemed harassment, and for the sake of ending this rationally, we'll ignore that last threat. For now."

Lola turned wide eyes in her direction, but Beth kept her own focused on Derek Paige. She may not work in the courtroom, but that didn't mean she didn't know how to wield the law when necessary. Defending Lola felt necessary.

Mr. Paige nodded. "Thank you for your time, Ms. LeBlanc. Sorry to bother you."

When the chimes faded into silence, Beth slumped back in her chair and Lola did the same beside her. "Child, I don't know whether to kiss you or ask to see your credentials. That was beautiful."

Beth exhaled. "My credentials won't get you far, but I couldn't let him threaten you like that. What does Tad Wheeler want with this island?"

"That evil man has been trying to buy us out for months now. Wants to turn Anchor into some rich people's playground. Do you know him?"

"Not personally, but I know of him." Beth's stomach turned. "He's a client of my law firm."

Lola looked even more impressed. "That must be one fancy firm based on what I know of Mr. Tad Wheeler. Which isn't much, but I can tell by his letterhead he's not your neighborhood contractor."

"No, he isn't. And based on office gossip, he's used to getting what he wants. Regardless of the obstacles in his way."

"Well, he's not getting this island, I can guarantee you that." Lola stood up to pour two glasses of iced tea.

"I'm sure you're right, Lola," Beth said. Then thought to herself, *But I wouldn't count on it.*

CHAPTER FIVE

By the time Joe followed Sid into the pub, he'd lost his appetite. The "working" part of Cassie's vacation had to mean doing dirty work for her daddy. Tad Wheeler had been courting various business owners for months to sell out. With the businesses gone, tourism would die and the cabin owners would have to sell.

And sell cheap.

It wasn't hard to see what the man was up to, and at the last Merchants meeting, they'd all agreed to stick together. He hoped Wheeler would lose interest, but past experience taught him not to underestimate the man.

"It's about time you got here," Joe's dad yelled from behind the bar. "Grab an apron and start clearing tables."

Joe looked around the crowded dining room. Families, college students, and middle-aged fishermen filled the tables and booths. "Where the hell'd they come from?" he asked, pulling an apron off a peg inside the kitchen.

"I have no idea, but they've been rolling in like waves for two hours."

"Need me to grab a tray, Tom?" Sid asked.

A beer mug slid down the bar and another glass appeared in Tom's hand. "No, we're good for now. Georgette's got most of the room and Elizabeth has been a lifesaver. Awful waste of a law degree if you ask me. She'd be worth the money to get her on permanent."

Sid and Joe both stood frozen, watching the tiny brunette work her way around the tables. If Joe didn't know better, he'd swear she'd been waitressing all her life.

"Where's Annie?" Joe asked, keeping his eyes on Beth. He didn't know where she got those cutoff jean shorts, but no doubt she'd set a record for tips by the end of the night.

"Her boy's down with an ear infection." Tom slid two more beer mugs and a margarita down the bar, where Beth arrived to pick them up.

"Three Bud Lights in the bottle on the tab for table twelve, and two iced teas for the elderly ladies in the corner. I also need to cash out table nine. I'll pick up the check after I deliver these."

Without so much as a glance in Joe's direction, Beth sailed through the tables once again, drawing every pair of male eyes in the room.

"That's Elizabeth? That's Lucas's fiancée?" Sid asked. "I thought she was a lawyer?"

"She is," Tom said over the ringing of the register. "Turns out she worked her way through college waiting tables."

Sid punched Joe in the arm.

"What was that for?" he asked, rubbing his shoulder.

"For making her sound like some plain Jane this morning. Now I see what you weren't telling me."

"You're crazy. I barely said anything about her this morning." And if Sid hit him again he was going to strangle her with his apron strings.

"And now I know why." Sid turned back to Tom. "Bud Light when you get a chance. I'll be in the pool room."

"Alvie Franklin is back there, and I don't want you hustling him at pool again," Tom said. "He's too drunk to know what you're doing, and if he breaks another cue, you're paying for it."

Sid raised her hands in innocence as she walked backward toward the sound of clashing pool balls. Fat chance she'd follow his dad's orders. A clearing tub in hand, Joe headed onto the floor. He'd cleared three tables before crossing paths with Beth.

"Oh," she exclaimed when they nearly collided. "I didn't know you were here."

Joe ignored the weight of the full tub. "I didn't know you could wait tables. You look like a natural."

Beth's head tilted to one side. "Are you paying me a compliment or setting me up for some smart-aleck remark?"

So much for trying to be nice. "Forget I said anything. Damn." He tried to go around her, but she stopped him with a hand on his arm. The burn was instant, and she pulled back as if she'd felt it, too.

"I'm sorry, I shouldn't have said that."

Joe shrugged, pretending being so close didn't affect him. "Where's Dozer?"

"In your backyard. Patty told me where to find the food by the back door, so I filled his bowl and made sure he had water before I left." She bit her bottom lip. "I hope that's okay."

"That's fine. Thanks for keeping an eye on him." Someone a few tables away called out, "Miss?" and Joe said, "We'd better get back to work."

"Sure," she said, staring at him through big green eyes. "Back to work."

~

Beth tried to shake off her brush with Joe before reaching the bar. A long-lost memory came to mind. Five naive girls sitting around a college dorm talking about what they called the "spark factor." The romantic notion that when the right guy came along, there should be fireworks and blinking neon signs.

In the brief second their bodies had touched, there were fireworks galore, and not of the minor sparkler variety. She got *zip* along with some *zing* and a *kapow*. Alarm bells echoed in her brain. Touching Lucas had never sent a light show dancing through her bloodstream. No bottle rockets. No Roman candles. Not even a hint of firepower.

She squashed her disloyal thoughts, focusing on her fiancé's positive traits. Lucas made her smile. He was sweet and generous and took care of her. She never had to worry or solve a problem because Lucas handled everything. Just as her grandparents had done for most of her life. No question of where to go. Who to be.

That's what she wanted. That's where she felt safe.

Joe didn't make her feel safe. Joe made her mad. Made her feel…unanchored. Ironic considering they were on Anchor Island. That zing stood as clear evidence Beth needed an anchor. Or something just as heavy to smack her upside the head.

"This beer goes back to Sid in the pool room," Tom said, sliding a longneck Beth's way.

"Who's Sid?" The name sounded vaguely familiar. Maybe Patty had mentioned him.

"Works with Joe. Just holler the name from the doorway."

"Got it," Beth said, dropping her now empty tray by her hip and carrying the bottle with her free hand. Sid sounded like a name that should belong to a large man. Shouldn't be that hard to find.

When Beth entered the pool room, she glanced around for a man towering over the others but didn't see one. "I've got a beer for Sid!" she yelled over the Buffett song pouring from the jukebox.

"That's me," came a female voice from Beth's right. She turned and met dark brown eyes belonging to one of the most gorgeous women she'd ever seen.

The body belonged in a centerfold layout, but the clothes looked more like something from the agri co-op in the small farm town where Beth grew up.

Not a speck of makeup on her face, but she didn't need it. Her skin was pale and flawless, eyelashes long without the aid of mascara, and lips Beth imagined sent men to their knees.

An instant feeling of inadequacy slid down Beth's spine. "You're Sid?" So much for making assumptions where names were concerned.

"That's right, princess." The brown eyes narrowed, and a dark ponytail flopped to one side as the woman stuck out her hip and tilted her head. "You going to hand over that beer or do I have to wrestle you for it?"

That was uncalled for. What had Beth ever done to this woman? She'd definitely never met her, even if the name sounded familiar. No woman would forget the bombshell who made her feel as if she should hand in her girl card.

"Did you say wrestle me?" Beth asked. Though Sid's head barely reached Beth's nose, her rolled-up sleeves revealed well-muscled arms. For a woman anyway. Not that Beth intended to wrestle her for anything. She'd never been in a cat fight in her life and didn't intend to change that fact now.

"For a lawyer, you sure are dense." The woman invaded Beth's space, slamming her pool cue down inches from Beth's blistered toes.

The Band-Aids together with Aunty Claudine's magical ointment were working so far, but she doubted they'd protect her against a solid stick of wood.

"Somebody needs to blow in your ear and give you a refill."

While Beth processed that insult, a figure appeared on her left.

"Back off, Sid." Joe moved in closer until his body stood between Beth and her aggressor. "She's just bringing you a beer. Go back to your game."

Sid let out a breath, staring hard into Joe's eyes. Then she shook her head and said, "Rack 'em up boys, and get out your wallets."

The standoff lasted several more seconds with the sound of pool balls being gathered on the table. When Sid turned away, Beth saw Joe's shoulders relax. Surely he wouldn't have hit a woman.

"You okay?" he asked, taking the longneck she'd forgotten she was holding.

"I'm fine. What was that all about?"

"That's Sid."

"Yeah, I got that. Who is Sid, and how does she know I'm a lawyer? For that matter, why does she hate me?"

"She doesn't hate you. She's just..." He seemed to be searching for the right word.

"Bitchy?"

"That works."

Beth glanced over Joe's shoulder. Four men, all in denim and flannel (the clear island dress code), lingered around the table as Sid bent over to break. None of them were paying her body any attention.

"Why are those guys treating her like that?"

"Like what?" Joe turned toward the men in question.

"Like she's one of them."

"She *is* one of them." If Joe's face hadn't been completely blank, Beth would have sworn he was messing with her.

"Come on, she's gorgeous. Guys in Richmond would be drooling right now."

Joe's brows shot up, and he turned as if expecting to see someone new behind him. "Sid?"

"You'd have to be a eunuch not to see that." Joe looked insulted by that insinuation. "You know what I mean. Who is she anyway?"

"She's my boat mechanic. A pain in the ass, but she can fix anything you put in front of her."

Beth couldn't respond. She'd need to lift her jaw off the floor to do that.

"What?" Joe asked, looking perplexed again.

"*That* is your boat mechanic? You work with a woman Hugh Hefner would pay a million bucks for, yet you claim not to notice she's the slightest bit attractive?" Beth pulled the tray to her now inferior-feeling chest and wrapped her arms around it. "Is that why you're so cranky all the time?"

Joe's mouth clamped shut and his eyes narrowed. "You're out of your mind. Sid isn't..." He trailed off as he looked again to the woman in question and got a straight shot of a well-shaped bottom. "You're nuts," he said, stomping out of the room.

Before Beth could follow behind him, he leaned back in to yell, "And I'm not cranky!"

~

Cranky my ass, Joe thought. He was a happy guy. Maybe not in a dance-around-smiling-and-spreading-sunshine kind of way, but what goofy idiot wanted to do that? He didn't have to take this shit. If he was cranky it was her fault. Nobody else pissed him off this easy.

"Hey, Joe!" shouted a voice behind him.

"What?" he yelled back as he swung around and just missed smacking a customer with his clearing tub.

"Dude, what's your problem?" asked Phil Mohler. Another charter boat operator on the island, Phil was Joe's least favorite competitor. They'd gone to high school together, and even back then, the two hadn't gotten along.

"Nothing. What do you want?" If he thought Joe would be running to get him a refill, Mohler would be waiting all damn night.

"Who's the new chick, and what do you say I get an introduction?"

"What new chick?" Joe asked, looking around for a pretty tourist.

"The one you were just talking to back by the pool room. Haven't seen a swing like that in way too long." Phil elbowed Buddy Wilson sitting next to him, and the laughter carried round the table.

Crankiness turned to white-hot anger. "She's off-limits, Mohler. Unless you want your ass flung out the door, you'll keep your eyes and your comments to yourself."

"Hey, man," Phil said, throwing his hands in the air, "I didn't know you were banging her already. Warn a guy next time."

Joe dropped the tub on the table, knocking over three bottles. The men scrambled to avoid the rivers of beer. "That's Lucas's fiancée, and I said keep your comments to yourself." His jaw clenched so tight, Joe could feel his teeth grinding. He'd rather grind Mohler's face.

"What's going on here, boys?" asked Joe's dad, sliding up to the table with three longnecks and a bar rag. "Looks like we had an accident."

"You need to teach your boy some manners, Dempsey. I just asked a simple question and he got all bent out of shape." Mohler kept his eyes on Joe though he was talking to Tom.

Joe's grip tightened on the tub. Hauling Mohler out of his chair in the middle of a crowded dining room wouldn't be a good idea. Though it would feel damn good.

Tom dropped the rag on the table and leaned down into Phil's face. "You know one of the perks of owning this place, Mohler? It's that I can refuse service to anyone I want. I've replaced the beers you paid for. You intend to have any more tonight, you'll have to buy them elsewhere."

Silence loomed over the surrounding tables as Joe waited to see what Mohler would do. His face turned red, but he wasn't brave enough to challenge Tom Dempsey. There was a reason the bar didn't employ a bouncer.

They didn't have to.

"Come on, boys. The air in here is starting to stink."

Tom backed up far enough for the men to get up from the table and head for the door. As soon as they were out of earshot, he looked at Joe. "In the kitchen. Now."

Shit.

Could his night get any fucking worse?

"What the hell are you doing out there? I have a full dining room and you're trying to start a brawl?"

Joe crossed to the dishwasher and unloaded his tub. "I'm not an idiot. I wasn't going to hit him."

"You sure as hell wanted to," Tom growled.

"Hell yeah, I wanted to. I've wanted to for years." Though he'd always been able to ignore Mohler's asshole ways before. "But I didn't, so lay off."

"You know he's a prick. I don't know why you let him get to you like that."

"He said the wrong thing, that's all." Joe slammed two plates into the strainer, chipping the one in his right hand. "Fuck."

"I've lost customers, I don't need to lose my plates, too," Tom said, sliding the tub away. "What did he say?"

"He said Beth has a nice ass, that's what. I was defending Lucas's fiancée's honor, since he can't be bothered to be here and do it himself." Joe grabbed the tub and reached for two more plates, making an extra effort not to break them. "Anything else you want to know?"

When his dad remained silent, Joe turned to see his face. The look said everything Tom wasn't about to say out loud. Joe dumped the last of the silverware in the soaking water and headed back to the floor.

CHAPTER SIX

The relief of connecting her bottom to a chair drew a long sigh from Beth. A hot bath would be better, but by the time this night was over she'd have enough energy to crawl into bed and nothing more. For now, sitting on the bench outside Dempsey's would have to do.

The blisters she'd developed on her walk that morning were not happy about waiting tables. Turned out Aunty Claudine's ointment went only so far. She'd been able to wear the slippers, which were really just terry-cloth flip-flops, back to the Dempsey house, where she'd followed Lola's orders and soaked her feet in saltwater.

But the slippers weren't appropriate for the restaurant, so she'd switched to Keds, figuring the soft material would be her best choice. She'd been wrong.

With the first shoe half-off, the pressure eased, but removing it completely would mean brushing the opening across the blister. After taking a few fortifying breaths, then holding one in, she jerked the Ked the rest of the way.

"Cotton picken' fricken' fracken'."

"Is that your idea of cursing?" came a now familiar voice from her left. She looked up to find his eyes on her foot. "What the hell did you do?" Joe reached the bench in two strides, taking her ankle in hand. "Are these from tonight?"

"No," Beth hissed as Joe examined the bloody wound centimeters below her left pinky toe. "They're from this morning. I wore new sandals to walk the island. Not my best idea."

Joe sat down, then lowered her foot into his lap. Beth tried to pull away. "What are you—"

"Hold still, damn it. Why the hell'd you work the floor when you were hurt like this?"

"I had Band-Aids on them. I guess that one is still in the shoe." The more Joe ran his hands along her foot and ankle, the more Beth squirmed. She felt as if she'd spiked a temperature, certain areas feeling more heated than others. "I'm fine, really. I came out here to put on new Band-Aids, and then I'll clean them better when I get back to your parents' house."

Joe lifted her foot, stood, then gingerly lowered it down to where he'd been sitting. Returning to the entrance, he opened the door halfway and yelled, "Dad! We need the first aid kit."

Beth smacked her forehead. Great. Now the whole place would be outside in seconds to see what had happened. "Did you have to do that?"

"Do what?" he asked, lifting her foot and taking a seat again. Beth ground her teeth and tried to keep her foot hovering half an inch above his thigh.

"Everyone is going to come out here to see what the emergency is. You couldn't walk in and get the kit yourself?"

Before he could answer, she said, "Forget it. I'll put on these Band-Aids and I'll be fine."

"The hell you will," he said. "Bring the other foot up here."

"Why?" she said, bracing herself to bolt. "The other foot is fine." He cocked his head to one side and lifted a brow. Why couldn't she be a better liar? "You're insufferable, you know that?"

"The foot," he said, that damn eyebrow still lingering near his hairline.

She gave him her foot and called him a jerk. In her head.

While Joe untied the laces on her right shoe, Beth ignored the throbbing in her left thigh from holding that foot up off Joe's lap. If she let the limb drop, her heel would be much too close to a crucial part of his anatomy. A part she shouldn't be contemplating but the more she tried not to contemplate, the more she felt heat shoot to the tips of her ears.

"Does it hurt that bad?" he asked.

"What do you mean?"

"You're holding your breath."

Beth exhaled and let her foot drop but kept it as far down his thigh as she could. "I told you, it's not that bad."

Joe pulled off her right shoe.

"Shit and stickers!" she yelled.

"You're getting better at that." He set her foot gently on his leg and turned to face her. "Sorry."

Removing her nails from the wood of the bench seat and invoking her yoga breathing, Beth took almost a minute to speak again. "Not your fault." Another breath and the fire shooting up her calf eased. "Guess they're worse than I thought."

"They're bad all right." As Joe bent for a closer look, Tom stepped onto the porch.

"What happened?" his dad asked. Spotting the blood, he moved forward and kneeled before the bench. "Did this happen tonight?"

Beth shook her head. "This morning, but I guess I aggravated them running the tables." Uncomfortable with the attention, she tried to put her feet on the floor. "I really am fine. A couple new Band-Aids and I'll be ready to tap dance."

With a firm hand around her right calf, Joe held Beth in place. Ignoring her protest, he addressed Tom. "You have any peroxide in there?"

"Should have." Tom flipped through the first aid kit, drawing out a small brown bottle. "Let me find some cotton balls."

"That square pad there should work," Joe said, pointing into the plastic box.

Beth couldn't get over the way they were ignoring her as if the feet in question belonged to some lifeless mannequin. "I'm still here, you know. Why won't anyone listen to me?"

"Stop talking nonsense and we'll listen." Joe looked to Tom. "Might be best to pour the peroxide on. You got a towel?"

"I'll grab a clean one from the kitchen. Be right back."

As they sat alone in silence broken only by the sound of crickets and the occasional passing car, Joe cleaned the blood from around the blisters with an alcohol swab while Beth pretended not to be affected. Closing her eyes, she sent her brain elsewhere by focusing on the chirping crickets. The creaking of the Dempsey's sign swaying in the night breeze. The smell of salt and male in the air.

Her eyes shot open to find Joe watching her. "I thought you were nodding off."

As if she could fall asleep with him so close, wreaking havoc on her nerve endings. "I'm awake."

"Good," he said, sharing a half grin that turned her inside out.

"I brought two," Tom said, joining them again. "Toss 'em when you're done."

Beth reached out a hand. "I don't want to ruin your good towels."

Joe and Tom chuckled in unison. "Don't worry, darlin'. Bar towels are a dime a dozen. Literally." Tom leaned over her feet again, then looked at Joe. "I could have one of the other waitresses come out and do this."

There seemed to be a question in Tom's words, but Beth couldn't be sure. Being doctored by Joe did feel odd. Intimate almost.

"I've got it," Joe said, the command in his voice ending the unspoken debate.

Tom sighed as he rose to his full height. With a reassuring smile Beth's way, he nodded. "I'll leave you to it then."

Sliding one of the towels across his lap beneath her feet, Joe reached for the peroxide. "This might sting. I'll count to three then pour. You ready?"

Beth nodded then gripped the bench.

"One, two…" Without saying "three," he tipped the bottle. The sting made her eyes water.

"You didn't say three," she ground through clenched teeth. "You'd make a horrible doctor." She refused to cry over stupid blisters, but the tighter she closed her eyes, the more the tears threatened.

"My last doctoring was done on a turtle. I didn't hear him complain."

The laugh bubbled out before she could stop it. Her shoulders relaxed as the pain faded to a tolerable twinge. "Careful or I'll start a rumor that you have a sense of humor."

"Don't threaten the doctor while he's working."

Joe dried the peroxide that had run down her foot, his hands gentle as if trying not to cause her any more pain than necessary. "Thank you," she whispered.

"Don't mention it."

"I mean for earlier."

His hands stilled for a moment, then returned to their ministrations. "Those guys are idiots. I should have ignored them."

"What guys?"

Joe jerked, turning a gentle pat into a rough poke.

"Ow!"

"Sorry."

"Maybe I shouldn't talk to you while you're doing this."

"Whatever you want." He glanced up, met her eyes, then looked away. "Won't happen again."

She considered asking about the guys in question, but decided for the sake of her feet to move on. "I meant back there with Sid. You saved my life."

Joe snorted. "Sid isn't that bad."

"She threatened me with a pool stick. Though I'm not sure if she intended to beat me with it or shove it down my throat."

"She didn't threaten you."

"I know a threat when one comes my way. That was a threat." *Blow in my ear.* The nerve. "The woman needs a keeper."

"That woman is my friend. You shouldn't go around judging people you don't know."

The shock of his words hindered her brain function for several seconds. Then the anger came. "You amaze me. Until yesterday, you believed me to be a materialistic blonde bimbo serving as the latest acquisition in your brother's life-long goal to collect the most...crap. I'd call that judging someone you don't know."

Joe poured peroxide over her other foot.

"Good God, just kill me."

"Stop being dramatic," he said, setting the bottle on the porch and dabbing her foot with a corner of the towel. "And I know my brother."

"You what?" Beth asked. Chucking the yoga breathing, she started to pant.

Pulling a bandage from the kit, he squeezed gel from a yellow tube onto a small gauze square. "Hold still while I tape this on."

Between the cold gel and the pressure of the gauze, holding still became impossible. "Are you trained in torture methods or just practicing these techniques on me for fun?"

"That turtle was a better patient than you are. At least he held still."

"He was probably moving," Beth said, biting her bottom lip, "too slow to be noticed."

She'd finally gained his attention. "That might be the worst joke I've ever heard." But he smiled. His eyes dropped to her lips, the bottom one clenched between her teeth. Beth's heart beat an uncomfortable rhythm. "Bite any harder and I'll have to doctor that lip up next."

Beth licked her lips, then closed her mouth. She couldn't look away, even when he returned his attention to the task at hand. Or foot, as it were. Regardless of how much she provoked, his hands remained gentle.

"You're right," he said.

"I am?"

"I shouldn't have assumed that stuff about you." He met her eyes again. "But I had my reasons."

She leaned her head on the back of the bench. "What reasons?"

He ignored her question and asked one of his own. "Why didn't you call me on it?"

"I told you. I didn't want to embarrass you."

"Why not?"

She straightened and repositioned herself on the bench. "The reason I'm on this island is to meet Lucas's family. To make you all like me. If I'd embarrassed you before we'd even been introduced, then you might have never liked me."

His brows drew together and his eyes narrowed. "You think Lucas would change his mind if we didn't like you?"

"No. But I'm not doing this just for Lucas. I have my own reasons."

Joe applied a final piece of tape, then lowered her feet to the floor. "I wouldn't put the shoes back on. Dad should be leaving soon. He'll take you home."

Tossing the damp, bloodstained towels in the garbage can at the top of the stairs, Joe stomped down the steps and walked off into the night.

Beth didn't move. The sound of a motor turning traveled on the breeze, then tires on gravel followed by taillights fading in the distance. Something had just happened. Something she didn't understand. While part of her brain, the rational, practical side, told her not to go there, the purely feminine side sat back with a sigh.

Joe Dempsey had more layers than he wanted anyone to see. And he'd managed to peel back a couple of hers as well. *Be careful, my dear. You're walking on dangerous ground.*

CHAPTER SEVEN

Beth saw Joe briefly the next morning, and in the few seconds during which they shared the same space, he refused to make eye contact. Even when he said good morning in his gruff, grunting way, his eyes never met hers.

Lucas had left a message on the Dempseys' home phone while Beth was at the restaurant. Exhausted and edgy after a long drive followed by meetings into the night, Lucas had explained that the evidence was worse than he'd expected, which tilted the odds of winning in the prosecution's favor.

Though a selfish thought, Beth couldn't help but be more upset about what the new evidence meant for their vacation. She'd told herself throughout the day that Lucas would return. He'd come to his senses, let the rest of the team handle the case, and be back on Anchor the next night. But with one brief message he'd snuffed any hope of a quick return.

Patty had announced that morning that she'd be running over to Hatteras for her Sunday grocery expedition and asked if Beth would like to tag along. Since the trip would require riding the ferry, Beth did her best to refuse the offer as gracefully as possible. Which meant breaking out in a sweat and yelling, "No!" Something she was doing much too often on this trip.

Tom refused her help for the lunch shift, so Beth was once again left to her own devices. Though there were plenty of shops and sights to explore, the place she really wanted to be was hanging out with Lola. Which is why she was now sitting alone in the art store, making jewelry and hoping no one would try to buy anything before Lola returned.

Lola had needed to run a quick errand and after giving Beth a crash course on the antiquated register, assured her she'd be back in no time. Trusting woman, that Lola. So far on this vacation Beth had waited tables and was now holding down a brief gig in retail. She'd be irritated if she weren't actually having fun.

The tips at Dempsey's were good, and Tom had forced her to keep them. Wanting to put them back in the local economy, Beth browsed Lola's store, picking out items that spoke to her. The first had been a black-and-white patterned vase, larger than the purple one she'd purchased the day before. This one would be perfect for her living room, while the purple one would go nicely in her kitchen. According to Lola, both vases had been handblown by an artist up in Nags Head. The work was exquisite.

The second treasure was a pencil sketch of the Anchor Lighthouse. Beth had yet to see the landmark in person, but the sketch wove such light and shade into the image, she could almost hear the gulls above and the waves in the distance. She had to have it.

Her island booty, as Lola called it, wrapped and tucked safely behind the counter, Beth turned her attention to the large selection of gems and beads laid out in the far corner of the store. Worktables dotted the area so tourists could gather the pieces of their choosing and assemble them into their own unique designs.

Beth had dabbled in jewelry making during high school, but her grandmother discouraged anything that detracted from her studies. She'd surreptitiously managed to get her art supplies into her dorm room in college, but endless papers and pressure to maintain a high GPA stole her attention. Slackers didn't get accepted to law school, or so her grandmother warned often enough. She never did make another piece.

A spattering of tourists wandered around the artwork as Beth occupied a small workstation in the back corner, which afforded her a view of the entire shop. She'd chosen to make a bracelet using various shapes and sizes of beads. Shades of blue slid together, broken by the occasional silver faux pearl. As she assembled the clasp, she realized one of the stones matched the same powerful blue as Joe's eyes.

The memory of his smile filled her mind, followed closely by the steady dose of sparks his touch ignited in her system. Had she subconsciously chosen that blue on purpose?

The notes from the wind chime hanging off the front door saved Beth from pondering the question. A blonde draped in an expensive-looking black-and-white dress, espadrilles, and large Jackie O sunglasses entered the shop. Her hair was short and stylish, her nails white-tipped perfection, and Beth knew the clutch tucked beneath the customer's right arm cost more than Beth's car payment.

A sense of familiarity lingered, as if Beth had seen her somewhere before.

"Can I help you?" she said, as the woman stopped just inside the door.

"I'm looking for Lola LeBlanc." The pinched voice contained the lilt of money with the typical lack of generosity. Beth knew this kind well. They were usually married to one of the partners at the law firm.

"Lola had to step out, but she'll be back shortly. Is there something I can do for you, or would you like to wait?"

Beth slid behind the counter while doing her best impression of a servant ready to serve. The blonde glanced at her watch, and Beth noticed a ring of diamonds surrounding the tiny glass. The term *high maintenance* came to mind.

"When will she be back? I have an appointment in twenty minutes."

She'd set aside a whole twenty minutes for Lola. Must be important. Perhaps her next appointment was kidnapping puppies. "Are you here to pick up an item? If you'll give me your name, I can see if there's something in the back room for you."

"My name is Cassandra Wheeler, and what I need is to talk to Ms. LeBlanc."

Wheeler. Wheeler Development. In an instant Beth remembered where she'd seen this woman before. At the firm.

Coming out of Lucas's office.

"I—"

"Here's my card. Tell Ms. LeBlanc to call me at the hotel number written on the back. Assure her it will be worth her time to make the call."

Before Beth could say another word, Cruella left the store, subtle chimes and a touch of Chanel lingering in her wake.

Beth pursed her lips. What business could Lucas have with Cassandra Wheeler? She'd assumed the woman to be just another client on the two occasions she could remember seeing her exit his office. But Lucas didn't work on the Wheeler account.

The only connection between the two was Anchor, but Lucas would never help Wheeler buy out the island. Or would he?

Beth didn't like the disloyal thoughts running through her mind. She would ask Lucas about his meetings with Ms. Wheeler the next time they talked. There was sure to be a simple explanation. Or so she hoped.

~

A morning on the water would normally put Joe in a good mood. Perfect weather, plenty of fish, and satisfied tourists all before noon. This morning's group was so satisfied, they booked another trip out for Tuesday. But instead of riding the wave of a job well done and more business ahead, Joe couldn't stop thinking about Beth and the damn spark she'd shot through his system the night before.

Future family gatherings were going to be damned uncomfortable if he couldn't stop lusting after his little brother's wife. But then last night had been about more than lust. God help him but Joe was starting to like her. Her spunk, her laugh, her quiet strength. Even her determination to win over his family, though he didn't understand why their approval meant so much to her.

Sailing through the door of Dempsey's, Joe stumbled into a scene that pulled his focus away from his future sister-in-law.

"I've ignored Mr. Wheeler's attempts to contact me because I'm not interested in what Mr. Wheeler has to say." Joe's dad stared at a pretty boy in a suit standing across the bar. "If saying it in person is necessary, Mr. Paige, then consider this my official answer. I am not interested."

Joe grabbed a glass and poured himself a soda then leaned back on the cooler. His dad looked mad enough to turn his verbal answer into a physical one, and that would be a show worth watching.

"You're not looking at the big picture here, Mr. Dempsey. Working with Wheeler Development would be significantly more profitable than the situation you have now. Mr. Wheeler is prepared to—"

"Do you have a hearing problem, Mr. Paige?" Joe recognized imminent danger when his dad crossed his arms and started shifting from foot to foot. The suit clearly did not.

"If you'll look at the plans we've designed for the project, you'll understand the scope as well as the potential the island has to gain in this endeavor."

So Cassandra wasn't the only Wheeler representative on the island.

Tom slammed his fist on the bar before Wheeler's minion could spread out the papers he'd pulled from inside his jacket. In a low voice he snarled, "Take your plans and your potential profits and get the fuck out of my restaurant."

Joe smiled. Tom Dempsey didn't show temper often, but when he did, the results were legendary. Maybe Pretty

Boy would push a few more buttons. His dad flinging the asshole out the door would definitely send a message to Wheeler Development.

The papers disappeared back inside the suit's fancy coat as he took a step back. Pretty Boy was catching on. "You should think about this, Mr. Dempsey. Once your neighbors join in the project, Mr. Wheeler will no longer be so generous to those who make this difficult."

A direct threat. *Stick it up your ass, Pretty Boy.* Joe moved down the bar as the suit made his exit. "Guess I don't have to ask what that was about."

"Son of a bitch won't give up," Tom said, keeping his voice down. "A million other islands that bastard could go after and he picks ours."

Joe suspected Wheeler's sudden interest in Anchor had more to do with revenge than business development. Revenge on Joe. He'd put a ring on Cassandra Wheeler's finger, then backed out when she forced him to choose between her and the island.

The choice had been easy, but that didn't make him feel like less of a fool.

Cassie had a knack for manipulating her father, who would do anything to make his little girl happy. Though he couldn't prove it, Joe long suspected Cassie was behind the job offer her daddy had sent his way after they'd first broken up. Money, power, a corner office. He'd tried to buy Joe the same way he'd buy a car or a new boat. So what was buying an island to Tad "Big Money" Wheeler? Especially when that island could eventually make him a killing.

"You don't think anyone is really giving in on this, do you?" Joe said.

"The asshole is bluffing, or else the price would have dropped by now." Tom wiped down the bar. "But we have to be pissing him off if he's sending a lackey all the way down here."

Before Joe could respond, Tom dropped the rag and headed for the door.

"There's my girl," he said, throwing an arm around Beth's shoulders. "Have a seat at the bar. You're here to eat this time, not work." He glanced at Joe. "Don't just stand there, get the girl a menu."

What the hell? "I'm not here to work either."

"Then grab two menus and get your ass out from behind my bar."

Joe snagged the menus and joined Beth, leaving an empty stool between them. Without a word he slid a menu her way, then buried his face in his own as if unfamiliar with the options.

"Gee, thanks," she said, setting a cell phone on the bar between them.

"You're welcome."

The strip of denim he supposed counted as a skirt showed off more than enough leg when Beth was standing. When she perched on the bar stool the thing revealed enough thigh to threaten his physical well-being.

Shifting his weight, Joe kept his eyes above bar level.

"Is there really no place on this island I can get a cell signal?"

Joe looked up as Tom answered, "Afraid not."

"I wanted to call Lucas about something, but I guess it'll have to wait."

"You can use the phone in the kitchen."

Beth pursed her lips. Maybe she'd changed her mind about staying on Anchor without Lucas. "No, that's all right. He's probably busy anyway. I'll talk to him tonight."

"Order up!" came a voice from the kitchen.

"I'll be right back," Tom said, sliding the hot plates off the stainless-steel shelf. "The phone is always there if you want to use it."

"Thanks," she said, then turned to Joe. "What do you recommend?"

"Excuse me?" Joe asked. Did she really want his opinion on whether to use the phone? Or worse, if she should stay on the island?

"From the menu. What do you recommend?" She flashed him those big green eyes and his mind went blank.

"I don't know. Order whatever you want." He hid behind his menu again, considering putting his order in to go.

"Is it so horrible to have to talk to me?" The hurt in her voice made him feel like more of an ass. Why couldn't she be mad? He could handle mad.

Joe kept his eyes on the menu and considered his answer. "I told you once, I'm not much of a talker. You want to know something just ask me."

"I did."

"You did what?"

"Just ask you."

"Well, I don't know what you like." The more he defended himself the more he felt like he was losing an argument he hadn't seen coming. "How am I supposed to tell you what to eat when I don't know anything about you?"

"You'd know something about me if you stopped walking away."

Such a woman thing to say. "What are you all wound up about? And don't tell me it's because I didn't recommend you order the hamburger."

"You're right, it's not. We were almost cordial to each other last night, and today you go back to acting like I have some kind of…cooties."

"Did you just say 'cooties'?"

Beth rolled her eyes. "Oh my gosh, you know what I mean. Why don't you like me?"

"I never said I don't like you." Life would sure as hell be easier if he didn't. "And why is it so damn important that people like you?"

She looked as if he'd asked her how to get from Anchor to Mars in a rowboat. "Because…it just is. Don't you want people to like you?"

As long as he was left alone, Joe didn't give two shits who liked him. "No."

"You're lying," Beth said, turning to face him.

"I am not. If I was going to lie, I'd tell you what you want to hear so you'd like me." He wasn't sure where that defense came from, but felt impressed he'd thought of it.

The green eyes narrowed as she tapped one finger on the menu sitting in front of her. "You're totally serious."

"Yep."

"This explains a lot, actually." She opened her menu as if trying to pretend she didn't care whether he liked her or not, but he could tell from her voice she still did. "I was just hoping that if I was going to be part of the family we might get along. Never mind."

Now she really thought he didn't like her. Part of his brain told him to let her believe it. But the other half, the one that was clearly insane, made him feel as if he'd just kicked a puppy. Twice.

"Fine."

"Fine what?" Beth asked.

"I like you just fine." Admitting it wasn't nearly as difficult as it should have been, and "fine" was an understatement, but she didn't need to know that. "I have another charter to run this afternoon, but I'm off tomorrow. You want to see more of the island?"

He'd officially lost his mind.

She blinked as if he'd thrown sand in her eyes. Then she glanced behind him, leaning out far enough to teeter on her stool.

"What are you doing?" he asked.

"Looking for the gun being held to your back."

"Nobody likes a smart-ass. If you don't want to go, say so." It wasn't as if playing tour guide would be a treat for him. "But don't say I didn't offer."

"No, no. You're right. You're being nice and I shouldn't give you a hard time." Beth shot him a genuine smile that lit up her face and did unwelcome things to his solar plexus. "But you can't blame me for being unfamiliar with the kinder, gentler Joe. I've seen so little of him."

That had to be the nicest way anyone had ever called him an asshole. "I did save you from Sid last night. And bandaged your blisters when you were less than cooperative."

She opened her mouth, presumably to argue, but he didn't give her the chance. "That's probably the nicest thing I've done in at least six months."

Beth laughed and Joe couldn't help but chuckle with her. The feeling was unfamiliar but not unpleasant.

"I bought a sketch of the lighthouse at Lola's shop today. I'd love to see the real thing. Could you drive me over there tomorrow? I promise to be on my best behavior." She scooted onto the bar stool between them, brushing her thigh against his then jerking away. The smile left her face.

Damn sparks.

"I'll take you. You interested in seeing the wild horses, too? They're too far up the island to walk so we might as well go while we're driving around." He needed his head examined. Or his other head put to sleep. Before tomorrow.

"I'd like that." Her smile returned, more tentative than before. "Thanks, Joe. I was hoping we could be friends."

"Right. Friends. We can do that." Provided she didn't touch him. Or until he gave up and threw himself off the pier.

CHAPTER EIGHT

Between the zing every time they touched and that lethal dimple, winning over her future brother-in-law was starting to feel like working on a mob case. Dangerous to her well-being. So there was a physical attraction. Not the end of the world. It wasn't as if she liked anything about him. The man was opinionated, cranky, and obtuse.

But when his face softened, and he let his guard down, she seemed to forget his faults. Spending time with Joe was like walking too close to the edge of a cliff. One wrong step and she could fall. No. She couldn't think like that. There was nothing wrong with liking her brother-in-law. In a friendly sort of way. They were going to be family when she married Lucas. They should be friends.

After an amicable if mostly silent lunch, Beth had watched Joe drive off for an afternoon on the water, the thought of which made her queasy, then rode home with Patty, who'd returned from her grocery shopping.

"The last of the meat is wrapped and in the freezer," Patty said, joining Beth on the porch.

"I wish you'd have let me help."

"You've done enough work already. This is supposed to be your vacation, not a summer internship." Patty set a tall glass of iced tea on the table next to Beth then dropped into an empty Adirondack chair. "How was your morning?"

"Good. I went to see Lola again, and I made this bracelet." Beth held up her right wrist.

"That's beautiful," Patty said, spinning the piece. "That blue one there looks just like Joe's eyes."

Beth dropped her arm. "You think? I hadn't noticed." Picking up her iced tea, she breached the subject of Cruella. "A woman came into the store today while Lola was out running an errand."

"For Lola's sake, I hope more than one woman came in."

"Of course, but this wasn't your usual tourist looking for a high-end souvenir. Her name was Cassandra Wheeler."

Patty nearly poured her own iced tea into her lap. "Cassie is on the island?"

"You know her?" Beth asked.

"Oh, we know Cassie Wheeler. Though Joe knows her better than anyone else."

"Joe?" Since Cassandra matched the description of the fiancée Joe expected Lucas to bring home, and he'd made it clear the "blonde bimbo" wouldn't be welcome, Beth assumed the Wheeler woman would be no friend of Joe's.

"She was his fiancée."

If Beth had been taking a drink, Patty would have gotten a face full. "Joe was engaged to Cruella de Vil?"

Patty laughed. "She does have that air about her, doesn't she? They met a couple years ago when Cassie spent the summer working for the parks department."

"But isn't her father Tad Wheeler?" Picturing Miss Hoity-Toity doing menial labor did not compute.

"He is, but how do you know that?"

Beth scrambled for an answer. Lying to her future mother-in-law twice in as many days had to be bad. But she couldn't mention Cassandra's meetings with Lucas. Not before she'd talked to him about them. "Her business card said Wheeler Development, and I put two and two together."

"That makes sense." Beth exhaled as Patty went on. "But he wasn't always wealthy, and he decided his daughter needed to understand what it meant to do real work. Of course, he paid for her to live in one of the nicest cabins on the island, and made sure she had all the money she needed." Patty crossed her arms. "Not exactly character-building circumstances."

This still didn't make sense. "What was Joe doing with someone like her?"

"For one, she's gorgeous, as I'm sure you noticed. They would have made beautiful babies." Patty got a faraway look and Beth felt nauseous. "I'm also guessing Joe was the kind of guy who would drive her daddy nuts. He likely wanted her to marry a doctor or a lawyer, which is another reason she picked Joe instead of Lucas."

"She knows Lucas, too?" A loaded question since Beth had seen the woman come out of Lucas's office on at least two occasions in the last month.

"He met her briefly the one time he came home during that summer. Lucas is married to his work, so he wasn't here long." Patty seemed to realize what she'd said. "I mean—"

"It's okay," Beth said. "I know how much time Lucas spends at work. He's determined to be the youngest partner the firm has ever had, and that requires sacrifices." He'd given her the "sacrifices" speech so often, Beth could quote it verbatim.

"Once you're married, I'm sure that will change."

Beth was under no such illusions, so she swung the topic back to Joe the hypocrite. "What happened with Joe and this Wheeler woman? Why aren't they married?"

Patty shrugged. "No one knows. He went to visit her in Richmond, and when he came back, he just said it didn't work out. Less than a week later the ring arrived in the mail." No surprise Cassandra Wheeler wasn't the sentimental type. "As far as I know, Cassie hasn't been back to the island since, which is why I was so surprised when you mentioned her."

"I'm pretty sure she's not here on vacation. She looked ready to storm a boardroom this afternoon." And then steal a litter of puppies for her fur coat.

"I wonder if Joe knows she's here. I don't think we'll see him tonight, since he asked me to feed Dozer for him." Patty tapped a finger on the arm of her chair. "Maybe I should leave him a note."

"He's driving me around the island tomorrow," Beth said, attempting not to grind her teeth. "I'll make sure I tell him first thing in the morning."

"He's driving you around the island?" Patty looked as surprised as Beth had felt when Joe made the offer. "Did Tom tell him to do that?"

"I don't think so. He offered during lunch today." How she'd jumped at the chance to get to know Lucas's mysterious brother and win his approval. Now she longed to tell him where he could stick his approval.

"Amazing." Patty leaned back and crossed her arms again. "He's just full of surprises these days."

"He's full of something," Beth said, relieved when her fiancé's mother smiled.

~

Joe parked the Jeep between his house and his parents' place, then noticed his gas gauge floating close to E. They'd have to get gas in the morning.

They. Shit.

He'd been waging a war in his head since leaving Beth at Dempsey's. As if getting distance from the source of the sparks would allow his brain to function again.

What in the hell was he thinking?

Stepping from the Jeep, Joe heard Dozer's dog tags rattle from the porch. He should have been in the house, not outside.

"Dozer?"

"I've got him," came Tom's voice out of the dark.

"Dad?"

"Who else would it be?"

"I don't know," Joe said, climbing the stairs. "People don't usually hover in the dark on my porch." Dozer stood up, tail wagging, and Joe scratched around his ears. "Hey, boy."

"Sit down," Tom said. "We need to talk."

"That statement is never good." Joe slid into one of the large white rockers he preferred to Patty's colorful Adirondack collection. "What did I do now?"

"Nothing. Yet." Tom hesitated as if buying time. Joe hoped this wouldn't take long. He needed a hot shower and a cold Bud. "Patty says you're taking Elizabeth sightseeing tomorrow."

"I offered, sure." The Bud changed to a shot of Jack. "What about it?"

"You called her Beth last night. I saw the way you looked at her today." Leave it to Tom Dempsey not to pussyfoot around an issue.

Joe ran his hands over his face. "She told me the first night she was here she preferred Beth. So that's what I call her. Ask her if you don't believe me."

"What about today?"

"What about it? We had lunch. You were there."

"And I saw how you looked at her," Tom repeated. "She's a great girl, I get that. But she's your brother's fiancée."

"Trust me, I know. Whatever you think you saw, it's nothing." Maybe he should save everyone some time and jump off the pier now. "I'm calling it a night."

Joe stood up and Tom followed suit. "Just be careful. That's all I'm asking."

"Got it." He watched his dad walk down the steps then stopped him at the bottom. "Hey. Did you tell Patty about this?"

Tom held out his hands. "Nothing to tell, right?"

"Right." Joe ran a hand through his hair. "Just checking. I don't want her saying anything. You know."

"Yeah," Tom smiled in the moonlight. "I know." Then with one word, he summed up the situation. "Women."

"Exactly," Joe agreed.

⌇

The next morning, Joe found Beth waiting on his parents' porch. Dozer reached her first, receiving a chin scratch as a greeting. One leg thumped the floorboards in canine bliss, and Joe ignored the spike of jealousy.

"You ready to go?"

She turned and smiled, though something in her eyes looked…different. Like a woman with a plan. Not the most comforting look in the world. "Ready when you are." She gave Dozer one last scratch, then hopped out of her chair.

A short white skirt that looked as if it should have been a tube top hugged her hips. Joe's mouth went dry. The simple V-neck T-shirt was a sea-foam green, which brought out her eyes.

"Dozer's coming too, right?" she asked, with the dog following her as if in a trance. So much for loyalty. Damn dog.

"Yeah, he's coming." Joe opened his Jeep door. "Get in, Dozer."

The dog continued to sit next to Beth, tongue lolling to the side. Beth gave Joe another smile. "I think he's with me." She opened the door on her side and the dog jumped in without being told.

"Keep it up, buddy. Keep it up." Joe climbed in as Beth clicked her seat belt on. "That treat jar can disappear real quick."

Beth reached up and scratched under the canine's chin once more. "Don't you worry, Dozer. I'll give you treats."

"You don't even know where they are."

She looked toward his little cottage and shrugged. "It's not a big place. They can't be hard to find."

"Let me guess, along with waiting tables, you did breaking and entering to work your way through college?"

She raised one brow. "There's a key inside your parents' kitchen door."

"Spoken like a true criminal." Joe dropped the Jeep into reverse and threw gravel as he backed onto the street. "First stop, gas. Then the lighthouse."

And then the horses and his obligation was done. The sooner he got this over with, the better.

"So I met a friend of yours yesterday," Beth said.

He knew everyone on the island, so she'd have to be more specific. "Who was that?"

"A woman," she answered.

"Can you narrow that down? I know a lot of women."

"A lot of women?"

"Did Patty put you up to finding out about my love life or something?"

Beth picked invisible lint off her skirt, drawing his attention to more exposed thigh than he needed to see. The Jeep swerved, throwing Dozer off balance.

"What was that?" she asked, reaching back to steady the dog.

"Squirrel." Seemed like a good answer. "About all these questions?"

"Nothing to do with Patty, though she's the one who enlightened me about the—how shall I describe her?" She tapped her chin, feigning deep thought. "I know. A tight-assed blonde bimbo. And though I didn't actually look out-side, I'll bet she was driving a fancy car."

Shit almighty.

"I'm sure she was." He looked over to see the sweet smile had disappeared. "Where did you meet Cassie?"

Beth ignored the question. "You were engaged to exactly the kind of woman you assumed I'd be that day on the ferry. You insulted me and your brother with the same stereotype that you almost married."

"When you put it that way…"

"Wait." She turned as far as the seat belt would allow. "You're not surprised to know she's on the island. You knew she was here."

"She paid me a visit at the dock on Saturday."

"How nice." She flopped back around to face forward. "I'm sure you had a great time catching up. I hope you dis-cussed what a hypocrite you are."

"Look, I'm sorry. It's not like you said, 'Hi, my name is Elizabeth and I'm your brother's fiancée.'"

She turned again. At this rate she'd have rope burn from the seat belt before they reached the gas station. "I didn't even know who you were. And I told you, after you gave the oh-so-complimentary description of what you expected me to look like, I didn't think it was a good idea to introduce myself as the person you'd just insulted."

"Amazing."

"Wha…what?"

"You don't have a problem calling me out on shit right now. And you didn't mind hurling insults at me while I was taking care of your blisters. So forgive me if this 'I didn't want to embarrass you' thing isn't working for me."

"Because. Well. I just don't do that."

"Really?" he snorted. "You could have fooled me."

"I'm not rude, unlike some people we know."

Joe pulled the Jeep off the road. "I didn't sign up for this. I've apologized for making assumptions. I would apologize for the woman I nearly married, but I don't see how that's anything to you. And trust me when I say I've more than paid for that mistake."

Beth's mouth resembled a fish gulping for air, while Dozer whined in the backseat.

"It's okay boy," Joe said. "Are we going to do this or am I taking you back to the house?"

"You can't back out now."

"I can if you're going to chew my ass all day. What are you so pissed off about, anyway?"

"She's just…" Beth crossed her arms. "You were engaged to Cruella de Vil."

Now she'd lost him. "I was what?"

"You work on a fishing boat. You wear"—her hand gestured up and down in front of his chest—"khaki shorts and old flannel. You drive a Jeep." She pointed to Dozer. "You even own a giant mutt. What would a guy like you be doing with, well, a tight-assed blonde bimbo?"

In two years he hadn't been able to answer that question. "Hell if I know." Then he turned to face her. "You're smart. Or seem to be. You wait tables like a professional, so you know what work is. You like my dog, so you have taste. What are you doing with a self-absorbed, overly ambitious workaholic?"

"How can you say that about your own brother?"

"Because it's true." Joe looked out over the water. "I love my brother, but that doesn't mean I understand him. He's running after something, and you don't look like the run-alongside type. You look more like the type to get run over."

"Lucas is sweet and generous, and he loves me." She waited until he met her eyes again. "And there's nothing wrong with being ambitious."

"Nothing wrong with it at all," he said, adjusting his mirror. "So long as you keep your priorities straight."

"And what makes you think Lucas doesn't have his priorities straight?"

He turned to meet her eyes. "He's not here, is he?"

Beth clamped her mouth shut, causing a muscle below her left ear to twitch. Breaking eye contact, she faced forward and crossed her arms. "You don't understand."

"You're right, I don't."

The look on her face told him he'd hit a nerve. Possibly one she'd been ignoring. "You ready to do the tourist thing?"

She glared at him once more then dropped her hands into her lap. "Let's go see a lighthouse."

CHAPTER NINE

Beth argued with Joe while he filled the gas tank on the Jeep and continued all the way to their destination. On the inside. On the outside she remained quiet and calm. Which meant the argument wasn't really with Joe. It was with herself.

Why isn't Lucas here?

You know he had to go back for that case. His work is important.

So are we. We're important. When are we going to come before the job?

We are important, and Lucas shows us all the time. He's sweet and generous and takes good care of us.

What are we, four years old? We don't need to be taken care of. We need to come first. Who cares if he makes partner?

Lucas cares, and that means we care now, damn it. We are not going to think bad thoughts about Lucas when he's not here to defend himself.

He's never here and he never asks what we're thinking, so what's the difference?

"That's enough." Beth didn't realize she'd said the words aloud until Joe hit the brake, jerking them all forward.

"What's enough?"

Stupid brain. Now look what you've done.

"Nothing. Sorry. I was thinking about something else." Focusing on the distance, Beth realized she could see the top half of the lighthouse rising up behind a row of trees. "Are we here?"

Joe undid his seat belt. "We're here."

Beth turned to unhook herself and caught the view of Joe's khaki shorts pulled tight over his butt as he climbed out of the Jeep. No guy with a butt that good should wear baggy pants.

We are not looking at Joe's ass.

What? It's a really nice ass.

"Are you getting out?"

Beth jumped in her seat when Dozer stuck a damp nose against her ear. "Yes. Of course," she said, wiping her ear on her shoulder. Joe opened her door, giving plenty of room for her to hop out without the threat of bodily contact. At least they were on the same page with that aspect of the day.

Joe headed around the back of the vehicle to what looked to be a long, railed pier on land. Following behind, in an effort not to focus on Joe's stellar butt, Beth worked up a mental picture of Lucas's butt in his dress pants. She'd always liked a man in a suit, and Lucas always looked good in his. Which made sense since he spent a great deal of money making sure they were perfectly tailored.

So what if Lucas wasn't there? So what if Joe seemed to know where Lucas should be when Lucas didn't?

No. Lucas needed to be in Richmond, and she would not fault him for that. His dedication and ambition were two qualities she loved about him. But there was more to her fiancé. He protected her, taking command of any situation. No need to stress about how to handle things or what choices to make, because Lucas handled everything. No worries. No questions. No doubts. No one pushing her out of her comfort zone.

Your comfort zone is boring.

Shut up.

Moving her eyes higher, Beth also noticed Joe had really broad shoulders. Solid. Wide. Lucas's shoulders weren't quite so broad, but he was leaner than Joe. Not that she was comparing the two. Though broad shoulders were nice to hold on to.

Okay. Time to find a new focus. Which was easy with a majestic white tower standing less than fifty yards before her. The lighthouse was wide at the base and tapered to a narrow top, upon which sat a small glass enclosure. A black railing wrapped around the top, creating what must be an amazing observation deck.

Made of whitewashed bricks, broken only by a small window near the bottom and another midway up, the structure looked to be taller than the five-story office building in which she worked back in Richmond. Even from a distance, Beth had to tip her head back to see to the top.

"Can we go up there?"

"Nope, no climbing."

"Why not?" she asked.

Joe held his hands up in the international sign for innocence. "Don't look at me. The Park Service deemed it unsafe years ago. During the season you can check out the base, but that's not for two more weeks. You'll be gone by the time they open to tourists."

Beth tilted her head back again and watched a pair of seagulls perform a flying dance around the point. Beth never imagined she'd envy a couple of seagulls, but in that moment she did.

Joe walked on, leaving her staring like a gaping tourist. She hurried to catch up. "Does the light still work?"

"It does, but it's not the spinning light you're probably thinking of. This one gives off a steady beam you can see about fourteen miles out."

The closer they walked, the more difficult it became to look up and keep her balance at the same time. But she couldn't take her eyes off the brick structure. Other than a brief glance at what she believed to be the Cape Hatteras Lighthouse the day she drove down, she'd never seen a lighthouse in person before.

The artist responsible for the pencil sketch she'd bought from Lola had done a beautiful job capturing the details of the brick and stone and small outbuildings. But a picture couldn't compare to the real thing. To see buildings this tall in a city packed with skyscrapers felt natural. A structure this high and solid standing guard on a tiny island held more wonder. As if God himself had planted the tower in this spot.

"When was it built?" she asked Joe, further breaking her promise not to act like a tourist.

"The original one was just a pole, and it stood on a different spot. That was in the 1700s. The shifting of the channel kept making the light obsolete, forcing the early settlers to relocate it several times." Joe gave her a gentle nudge to the right, saving her from tripping over an unnoticed branch. "One of them was struck by lightning, but I can't remember when. This one went up in the early 1820s."

"Amazing. I'm not sure which is more fascinating, the lighthouse itself or the history behind it." Beth imagined the generations of sailors, not to mention pirates, who must have used this beacon to safely reach land. For some odd reason, strolling the same ground as pirates gave her an unexpected thrill.

"You like history?" Joe asked, sounding slightly less bored.

"Love it," she said. "My favorite field trips in school were our yearly treks to Jamestown and Williamsburg."

"Did you grow up in Richmond?"

Beth hadn't intended the conversation to become about her. Even Lucas didn't know the details of her early years. Mostly because he'd never asked, but she'd also never volunteered the information. She'd tell her fiancé. Someday. Didn't mean she had to tell his brother.

"Around there. Do you use this light to navigate when you're out on the water?"

If he caught her deflection, Joe didn't mention it. "Nah. We've got modern navigation equipment. We don't need the lighthouse anymore."

"Oh." Beth realized Joe was smiling with the effort not to laugh at her question. Which was a pretty stupid question now that she thought about it. She couldn't help but smile back.

~

If Beth shot him any more of those smiles, Joe was going to have to end the tour and head home for a cold shower. Not that the woman could ever look hard, and she wasn't very good at angry either, but when she smiled like that, like she actually liked him, her face softened and her eyes glowed like lightning bugs dancing over the water on a warm spring night.

Good God. He'd just compared her eyes to lightning bugs. Next he'd be writing love notes and drawing little hearts over the *i*'s.

Giving Beth distance to explore what felt like his own backyard, Joe pondered his brother's catch. The woman continued to destroy every assumption he'd made about the kind of woman who would marry Lucas. An interest in history usually meant an interest in people more than things.

A woman attracted to Lucas should have been more interested in shopping and getting off the island as soon as possible. Beth ignored the shops, except Lola's, as far as he knew, and had yet to give an excuse for why she should head back to Richmond. Something she could have easily done with Lucas gone.

If he didn't know better, Joe would say Beth liked Anchor Island. Which made no sense at all, so he ignored the thought. But what he couldn't ignore was Beth's unwillingness to talk about herself. His question about where she grew up seemed simple enough, but she'd changed the subject faster than a bluefin hitting fresh bait.

What didn't she want him to know? And was she keeping the same details from Lucas?

Asking Lucas what he knew about his fiancée wasn't an option. Asking Patty what she'd learned would send up more red flags with his dad. Joe would have to dig for answers another way.

"I think I've gotten all the pictures I wanted," she said, sliding her cell phone into her pocket. "The horses are next?"

"The horses are next." Joe reached for the small of her back as they moved toward the parking area, then realized what he was doing and shoved his hands in his pockets. "I'll warn you now, if Chuck isn't working, we'll be stuck on the small observation deck like the other tourists."

"Who is Chuck?" she asked as she climbed in behind Dozer.

"Chuck Brighteyes works with the horses. His ancestors go back to before the colonists landed around Roanoke Island."

"Is that where the Lost Colony was? I saw that in one of the flyers Patty gave me."

"They call it the Lost Colony, but they were never lost; they simply moved before others came back for them." Joe made a right onto Highway 12. "The myth keeps the tourists coming, but like most of history, it's twisted for modern-day purposes."

"I'd still love to go see it," Beth said, sighing like a teenager talking about the latest heartthrob. "I can't imagine doing what those colonists did. Leaving their homes and all they knew to move to a primitive, unknown world."

Her words brought back a memory of the day Cassie had handed him an ultimatum. With a mocking laugh, she'd declared she'd rather die than live on his primitive island.

Since he'd rather die than live without it, the end of the engagement was an inevitable next step.

"They had their reasons. Besides, primitive just means simple. I, for one, prefer simple." Joe could feel Beth looking at him, but kept his eyes on the road.

"I didn't mean it as a bad thing. I just think they were brave for doing it."

"Yeah, they were."

Silence fell over the Jeep for the rest of the short drive up the island. Joe went back to figuring out how he'd get Beth to talk about her past. Like when coaxing an animal to cooperate, he'd need to gain her trust. But that would mean spending more time together. Not the most comforting thought.

Then he got a better idea. Sic Sid on her. Girl talk wasn't Sid's forte, and since she already didn't like Beth, convincing her to play friendly wouldn't be easy. But, if she understood she was doing it for Lucas, she'd go along.

Sid could find out what Beth was hiding, then if there was anything Lucas needed to know, Joe would tell him. A man deserved to know who he was marrying before getting to the end of that aisle. However Joe felt about Cassie, at least she'd revealed her true bitch nature before he found himself shackled for life. For that he'd be forever grateful.

Pulling onto the dirt road next to the horse pens, Joe knew the absence of trucks parked by the barns meant no getting past the gate. "We're not getting close to the horses today. At least not this morning."

"Your friend isn't working?" Beth asked, straining to see over the pen walls. "Can I still see the horses?"

"Sure," Joe said, pointing toward the raised deck to the right, "you can climb up there and take all the pictures you want. Just let me park in the lot across the highway so I don't block the gate."

As soon as he killed the engine, Beth's feet were on the ground. At the back of the vehicle she turned to Joe, still sitting behind the wheel.

"Are you coming?"

"I'll stay here with Doze. You go on over."

"Oh. All right then."

Joe took a seat on the back gate of the Jeep and barely noticed Dozer panting in his ear. Beth's white skirt, what there was of it, swung from side to side, then tightened across her ass as she climbed onto the platform. So much for thinking distance would put his body back in check.

"She's hiding something all right. But she's not hiding it in that skirt."

Dozer barked.

"Right. Eyes off the skirt. Got it."

~

Beth snapped pictures with her cell phone as the horses grazed and snorted, oblivious to her presence. She could feel Joe watching her, which made her body tingle in places she shouldn't be tingling. She'd turned once, and instead of pretending he wasn't looking, Joe waved. Dozer raised a paw and did the same.

She could get used to having these two in her life.

Not that they'd be in her life once she went back to Richmond. Her chest tightened at the thought, so she focused harder on the horses. The term *wild* had led her to think they'd be running across a wide, open field, manes flying in the wind, basking in their freedom.

Instead they were in a pen, or what looked to be a series of pens, with little room for running. What was the good of being wild when they couldn't be free? The questions related to her own life as much as to the horses' lives. Even with the fences gone, after her grandparents had passed and were hopefully enjoying the afterlife, Beth continued being what they wanted her to be.

Beth shoved down the threatening resentment and headed back to the Jeep. Her grandparents had scrimped and saved to send her to college, and she owed them for those sacrifices. Other than thanking Joe for showing her around, she didn't say much on the way back to town. Until Joe parked in front of Dempsey's.

"What are we doing here?"

Joe shrugged. "Patty told me to drop you off when we were done. She and Dad are both working, and she didn't want you left at the house alone."

Beth ignored the trace of disappointment that Joe wasn't stopping for lunch. He'd promised to show her the lighthouse and the horses, not spend the whole day with her.

"Dozer needs water, so I'll take him back by the kitchen door, but you go ahead." At the mention of his name, the mutt squeezed himself between the seats and drooled on Beth's shoulder.

"Yes, that's you," Joe said. "Let's go, bud."

Beth followed the pair onto the deck that ran across the front and down the side of the restaurant. As Joe and Dozer reached the top step, the dog froze, emitting a growl that vibrated the boards beneath her feet.

Finding the source of his agitation was easy enough. Between the step and the entrance stood Cassandra Wheeler, shooting Dozer a look that said she'd be wearing him by winter.

CHAPTER TEN

"Easy, Doze," said Joe. The dog grew quiet, his body still ready to pounce.

Beth climbed the last two steps to take the spot on the other side of Dozer, but when she did, the dog moved in front of her as if protecting her from the dangerous blonde. Joe said his name again and the dog sat, never looking away from Cassie.

"I see all your heathen creatures are still the same," Cassandra taunted, looking unamused. "You really should learn to keep them on leashes."

Beth didn't think Joe had other pets, so she had no idea what that comment was about.

Then Cassie looked at her. "You look familiar. Who are you?"

"This is—" Joe started, but Beth interrupted him.

"I was working at Lola's store when you came in to see her. You left your business card with me."

"That's right. She hasn't called me yet either." Cassie tucked a clutch under one arm and stuck a hand on her hip. "Did you give her my message?"

"I did." No need to admit Lola threw the card in the garbage. "I can see you're on your way out. Don't let us stop you." Beth stepped to the right, forcing Dozer and Joe to do the same.

Cassandra narrowed her eyes, clearly not missing Beth's dismissal. "My offer still stands, Joe. Call me when you're ready to talk."

Beth could have won an Oscar for her casual response to Cassie's words. Cruella must have assumed that she and Joe were together, hence landing a parting shot. Dozer continued the growl as Cassie passed by, putting as much distance between herself and the mutt as possible. For a moment Beth imagined Dozer chewing one of Cassie's expensive heels. Drool would do a number on that silk skirt, too.

"Let's go, Dozer," Joe said as Beth watched Cassie climb into a Mercedes. "What was that all about?" he asked.

She doubted Joe was talking to Dozer, so she turned around. "What was what about?"

"You stopped me from introducing you as Lucas's fiancée. Why?"

Beth had actually been saving him from mentioning where she worked. The last thing she needed was Cassie knowing a rep from her daddy's law firm was on the island. One call and Beth could be forced to become one of Cassie's minions.

She also had yet to ask Lucas why Cassandra Wheeler had been in his office. Until she knew for sure, she wasn't about to tell his family about the connection. If Lucas was helping the Wheelers, the Dempseys would be devastated.

"I was just telling her where she'd seen me before. I didn't mean to interrupt you." Joe didn't look convinced.

"Weren't you getting Dozer some water? He looks like he needs it." On cue, the dog plopped down on his stomach, tongue lolling to the side. "I'll see you inside."

Before Joe could respond, Beth slipped through the door into the rush of a busy lunch hour.

"I thought the crowds came after Memorial Day," she said to Tom as she slid onto a bar stool.

"That's how it used to be," he said, reaching for a glass behind him. "Seems the season starts earlier every year."

"Do you need my help?"

"Nah. Daisy is back, and Annie is working the back section. They can handle it." He set the glass of soda next to two others already waiting on the bar. "Where's Joe? I thought he was with you?"

"He's getting Dozer water. We ran into Cassandra Wheeler on the way in."

Tom hesitated and looked up from filling a draft. "How did that go?"

"Dozer doesn't like her much, does he? I've never heard him growl like that."

Tom chuckled. "He never did like Cassie. I'm pretty sure the feeling was mutual. Goes to show, animals are a better judge of character than people are."

"I admit, I agree with Dozer."

"You agree with Dozer about what?" Joe asked, taking a seat two stools down.

"She's saying she doesn't think much of your ex-fiancée." Tom threw his trusty white bar rag over his shoulder. "I think we'd both agree Lucas did a better job in that area than you did."

The two men exchanged a look Beth didn't understand, but Joe didn't confirm or deny Tom's statement. "What was she doing in here? She wasn't giving you the Wheeler bullshit again, was she?"

"No. She was having lunch with Phil Mohler. The man was drooling on himself sitting across from her." Tom slid a glass of iced tea in front of Beth and passed a soda to Joe. "I don't know what she wanted with him. Other than his house, he doesn't own property on the island."

"She's probably looking to recruit locals. Mohler is dumb enough to be the perfect pawn."

"What exactly does this developer want to do with the island?" Beth asked, trying to figure out why Tad Wheeler—the man who practically coined the phrase *Go big or go home*—would set his sights on such a small, remote island.

"The initial offer came with a design plan that showed the island as one giant resort," Tom said. "Nearly all the homes and business would be leveled to make way for the main lodging, a pool, a spa, and various other Vegas-style services all tied to the property."

"That's awful!" she exclaimed. This beautiful, tranquil island being turned into a shallow, characterless resort was unthinkable. And exactly what she'd expect from Tad Wheeler. "But what do you mean 'pawn'?" Beth asked. "If this Mohler person doesn't own a business with land, how can he help her?"

"The Merchants Society," the men said in stereo.

"Someone needs to elaborate on that one." Beth took a drink of her iced tea, trying not to sound too interested.

"We don't have a mayor or a formal government on this island," Tom said, "but we do have a Merchants Society so we can work together on promotion, marketing, festival planning. That sort of thing."

"I've got two orders down here, Tom," yelled a pretty redhead from the far end of the bar.

"I'll be right back."

Beth watched her future father-in-law walk away, then turned to Joe. "What does Mohler have to do with the Merchants Society?"

"Are you really interested?" he asked. "This small-town stuff must be boring to a big-city lawyer."

"I'm far from a big-city lawyer," Beth said, tapping the side of her glass. "I do research for the lawyers who try cases. And Richmond isn't exactly New York City."

"You don't like it up there?"

"I didn't say that. But I like this island and I don't want to see you guys lose it."

She must have said the magic words, because Joe visibly relaxed. "We know Wheeler is courting the merchants on the island. So far, we've all agreed to hold our ground, but his offers keep going up while the money coming in isn't what it used to be. The season starts earlier, but the crowds aren't the same."

"I'm still not seeing how Mohler can help her."

"He's an ass, but he's a native. That means other natives will listen to him. If he sells his measly property and plays this up as a good thing, the ones who are wavering might take the deal." Joe downed half his soda, then wiped his upper lip. "That could create a domino effect. It's hard to know for sure."

"Let me get this straight. You've all held out against Wheeler Development for months, but you think this one guy, whom you declare an ass, could sway them to change their minds?"

"Not by himself, but he's a talker. He could find some allies to start working on the rest."

Beth took a moment to assess the situation. If talking up Tad Wheeler and his island-leveling plan could make a difference, then so could talking it down.

"Does this society have regular meetings?" she asked.

"We do."

"When is the next one?"

"Friday, why?"

"Then that's when we launch Operation Save Anchor." Beth wished she had her notebook and pen. "Is there any paper around here?" She stood up on the cross legs of her stool to look over the bar.

"Wait a minute. What are you talking about?" Joe grabbed her stool as it teetered forward. "Sit down before you break something. No one is launching anything."

Beth plopped back onto her seat. "We have to. Don't you see?"

"What I see is a crazy woman talking in circles about something she has nothing to do with."

"Hey. My last name is going to be Dempsey. That means I have plenty to do with this." The plan would go nowhere without Joe on board. "If something happens to your parents, does this place go to you and Lucas?"

"That's a morbid question."

"Does it?"

"Sure."

"Then this is my fight, too." Beth stood up again, looking for paper.

"Sit your ass down. I'll get the damn paper." Joe walked around the bar and pulled a steno pad and pen out of the drawer beneath the cash register. "Here," he said, sliding it toward her.

Beth flipped the cover around to the back. "We need to figure out who we can count on for support. I know Lola for sure. I'm guessing your Sid person will side with you." Excitement had the pen flying across the page. For the first time since driving onto the ferry, Beth felt in her element.

"She's not my Sid person, but yeah, you can count on her. And her brother."

Beth's hand slipped, sending a line of black ink down the pad. "Sid has a brother?"

"Why is that a surprise? You need to give Sid a break. Get to know her some." Joe returned to his bar stool. "You should have one of those girls-night-out things. Or whatever you call 'em."

"You want me to have a girls' night out with Sid?" Oh, to be a fly on the wall when he suggested this to the female terror in question. "She'd club me with a pool cue and throw me in the ocean. Which is probably her idea of a good time."

"She's not that bad. Are you afraid to sit next to her in a bar?" Joe raised one brow in challenge.

"If you mean afraid of a right cross, then yes." Beth felt as much as saw Joe's eyes slide down to her breasts, and realized the fear of bodily harm was not what he meant. She crossed her arms to cut off his view and hide her body's unexpected reaction.

The girls were practically basking in the attention.

"Are you insinuating that I'm not as attractive as Sid?" Beth knew her body didn't hold a candle to Sid's, but that didn't mean she wanted the fact confirmed by a man.

"No. I'd say you're hotter."

~

Shit.

Green eyes wide, Beth stared at Joe in stunned silence as a pretty shade of pink traveled up her long, slender neck. "I...uh...well...You really think I'm hotter?" she asked.

Where the fuck did he go from here?

"Not that I think Sid is hot to begin with, but..." The look on her face told him this was not the right response. "I mean, you dress more like a girl and..." Her eyes narrowed. Where was a shovel when he needed one?

"What are you guys doing?" asked Patty from behind the bar.

"Nothing," they said in unison, both turning back to face her. Joe kept his eyes on his drink, resisting the urge to press the cold glass to his forehead.

"Am I interrupting something?" Patty asked.

"No," Beth said, clicking the pen like a hyper squirrel with a nervous tic. "Maybe you could help us."

Holy shit, if she asked Patty to clear up the "Who is hotter?" question, he was making a break for the door.

"Help with what?" Patty said. Then she tapped the legal pad. "Are we making a guest list for the wedding?"

Nothing like a subtle reminder from the universe. A quick glance to his right revealed Beth gnawing on her bottom lip. Was that a look of guilt on her face?

"No, I guess I haven't thought that far yet."

"Oh." Patty's shoulders dropped along with her instant enthusiasm. "Then what do you need?"

"Beth wants to organize the merchants to save the island," he said, going with the safer topic.

"Yes." Beth sat up straighter, pulling the thin shirt tight across her chest. Joe went back to staring at his soda. "So far we have Lola and Sid. Then Joe mentioned Sid has a brother."

"Randy Navarro," Joe said.

"Wha...um...who?"

"Sid's brother. He owns the water sports setup on the harbor, and the fitness center off Ocean Road." He glanced over in time to watch a drop of condensation drop from her glass and disappear between her breasts. His palms went damp.

She belongs to Lucas, douche bag.

Writing down Randy's name, she asked, "There's a fitness center on this island?"

"We have lots of little businesses you wouldn't expect," Patty responded. "Like the day care center. That's Helga Stepanovich. She lives for the kids, so I can't imagine her selling out."

"That's good." Beth started writing, then hesitated.

Patty tapped a finger on the page. "Stepanovich. Just like it sounds."

Beth smiled. "Thanks. Who else?"

"Eddie Travers runs the coffee shop, and his wife, Robin, runs the pottery place," Joe said. "Good people who've been here a long time."

"Is that the pottery shop with all the wind chimes on the porch?"

"Yeah, that's the one. You've been there?" Other than where he'd taken her today, Joe had no idea where Beth had visited.

"I walk by it on my way to Lola's. The chimes echoing together make me think of a fairy garden."

"I have some of those chimes hanging on my back porch," Joe said, affronted. "Let's not throw around the term *fairy garden*. What about Floyd Lewinski?"

"I'd put him on there." Patty filled herself a glass of iced tea. "His wife is buried on this island. He'd stand in front of a bulldozer before he'd let Wheeler have the place."

"What does Floyd run?" Beth asked.

"The Trading Company. It's on Back Road, not far from Lola's place."

"I saw that the first day, too. Okay, looks like we have a good list to start with."

"What do we do now?" Joe asked. "In fact, why are we listing the people we know will hold out instead of the ones in danger of caving?"

"That's simple," Beth said. "We're recruiting."

"Recruiting?"

"Recruiting for what?" asked Patty.

"Supporters to the cause."

Joe glanced at Patty, who looked as confused as he felt.

Beth tapped the pen against the bar. "Wheeler sent Cruella and that fancy suit guy to talk up the deal, right?"

"Right," Joe and Patty said together.

"That's two against the whole island. We already have seven. Add you three and that's ten. They're outnumbered, and we're just getting started." Beth beamed, hugging the notepad to her chest.

"We have ten people," Joe said. "Wheeler has millions of dollars. I'm not following."

"Don't you see? Cruella and her lackey won't stand a chance. It's like a blockade of willpower."

"Blockade of willpower? Did you just make that up?"

"I did. Sounds cheesy, I guess, but it makes sense."

"We recruit these others to help spread the word and batten down the hatches, so to speak," Patty said, her enthusiasm returning, "and Wheeler won't have a choice but to give up. This could work."

"What could work?" Tom asked, sliding up next to his wife.

Patty turned and planted a kiss on his cheek. "Our future daughter-in-law has come up with a plan to get rid of Wheeler."

Tom winked at Beth. "So she's as smart as she is pretty. What's the plan?"

"You two decide what you want to eat and I'll explain the plan to Tom in the kitchen." Patty slid two menus across the bar. "Nice to see you two getting along." Turning to Beth, she said, "You're good for him. He's never this nice for this long."

CHAPTER ELEVEN

Tom threw Joe a look over Patty's head, which Joe pretended not to notice. By the time Joe had buried his nose in the menu, Patty had hauled Tom into the kitchen.

"Great," Beth said, leaning from side to side trying to tug down her skirt. Which didn't need tugging down at all. "I can talk to Lola this afternoon. She might have some ideas about who needs the most convincing." Turning to Joe, she asked, "Could you drive me over there?"

"Sure. We can drop Dozer at the house and I'll come with you."

"No, no!" Beth said, as if he'd suggested they take off their clothes. Not a bad idea if the situation weren't so fucked up. "I mean, you need to start with one of the others." She glanced at the notepad. "You can start with Floyd, since he's right there by Lola."

If Beth's life ever depended on her telling a convincing lie, she'd be in serious trouble. "Why don't you want me coming to Lola's with you?"

"It's not that I don't want you with me," she said, wringing her hands. "I just know Lola is going to want to sit and chat and have tea, and you don't strike me as the tea-and-chat kind of guy."

She was lying, but he let it go. "You're right, I'm not. I'll talk to Floyd."

"You said the next meeting of this Merchants Society is Friday?"

"Yeah, why?"

"That doesn't leave much time to talk to everyone on this list and get them all in one room before the meeting."

"Why all in one room?" Joe asked. "You just said we would talk to them separately."

"Sure, but we can't go into that meeting thinking we have a unified front without everyone sitting down together so we know the strategy. A lawyer would never present a case without making sure everyone on the team was on the same page."

For the first time since they'd met, Beth sounded like the lawyer she was. Joe couldn't help but find the take-charge tone sexy. What was it with him and bossy women? That weakness was how he got the island in this mess to begin with.

"Is this what you're like when you present a case?" Watching her work a courtroom might be worth committing a crime.

Beth shook her head. "I don't work in the courtroom. I told you, I do research."

Sounded like a waste of law school tuition. "I don't know much about being a lawyer, but I thought working cases was the whole point."

She studied the menu as if she'd never seen it before. "I do the research to back up the cases other lawyers present. I'm better behind the scenes."

A pinched mouth and the eyes darting from burgers to seafood to side dishes said she wanted to drop the subject. Something made him push. "I don't believe you."

"Believe what you want," Beth said, ending the conversation by yelling toward the kitchen. "We're going, Patty. If Lucas calls, tell him I'll call him later tonight from the house."

Before they reached the door Patty yelled, "But you haven't eaten!" through the service window.

Without missing a step, Beth replied, "We'll get something later."

Joe ignored the growl from his stomach as he followed her through the door.

～

On the thankfully short drive to Island Arts & Crafts, Beth held her breath to keep from screaming, "Shut up!" at the voice in her head. The voice that kept repeating, *Joe thinks we're hot, Joe thinks we're hot, Joe thinks we're hot.* She hoped her mad dash from the moving vehicle came off as excitement to see Lola and not the panicked flight of a woman trying to outrun her traitorous hormones.

"Heavens, woman. What has your sails all aflutter?" Lola asked as Beth dropped into a chair behind the counter. "Nothing but a man can put that look on a woman's face." The accuracy of Lola's observation did little to calm Beth's nerves. "Would this have anything to do with how you hopped out of Joe's Jeep and ran through this door like the hounds of Hell were on your heels?"

Beth clearly sucked at acting nonchalant. "I'm more comfortable talking about the real reason I'm here."

"You mean something besides my sparkling personality brought you my way?" Lola's smile assured Beth the words were meant to be a joke.

She laughed, feeling in control again. Mostly. "Your sparkling personality is going to be the hardest thing to leave behind when this vacation is over."

"Good," Lola said. "That means you'll come back."

"And we're back to why I'm here. Making sure there's an island to come back to." She waited for Lola to take the seat opposite her. As the only person who knew Beth's law firm represented the Wheelers, she needed to ensure Lola kept the information to herself. "Before I get to that, I have to ask a favor."

"Anything for you, honey."

Beth blurted the words before guilt could stop her. "No one can know I work for the law firm that represents Wheeler Development. Can you keep that to yourself?"

Lola's eyebrows shot up. "Sure, but why the secret?"

"Not a secret, necessarily." The word *secret* made keeping the information quiet feel that much worse. "It's just that I'm afraid if the people on the island know, they won't trust me. And if Cassandra Wheeler finds out I'm helping throw up roadblocks to this project, I have no doubt she'd get me fired with one phone call."

"That does put you in a tough position." The older woman tapped her chin then leaned forward. "Are you sure you want to do this? Put your career on the line for people you don't even know?"

"I know you. And the Dempseys. But even if I didn't, this island is worth saving." Beth bounded from her chair to pace the narrow space. "I've been on Anchor less than a week and already see why people leave their lives behind to start new ones here." Though she hadn't consciously realized what was happening, the words were true. Life was different on Anchor Island. A smaller world, in a good way.

"This place does have a way of growing on a person, I'll give you that. I came here on vacation and never left." Lola's laugh matched the chimes that filled the air whenever the front door opened. The entire shop was a really just a reflection of the vibrant, colorful woman who gave it life.

No wonder Beth liked it so much.

"Then you see what I mean. We can't stand by and do nothing while Wheeler destroys the island," Beth said, getting back to her mission. "That's why we've come up with a plan."

"A plan. I like the sound of that." Lola waved a fist in the air, prepared to do battle. "Where do we start?"

"The people," Beth said. "I don't know if you've talked to your neighbors, but as far as we can tell, Wheeler is increasing his offer to most of the merchants. Maybe all."

"I haven't asked anyone else, but it would be silly for Mr. Big Man to send his fancy suit down here just for me. He's certainly offering more than this place is worth if you go by property value alone, but this store is more than a piece of property. It's my life."

Lola's words strengthened Beth's resolve. "That's how the Dempseys feel as well. If we make it clear nothing is for sale, no matter how much he offers, Wheeler will have to give up."

"Well, honey, if you're here to recruit me, consider it done, but tourism isn't what it used to be. This year is looking good so far, but later in the season when it warms up, the kids want amusement parks and water slides. Makes it hard to compete. I know several on the island are struggling. Makes the kind of money Wheeler's offering hard to resist."

Beth scooted to the edge of her chair. "That's why we're starting with the Merchants Society. One or two businesses alone are worthless to Wheeler. He needs the majority of them, as well as the cabins, to clear the way for the kind of resort he wants to build." She raised the legal pad from her lap.

"What do you have there?" Lola asked, leaning closer.

"These are the names the Dempseys gave me of merchants they were sure would stand against Wheeler. The plan is to start with these and gather others as we go." Turning the paper to face Lola, Beth asked, "Is there anyone you'd add? Someone you know for certain wants nothing to do with selling?"

Lola slid a dark finger down the page as she read the names. She stopped when she reached Floyd's name. "His wife is buried here, so I know Floyd isn't going anywhere. Especially if Helga stays put, too."

"What does Helga have to do with Floyd?"

"He's been courting her for a year now, though Helga pretends he's just being friendly." Beth had yet to meet these people, but couldn't resist a potential love story. "I thought Floyd was devoted to his dead wife? You just said so yourself."

"He loved that woman like a sailor loves the sea, but old Floyd isn't the kind to stop living. Mabel's been gone five years now. Even us old folks get lonely and need someone to spend our days with." With a wink, Lola added, "And our nights."

Beth sat back in surprise. "I don't know Floyd or Helga, but I'd rather not think about how they do or do not spend their nights. And not to step too far into your business, but that wink says Floyd isn't the only one looking for a companion."

She couldn't be sure, but the black woman appeared to be blushing. "The man for me is miles from this island. More's the pity."

"Where is he?" Beth asked. "Is he back in New Orleans?"

"Oh, you don't want to hear this old lady's sad tale," she replied, squeezing Beth's knee. The fragile grip reminded her of Granny and how she missed their talks on the old porch swing.

"Now I have to hear it." The notepad dropped to the floor as Beth gave Lola her full attention. "I wouldn't be surprised if you left a lot of broken hearts behind you."

Lola shook her head slowly and her eyes gentled. "There were men I might have left a little bruised, but when it comes to Marcus, I broke my own heart."

"Oh," Beth said, instantly regretting pushing the question. "I shouldn't have pried into your personal life like that."

"Don't be silly. It was a long time ago, and I really am too old to be pining like a schoolgirl." Settling back into her chair, Lola crossed her legs, bouncing one foot as if tapping to the beat of a song only she could hear. "Marcus Javier Granville was a fine man, but I was young and wild and thought I was doing the right thing. You see, my best friend, Dorothy, had been in love with Marcus for years. Well, we were all a little in love with Marcus, but Dorothy believed him to be the very air she breathed."

Beth remained quiet, not wanting to interrupt the story.

"I'd have done anything for Dorothy. We grew up together, and she was there for me when times were hard. More like a sister than a friend." Lola looked as if she were floating back in time. Wherever she'd gone, the memory didn't appear to be a happy one.

Beth squeezed her hand again. "You don't have to tell me the rest." Though not knowing what happened to Marcus Granville would drive her nuts, she'd rather Lola return to her sweet, peaceful self than see the pain now lingering in her eyes.

"No, no, I'm fine," Lola said, her smile returning. "Dorothy was like a sister, so when Marcus declared his love for me, I did a terrible thing."

"What did you do?" Beth asked, holding her breath.

"I lied. I told him I didn't love him and never would. Now, mind you, Marcus and Dorothy were never an item. He knew she had a thing for him and he never abused her attentions, but he never pretended to return them either." The smile dimmed again. "But I knew following my heart would break Dorothy's. I couldn't do that to her, so I lied, and shortly after left New Orleans and Marcus behind."

The finality of Lola's words, how hard it must have been to walk away, tightened something in Beth's chest. "You said he isn't that far away. Does that mean you know where Marcus is now?"

"I do." The happy Lola returned, a sparkle in her eye making her look younger than her sixty years. "Can you believe he found me on the Internet?"

"No," Beth said. "Where is he? Are you going to see him? Is he married now? Tell me he isn't married."

Lola laughed. "He's living on the Eastern Shore, and no, he isn't married. His wife, who was not Dorothy, by the way, died a few years ago. He's mentioned coming for a visit, but I don't think that's a good idea."

"Why not?" Beth nearly tipped forward on her chair. "Of all the places he could have ended up, he's a few hours away from you. That's a sign."

"I haven't seen the man in almost forty years. A quick glimpse in the mirror is my sign." The woman rose from her chair to fiddle with flyers on the counter. "Best to leave the past in the past, I say."

Beth wanted to argue but instead thought about what she would do in the same situation. The pain of the choice shone clearly on Lola's face. She'd loved the man once upon a time.

"Have you told him?" Beth asked, keeping her voice soft.

Lola kept her back turned. "Told him what?"

Beth rose and joined Lola at the counter. "Told him that you lied. Does he know that you loved him?"

No answer came, nor did Lola meet her eyes. Beth worried she might have crossed a line, but then the woman turned and laid a hand against her cheek.

"Some choices can't be undone. Some wounds can't be healed. Telling him now won't change anything." Narrowing her eyes, she added, "Let my story be a lesson for you. Real love comes along once in a lifetime. When you find it, don't ever let it get away."

Lucas appeared in Beth's mind, but the face shifted to one with blue eyes and a rarely seen dimple. Beth blinked the image away. "I won't. I promise."

CHAPTER TWELVE

Convincing Floyd Lewinski to join the anti-Wheeler movement took little effort, as Joe expected, but his insistence they involve Helga Stepanovich came out of nowhere. After reassuring him Helga was on the list to contact, Floyd said he'd take care of bringing Helga up to speed, then proceeded to tell Joe no less than three stories about the "good old days." All of which he'd heard before.

Unlike most men Joe knew, Floyd was a talker. He'd been on the island since before the Dempseys arrived, twenty years before, and considered himself an expert on the good old days. No one had the heart to remind Floyd that little had changed on the island in fifty years. Joe took advantage of a newly arrived customer to make his getaway. Minutes later, he swung by the art store to pick up Beth, who, other than to say Lola was on board, remained silent on the short drive to the house. He wondered what she and Lola could have talked about to put such a distracted look on her face.

More than once she glanced his way wearing a thoughtful but confused expression he couldn't interpret. Something deeper than thwarting a real estate deal was on her mind, but Joe knew better than to ask a woman what she was thinking.

The restaurant was quiet enough on Monday nights for Tom and Patty to both take the night off, which meant a family dinner at the house. Beth was as quiet during the meal as she'd been in the Jeep. His stepmother shot him an accusatory look. Joe shrugged in response. He had nothing to do with this mood swing. Nothing he could think of anyway.

Tom drew Beth into the conversation when he brought up the plot against Wheeler, but she fell silent again after Joe had to pass along bad news. Running two charters a day for the next three days was good for business, but left Beth on her own to deal with the locals and move the plan along.

She should have been happy to have him out of her hair, considering how well they got along, but just when he thought he had her figured out, Beth changed the rules and kept him guessing. Patty volunteered to go with her, but Beth still looked disappointed, casting strange looks his way through dessert. How was he supposed to enjoy his pie with her making him feel guilty like that?

The guilt stuck with him as he boarded the boat the next morning.

"You look like someone stole your pecker," Sid said as they prepared for the first group of tourists to arrive. "Did right-hand Rosie tell you no again?"

"Where do you get this shit?" Joe asked, ignoring the question.

Now that Beth had given him a more feminine view of Sid, he was having trouble thinking of her as one of the guys. Spending a little time with Beth might be good for Sid. He'd get answers, and Sid could get in touch with the girl hidden under all the grease and profanity. "Forget the question. I don't want to know."

Double-checking the fishing rods for adequate line, he waded into the topic. "I need a favor."

Sid looked up from securing a hook, eyebrow raised. "What makes you think I like you enough to do you any favors?"

"Not for me so much as for Lucas." So he was using Sid's feelings for his little brother against her. Ferreting out Beth's secrets really was for Lucas's benefit.

His mechanic gave him her full attention. "If this involves making little lawyer chick disappear, sign me up." Her girly side really was buried deep. Like two hundred feet below the surface.

"I asked Beth about her background. Something simple like where she grew up. She dodged the question and changed the subject." Joe glanced over to Sid to make sure she was paying attention. She'd gone back to tying the hook, but he could tell she was listening. "I want to know what she's not telling and if she's also not telling Lucas."

Sid finished with the hook and reeled in the excess line. "Where do I come in to this?"

Joe shrugged. "Girls talk, right?"

"I'm talking to you, ain't I? What the hell are you getting at?"

He should have known being subtle would never work with Sid. "Take her out. Give her enough alcohol to loosen her up and start asking questions."

The rod in her hand hit the floor. "You're full of shit if you think I'm having a girls' night out with that tight-assed Goody Two-shoes. First off," she said, counting on her fingers, "I don't do girls' nights out, and you know it. Second, what would we talk about? The latest fashions? Maybe we could paint each other's toenails pink."

Joe started to laugh at the image of Sid with painted toenails, but the look on her face said danger, so he shifted to a cough. "I'm not suggesting you have a sleepover. Get some drinks. Ask her some questions. That's all." When Sid didn't look convinced, he went in for the kill. "Don't you think Lucas deserves to know who he's marrying before he's stuck till death do them part?"

She wanted to argue. Joe could see the war waging as she switched from grinding her teeth to chewing her bottom lip. As far as he knew, Sid didn't have any female friends. If convincing her to spend a little time with Beth would get him the answers he wanted and buff out some of her rough edges, all the better.

"If I do this, you're paying," Sid said, crossing her arms over her "Wench My Ass" T-shirt.

"Like what, washing your truck or something?"

"I mean you're buying the drinks. You want me to do this without interference, that means avoiding Dempsey's." Shooting him an "I dare you" look, she added, "I'll need cash up front."

He should have known she'd find an angle. "How much?"

Sid hesitated, clearly pondering how much she could take him for. "A hundred bucks."

Joe shook his head. "I said get her tipsy, not give her alcohol poisoning."

"Fine," she said with a huff. "Fifty bucks, but that's my final offer."

"You got it." Joe took the hand she extended, but threw in a caveat of his own. "But you have to convince her to hang out with you. If she thinks I've set this up, she'll be suspicious."

Sid pulled her hand away. "She's never going to believe I want to hang out with her. It's not like I've been friendly so far."

She had a point. What would make Beth spend an evening with Sid and not leave her wondering what he was up to? The answer was obvious. He'd already considered the idea of Beth helping Sid find her girly side.

"I'll tell her you're interested in a guy and need her help to look like a girl."

"Hey!" Sid yelled, poking him in the chest. "Are you saying I don't look like a girl?"

Joe raised a brow and looked her up and down. The dark-green carpenter pants had to be two sizes too big, and the work boots were covered in grease. He couldn't remember the last time he'd seen her hair in anything but a ponytail. As he brought his eyes back to hers, Joe put on his best unimpressed face.

Sid huffed. "You're a dick."

"You going to do this or not? Fifty bucks and one day of your life to make sure Lucas isn't fucked for the rest of his."

"If I'm going along with this stupid looking-like-a-girl story, the price goes up to seventy-five." Joe opened his mouth to argue but she cut him off. "She's going to want to buy me clothes. It's not like I have girly shit in my closet."

Of that he was sure. "Seventy-five. But you don't get the money until Beth says she'll go. I'm not stupid enough to give it to you before."

Sid fluttered her eyelashes, which looked about as natural as a trout on water skis. "Why, Joe Dempsey, don't you trust me?" Her fake Southern accent sounded like that *Gone with the Wind* chick on steroids.

"Beth doesn't have a shot in hell of turning you into a girl."

Voices sounded from up the pier as their first group of the day headed toward the boat. Sid turned her back on the tourists, giving Joe a determined look. "Now you've just pissed me off. I'll play your little game and find out what big-city girl is hiding. But an extra twenty-five bucks says I'll be the hottest thing in O'Hagan's Pub come Saturday night." Before Joe could apologize, Sid snatched the stack of fishing rods off the floor of the boat. "Now go greet your customers before I shove your nuts down your throat."

～

Beth paced the Dempseys' kitchen as she waited for Lucas to pick up on the other end. She'd tried to call three times the night before with no answer. Knowing Lucas, he'd turned off his cell phone ringer during a late meeting and never turned it back on. The fact he had yet to return her calls meant the ringer was probably still off. It also meant he hadn't thought about calling her on his own.

She tried not to be bothered by the fact her fiancé hadn't talked to her in days and showed no sign of missing her. But trying not to be bothered and not being bothered were two different things. Back in Richmond she could drop into his office when he didn't return her calls. Being ignored from two hundred fifty miles away left more of a sting.

"Hello?" said Lucas, finally answering his office phone.

"Hi, it's me." Beth struggled to sound happy instead of annoyed.

"Is everything all right?" Lucas asked.

Beth didn't realize something had to be wrong to give them a reason to talk. "I was about to ask you the same question. Haven't heard from you in a while, and you didn't pick up when I called last night."

Lucas sighed. She could picture him running a hand through his hair. "Yeah. Sorry about that. This case is kicking my ass. The whole team worked through the weekend."

Beth reminded herself again how important this case was to Lucas's career, but her patience was wearing thin. Lola's words played on a loop in her mind, poking at her conscience. Was Lucas really the one? The once-in-a-lifetime guy? Her brain gave one answer while her heart gave another.

"I know you're busy. I just miss you." She leaned on the counter, twirling the tea towel in a circle. "You haven't forgotten about me, have you?"

"Of course not. Why would you say that?" At least now she had his attention.

"Oh, I don't know. Because I'm more than two hundred miles away, spending our vacation by myself?"

"You're not supposed to be by yourself."

"I know. You're supposed to be here."

The sound of papers shuffling traveled through the phone, and Beth felt a twinge of irritation that he couldn't stop working long enough to talk to her.

"No, I mean my family is there with you. They aren't leaving you to fend for yourself, are they? Is Joe giving you a hard time?"

Beth bit the inside of her cheek. She didn't want to talk about Joe with Lucas. "No, no. They're being very sweet and I'm making my way around the island. Like I said," she sighed, "I miss you."

"I miss you, too, but you know these—"

"Kinds of cases are important for your career," Beth finished for him. "Yes, I know." She heard the papers shuffle again and knew he'd end the call soon. "Speaking of your career, you're not working on the Wheeler account, are you?"

The line fell silent for half a beat. "Why do you ask?"

She didn't appreciate the classic answer-a-question-with-a-question, but chose not to call him on it. "I saw Cassandra Wheeler coming out of your office a couple times recently," she said, letting the words drop like live grenades into the conversation.

"I didn't realize you knew Cassandra Wheeler." Still not answering the question. There was a reason Lucas was so good in court.

"I didn't until a couple days ago. She's here on the island."

More silence. She could almost hear his wheels turning, and her chest tightened.

"Has anyone told you Cassandra was once engaged to my brother?"

"Yes, they have."

"If she's there, it's because of Joe. You should stay out of it."

"Out of what, Lucas? You never answered my question." Pushing for answers wasn't Beth's usual way, but she wanted to know what Cassandra Wheeler wanted with Joe.

"I told you, Cassandra was engaged to Joe. She stopped in to see me as an old friend."

"So you're friends with your brother's ex-fiancée? Does Joe know about this?" Beth twisted the tea towel into a knot.

"I wouldn't call her a friend, and there's nothing for Joe to know." Lucas still hadn't answered the question, and he had the nerve to sound put out. "Look, I have another meeting in two minutes. It would be best if you avoided Cassandra and stayed out of Joe's business."

"Do you know she's here trying to talk people into selling their land to her father?"

"She's what?" A muffled voice sounded in the background, and Lucas said, "I'll be there in a minute, Pamela." Then back to Beth. "They're trying to buy up Anchor?"

"You didn't know? Cassandra didn't mention it during her friendly visits?" Beth felt her temper rise. The feeling was new and unfamiliar. "Tad Wheeler wants this island, and we're trying to stop him."

"What do you mean 'we'? As an employee of this law firm, you cannot work against the interests of one of our clients." Lucas's words came out in a rush, indicating he was rattled. "Maybe you should come home."

A voice inside declared, *I am home!* Beth rubbed her temple, unable to deal with that revelation. "Are you saying you don't care about this island and the people on it?"

"Of course I care," Lucas said, frustration in his voice. "But people have been on that island for three centuries, and I have no doubt they've faced bigger challenges than…" His voice lowered as if he was afraid to be overheard. "Tad Wheeler. Hell, Joe would man the torpedoes before he'd let anyone take that island. You need to stay out of it."

Beth disliked Lucas in that moment. "I'm helping the locals get organized. As of now, Cassandra Wheeler doesn't know who I am or where I work. My goal is to keep it that way." Unable to help herself, she asked, "Do you know what happened between her and Joe?"

An uncharacteristic snort came through the line. "No idea. The only thing Joe ever said was that he couldn't give Cassie what she wanted. He never told me what that meant, and I didn't push the issue."

"How well do you know her?" For reasons Beth couldn't explain, this answer mattered more than the others.

"Not well. The two times she came to see me in the last month were my first encounters with her since they broke up. The first time she said she was in the building and decided to stop by. I think we might have chatted about the weather. Mundane stuff. The second time she asked how often I went home—back to Anchor. After I said almost never, she remembered another appointment and left." Beth heard what sounded like a door opening, and Lucas said, "I really have to go. Just stay away from Cassie, okay?"

"I will," Beth said, since avoiding Cruella de Vil was the one thing they could agree on. "Call me when you get a chance. And good luck with the case."

"Thanks. I'm still trying to get back down there, but it's not looking good."

Beth sighed. "Just do what you can."

"And hey." His voice dropped again. "Try to keep Joe away from Cassie, too."

He wasn't telling her everything, but at least Lucas did care about his brother. "I'll see what I can do."

CHAPTER THIRTEEN

Beth expected the Power Center to look like every other Anchor business she'd encountered so far. Small, unassuming, laid-back. A machine or two hovering near a mirror and maybe an exercise ball for the ambitious. The dumbbells would be anchored by coconuts instead of actual weights.

She should have known better than to make assumptions.

Behind the large, ground-to-gutter window, a line of treadmills and elliptical machines stood in rows like soldiers prepared for a siege. Metal and chrome ready to take on the battle of the bulge. Crossing the threshold, Beth looked up as a bell jingled overhead. Maybe there was a "chimes on door" ordinance in place on the island.

"Welcome to the Power Center," said a perky redhead from behind the front desk. The turquoise color of her shirt matched the paint covering every surface within sight.

"I'm here to see Randy Navarro," Beth replied. "He's expecting me."

"Your name?"

"Elizabeth Chandler." Raising her sunglasses to the top of her head, Beth added, "I'm a little early, so I can wait if necessary." Joe had told her to be at the gym at eleven thirty to catch Randy on his lunch hour, but waiting around at the house was making her nervous, so she'd left earlier than she should have.

"I've got it, Abby," said a giant of a man who'd come around the end of the wall behind Abby's head. A white towel rested around a neck the size of Beth's thigh, while the massive breadth of his chest and shoulders made one wonder how he fit through doorways. Damp hair, dark as night, curled over his ears with one wayward curl settled on his forehead.

His brown eyes looked oddly gentle, and his smile, a perfect row of white teeth behind full lips, softened the menacing effect of his overwhelming stature. The resemblance to Sid was obvious, if one didn't count the noticeable difference in attitude. Where Sid was harsh and confrontational, this bear of a man looked welcoming and friendly.

Staring at him felt like getting an extra shot of estrogen in her latte. The man belonged on the cover of a romance novel.

"You must be the Beth Joe told me about," Randy said, extending a hand. She obliged, managing not to sigh when he brushed a kiss across her knuckles. "No wonder Joe warned me you're off-limits."

"I am?" Beth asked, an estrogen fog hampering her brain function. "Oh yes, I am. Engaged. Of course I am."

"Engaged?" Randy's brows drew together, and Beth forced herself to pull her hand from his.

"Yes. To Lucas Dempsey, Joe's brother."

"Lucas? Huh. That explains it." Beth was still processing that response when Randy said, "We can talk in my office. This way."

Her trek through the gym revealed two things. One, Anchor sported more than one Hulk-size individual if the two men lifting weights in the far corner were any indication. Each looked as if he could bench-press a bus without breaking a sweat.

And two, feeling like a bug that could be squashed at any moment was a nerve-racking experience. Not that she feared Randy Navarro, but his size and height, more than a foot taller than her five foot five, were flat-out intimidating. The fleeting thought as to what kind of woman would be attracted to this kind of man brought two words to mind.

Size matters.

Beth shut down that train before it left the station.

"Thank you for taking the time to see me. I know you're busy running two businesses here on the island."

Randy stopped before an open door, stepped to the side, and motioned her in. "When Joe mentioned the name Wheeler, I was happy to make the time. Having this chat with a beautiful woman instead of Joe's ugly mug is a bonus."

Beth took in the spacious office as she settled into the chair Randy indicated. The walls were covered with pictures of what looked to be a man hell-bent on killing himself. Glancing to a shot on her left, she realized that man was Randy himself.

Whether trailing a wilted parachute behind him, riding a giant wave on a surfboard, or standing atop a snowy mountain looking like the abominable snowman, the common denominator in every picture was joy.

Randy Navarro didn't just live, he attacked life with something between sheer joy and a death wish. Which begged the question: What was an adrenaline junkie doing on a tiny island known more for its history and laid-back lifestyle than heart-racing attractions?

"Would you like a drink? We have water, vitamin water, and a variety of sport drinks."

"No, thank you, I'm fine." Beth remembered what Randy had said before they moved to the office. "When you said 'That explains it,' what did you mean?"

"Why Sid doesn't like you," he said, pulling a red bottle from a small fridge behind his desk. "You're engaged to Lucas, so that explains it."

"I'm afraid I don't understand. Why would that matter to Sid?"

"Sid's been half in love with Lucas since high school. Joe should have told you so you'd be prepared. I know my sister can be a bit...abrasive at times."

Abrasive? Feral cats were abrasive. Sid the boat mechanic was downright mean. And she had a thing for Lucas. No wonder the pint-size playmate looked ready to kill her.

"Joe never mentioned it. Does Lucas know how Sid feels about him?"

"I doubt it. Lucas always had a one-track mind, and that was getting off this island as soon as possible." Randy took a drink and then continued. "I'm sure I don't have to tell you how ambitious he is. Ambition gave him tunnel vision, and Sidney Ann was never able to find her way into his line of sight."

"Did you say Sidney Ann?" The feminine middle name warred with the image of the tomboyish, hard-nosed woman Beth had met in the pool room.

"That's what we call her in the family. Needless to say, she hates it." Randy flashed a conspiratorial smile, giving a glimpse of an agitating big brother.

"Maybe it's good Lucas is back in Richmond, then," Beth said, struggling to imagine how any man could overlook a woman built like Sid Navarro. "But we should move on to the reason I'm here. I'm assuming Wheeler Development has been contacting you about negotiating a buyout?"

"They have, and it's damned annoying. Excuse my language. I've told the man no in writing, on the phone, and now in person to that little suit he sent down here." Randy pulled a stack of envelopes from his top drawer. "The offer gets bigger with each new contact. If he's doing this same thing with others, I won't be surprised if a few give in."

"That's what we want to prevent." Beth scooted to the edge of her chair. "By organizing the merchants to stand together as a solid no, we make sure Wheeler doesn't get a single business. If the weaker ones see a united front, they'll hold their ground."

Randy sat back, tapping a finger against the plastic bottle. "Sounds like a solid approach. Our Merchants Society is informal at best, but I'm positive no one wants to see this island turned into a money-sucking resort."

"We're having a meeting at Dempsey's Restaurant Thursday night to discuss how to present the idea to the rest of the merchants at the meeting on Friday. Will you join us?"

"I'll be there. Who else have you talked to?"

Beth pulled the list of names from her purse. "Lola LeBlanc and Floyd Lewinski. Floyd is bringing in Helga Stepanovich, and I'll be talking to Eddie and Robin Travers tomorrow to sign them up as well."

Randy leaned forward, setting down his drink and picking up a pen. "Sam Edwards runs three small hotels on the island. Some of us might survive if Wheeler gets his way, but Sam would have no choice but to start over somewhere else." He scribbled the name and a phone number on a yellow sticky note. "Give me an hour or so to give him a heads-up, then call to set up a meeting."

"I'll do that, thank you." Beth took the note, feeling good about adding another ally to the team. "We'll start around seven Thursday night."

As she stood to leave, Randy rose with her. "By the way, you have nothing to worry about from Sid. She's not nearly as tough as she'd like people to believe."

"Right," Beth said, not the least bit convinced. "I'll try to remember that."

∾

Three days on the water with some of the best action he'd seen in months put Joe in a damn good mood. A good-enough mood for him to ignore Sid's whiny-ass complaining all the way to Dempsey's.

"City chick is never going to fall for this," she said. Again. Sid had been repeating this statement for more than an hour.

"We're early enough to set this up before the others get here."

"This is a waste of time," she said, stopping at the bottom of the steps. "Why don't you just ask her what the hell you want to know?"

Determined not to lose his temper, Joe counted to ten as he walked back down the stairs. "We've been over this.

All you have to do is spend one night buying drinks on my dime, find out what she's hiding, and then you're free to go back to work boots and wifebeaters." Taking Sid by the arm, he pulled her up the steps with him.

Sid yanked her arm away and stormed past. "You're lucky this is for Lucas."

By the time Joe entered the restaurant, Sid was sitting at the bar, waving his dad down for a beer. What was her freaking problem? It wasn't as if he'd asked her to wear a bikini on the boat or rub up on Phil Mohler or something. She just had to be a girl for one goddamn night.

"I'll take one of those, too, Dad," he said, taking the stool beside her.

"He's paying for both," Sid added, turning her back on him.

Maybe bringing out Sid's inner female was more dangerous than he imagined. Crude, locker-room-style sparring was one thing. Cold shoulders and getting pissed about shit that was no big deal were two things he'd never seen from Sid.

"You two having a spat?" Tom asked, smiling until Sid glared at him. "The meeting starts in twenty minutes."

"Where's Beth?" Joe asked, wanting to get this Sid situation settled as soon as possible.

Tom nodded toward the private dining room in the far right corner. "She and Patty are getting the room ready. Beth typed up some kind of handout using a Merchants member list we had on hand. She's been doing research for two days, according to Patty."

"Researching what?" Sid asked. "Everybody on this island knows everybody else's business. It's not like we need her to tell us what we already know."

Tom shrugged. "I haven't seen what she put together, so I guess we'll find out."

Joe nudged Sid off her stool. "We'll go back and see if they need help." She could scowl all night if she wanted, but she'd agreed to this deal and her ass was doing it whether she liked it or not.

Sid's mumbling behind him said she was following, if reluctantly, so Joe kept walking. Inside the dining room, Beth stood next to a round table with a sheet of paper at each place setting. Examining a copy, she didn't look happy with what she saw.

"What's that?" Joining her, he lifted a packet from the table. "The Merchants Society has a letterhead?" In more than ten years, Joe had never seen anything this official-looking from the group.

"None that I could find, so I threw this together. What do you think?"

The small image of a seagull soaring through a sunset over a deserted pier anchored the top left side of the page while THE ANCHOR ISLAND MERCHANTS SOCIETY hugged the right along with an address. "I know this island like the back of my hand, but I don't recognize this address. What is it?"

One brow shot up. "The library. I was told that's where your meetings are held?"

"Oh." So he didn't know the address for the library. On an island the size of Anchor, saying "Meet at the library" was enough to know where to be. "What's the rest of this?"

"The front page is a list of society members and the businesses they own. The second is as much as I could find out about Wheeler's plans for the island so we'd know who would be most affected." Turning the sheets in his hand, she flipped to the last page. "This is a chart showing the tourism trends for the last five years and prediction indicators for the next five."

Joe was speechless. Where had she found this kind of information? Maybe there was more to their little library than anyone knew. "This is amazing."

Beth blushed. "It's what I do. Research and gather information for others to use. Like I said, it's just something I threw together."

"This is anything but thrown together." He never expected her to put this much effort into something she had no stake in. "Why are you doing all of this for people you don't even know?"

"These aren't people I don't know. Well, true, I don't know all of them. Or even most of them. But I know Lola, you, and your parents, and in the last few days I've gotten to know a few others." Flipping his packet back to the first page, she pointed to the list at the top. "Randy Navarro sent me to see Sam Edwards, and Sam sent me to see your friend Chuck Brighteyes. There's a chance the effect Wheeler's project would have on the horses could play in our favor."

"How do you figure?"

"The horses are still considered wild and protected, even if they can't run free. Protecting the horses and the historic landmarks could be grounds for declaring the island off-limits to Wheeler."

"You say 'could be.'" Joe struggled to follow the conversation with Beth pressed against his right arm. "No guarantee?"

"Well, no," she said, backing away a step. He fought the urge to move with her. "I can't research the legal aspects without a law library. I do know Wheeler could make a sizable donation and agree not to infringe on the historic sites to clear any obstacles. But the island would never be the same."

"No. It wouldn't." Beth had been on the island less than a week and already understood what some natives had yet to figure out. "If I didn't know better, I'd think you like this place."

"Of course I like it," she said, with more passion than he expected. "The people here are friendly and welcoming and they don't deserve to have their lives turned upside down just because some arrogant man with money gets a burr up his butt to take their homes."

Seeing her temper aimed at something besides himself gave Joe a glimpse of how hot she looked when she was mad. The flat line of her mouth and stubborn set of her shoulders made him want to kiss her until she couldn't remember why she was so angry.

Beth stared at the paper in her hand while Joe stared at her lips. Until Sid walked up behind them and coughed loud enough to jerk him back to reality.

"Is she okay?" Beth asked, eying Sid warily.

He turned to see Sid dropping napkin-wrapped silverware on the tables. Patty must have put her to work. A twinge of guilt hit his gut at the reminder of their plan. Beth was helping save his island and he was trying to dig into her past for something to hold against her.

When the only thing he really wanted to hold against her was himself.

This was for Lucas. He had to keep telling himself that.

"I hate to ask, seeing as you've done so much already, but I need a favor." Seeing her surprised expression he added, "Actually, Sid needs a favor."

~

Beth was immediately suspicious. Except to serve as a punching bag or live bait, what would Sid want from her? "What kind of favor?"

Joe took her elbow and pulled her away from the gathering crowd. "She has a thing for some guy, I don't know who, but he just sees her as one of the boys. Like you said that first night you met her." The suspicion grew. Especially considering what Sid's brother said about Sid having a thing for Lucas. "I thought maybe you could do whatever it is you females do to make her look more like a girl."

Beth's jaw dropped. "Unless you're hiding a magic wand, I don't know what you want me to do."

"You said she's gorgeous." He glanced at Sid as if trying to find some positive attribute. "Put her in a dress or something. Do her hair. Aren't women always doing each other's hair?"

What was this man's point of reference? Nineteen-sixties set musicals? "Sid and I are a bit old for the slumber-party scene. And since I don't have a death wish, I won't be trying to change out her cargos for silk anytime soon."

Beth tried to walk away but Joe cut her off. "Sid said you wouldn't do it. She said you were too stuck-up, but I told her she was wrong. Guess I'm the one who was wrong."

The parting shot was a low blow, and Beth knew he was manipulating her, but she couldn't help herself. Joe didn't make it two steps before she said, "Fine."

"What?" he asked, giving his best innocence-incarnate look. She wasn't fooled.

"I will attempt to turn your boat mechanic into a girl, but on one condition." Beth could play his little game. "You're paying."

The innocent look took on a green hue. "I'm what?"

"It's going to take more than a dress and a few hot rollers to transform Cinderella over there. If I'm helping, you're helping. With cash."

The green turned to white as Joe ran a hand through his hair. She hadn't thought to wonder if his funds were too tight to cover a makeover and girls' night out, but after another quick glance at Sid, he relented. "I'll give you fifty dollars to pay for whatever you need. If you two want to have a good time with drinks, you're on your own."

Having a good time with Sid sounded near impossible, but if the woman had a thing for someone on the island, that meant she'd given up the crush on Lucas. Not that Beth was worried about losing her fiancé to a woman more comfortable around twin engines than mundane dinner parties. That would be silly.

Maybe Sid's crusty outer shell really was softer than it looked, but watching from three tables away as Joe passed on the news, Beth was not encouraged. She made a mental note to verify her health insurance would cover any out-of-state injuries.

CHAPTER FOURTEEN

If Beth's coworkers were one-tenth as grateful as their little Defeat-Wheeler team, she might actually enjoy her job. Instead of the invisible girl from research, she was the brilliant soon-to-be Dempsey. She hadn't been called brilliant since winning the third-grade spelling bee, and being called a Dempsey meant even more.

On Anchor, being a Dempsey meant you were somebody. Beth had never been a somebody.

The meeting went better than expected, except for a brief tussle between her and Joe. Mr. Pushy insisted she explain the handout after she'd made it clear she would not be playing a speaking role. She refused, he called her "chicken" (in a whisper only she could hear, the jerk), and she relented.

If she were honest, she'd admit she enjoyed running the show for a while. Not that she'd ever admit that to Joe. By the end, they'd assembled a phone-tree-style contact list giving everyone a group of other merchants to contact before the regularly scheduled meeting the next night.

There was an awkward moment when Sam Edwards voiced the question everyone else was thinking: Why had Wheeler chosen their island? The tourist season didn't run year-round the way more tropical locations would, and what season they did have would always face the threat of hurricanes.

As theories were tossed about, Joe remained silent. In fact, he looked uncomfortable and changed the subject at the first chance.

Had Joe's breakup with Cassie put a target on Anchor?

Surely no man would buy an island to avenge his daughter's broken heart. Everything Beth knew about Tad Wheeler said the man was cunning, ruthless, and methodical about his investments. Not the type to make a financial decision based on emotion.

Maybe Joe's behavior stemmed from something else, but Beth had observed enough criminals during law school to recognize a guilty conscience when she saw one.

"So are we doing this or what?" Sid asked, snapping Beth back to the present.

She'd been staring out a window and hadn't heard Sid come up behind her. "Oh, sure." Beth nodded to the other side of the booth. "Have a seat." Best to find out what Sid expected from this little makeover.

"Fine." Sounding like a rebellious teen arriving in the principal's office, Sid plopped down and crossed her arms over a T-shirt that read, "Life's a bitch and so am I." That would have to go.

"Joe says you're interested in a man?"

"You sound surprised. Let me guess. You thought I was a lesbian."

The thought hadn't occurred to her, but Beth could see how the assumption might be made. "No, I didn't. But we need to get something out of the way right now."

"What? Are *you* a lesbian?"

Beth could only hope that the man upon whom Sid had set her sights was profoundly patient. And liked his women rough around the edges. "Joe asked me to do you this favor and, for some unknown reason, I agreed. But this won't work if you waste both our time insulting me and acting like an adolescent who's been grounded from her cell phone."

Sid loosened her posture and rested her arms on the table. "I might have an attitude problem now and then." At Beth's raised eyebrow, she conceded, "Okay, more now than then. I'll work on it."

That was more than Beth expected. "Good. Then we're on the right track."

"But I want to know something from you."

Beth waited for the question but nothing followed. "What's that?"

Sid crossed her arms. "Why did you agree to help me?"

An immediate answer didn't come to mind. There was the lure of a seemingly impossible challenge, but she doubted Sid would appreciate the "seemingly impossible" part. Nor would she be happy to know Beth was aware of her feelings for Lucas.

"As much as you don't like me, I have no reason not to like you. If you were brave enough to ask for help, I can be brave enough to give it." Seeing the skepticism on Sid's face, she gave one more reason. "Or maybe I think you're hot."

Sid's eyes went wide and she looked ready to bolt. Then Beth smiled and her opponent caught the joke. "Nice one, Curly. You're not so bad for a prissy city lawyer."

Not the greatest compliment, but it was a start.

~

Joe paced outside the Anchor Island library struggling to focus on the meeting at hand. He should have been thinking about the speech he'd be delivering in five minutes, but couldn't get the image of Beth's heated expression out of his brain.

If he'd known she was the one on the other side of the door, Joe never would have answered wearing nothing but jeans and wet hair. His own physical attraction was bad enough, but when he opened his door to find Beth gaping back at him like a woman about to dive into a hot-fudge sundae, all systems kicked into overdrive. He'd expected his father, not his brother's sexy fiancée wearing a skintight skirt, heels, and a blouse with one too many buttons undone.

With the mass of brown curls pulled into a loose clip on the back of her head, a pair of wire-rimmed glasses would have finished off the hot-librarian-looking-for-a-good-time fantasy. His body longed for a roll in the stacks, while his brain reminded his dick for the umpteenth time that Beth belonged to Lucas. Why the fuck couldn't Lucas be here to drive that fact home?

"Are you jerking off out here or what?" Sid asked, joining him outside the library entrance. "They're waiting for you to get this thing started."

Even if Beth put Sid in the hot librarian outfit, she'd never turn the heathen into a girl. "Aren't you supposed to be working on your feminine side?"

"I'm saving her for the big debut tomorrow." Sid's eyes dropped to the floor and for the first time Joe saw the hesitation. This wasn't just about getting information out of Beth. Sid actually wanted to be a girl.

The look she shot him when she realized he was staring at her said "pissed-off woman" way more than "sweet-natured girl." Since he knew Sid hadn't been on a date since before he met Cassie, he could only assume her feminine wiles were rusty.

"You aren't going to let me win that twenty-five bucks, are you?" Joe asked, knowing Sid could never back down from a challenge.

"Make sure you hit the ATM tomorrow, asshole. I expect payment immediately." Sid stormed into the library, the fire back in her eyes. For the first time Joe wondered if the tough act was just that. An act. Then he remembered the punch she'd thrown at Phil Mohler the prior Fourth of July for grabbing her ass after six shots of tequila.

Definitely not an act.

Joe passed through the door before Sid could slam it in his face, and the first person he spotted in the crowd was Beth. Standing in the back corner with Lola by her side, she glanced his way as if she'd been watching for him. After a brief word to the older woman, she headed toward him, walking with purpose. The heels did incredible things to her hips, and Joe wondered what it would be like to watch the skirt slide to the floor.

"We have a problem," she said, standing close enough for him to catch the scent of honeysuckle in her hair. He had a problem all right. "Lola says Derek Paige came to see her again today. They've doubled the offer."

"What?" His brain was drowning in the flowery fog. "Who doubled what?"

Beth bit out her answer. "Wheeler offered Lola double what he'd put on the table last week. Word has it he's increased his offer to several others."

That statement brought his brain around and sent his dick back to dormant mode. Mostly. "The timing is interesting. They must know about our meeting last night."

"We should have done it somewhere other than Dempsey's. Did you see Cassandra or Derek at the restaurant?"

"No," Joe said, shaking his head. He'd had Annie keep an eye out for the enemy and she'd assured him they never came in. "Someone must have told them."

Beth looked around the room. "Who would do that? We didn't begin the phone calls until this morning."

Before Joe could answer, the door opened behind him and Phil Mohler stumbled into him.

"Jesus, Dempsey, get the hell out of the way."

Joe's hands balled into fists in his pockets. Of course. "You haven't been to a meeting in months, Mohler. Why the sudden interest?"

"I'm a merchant, same as everybody else here. I can come to one of these things any time I want." The weasel puffed out his chest and tried to look taller but was still several inches shorter than Joe.

"You're right, Mohler. Have a seat."

Suspicion clouded Mohler's eyes. He looked as if he wanted to continue the argument, then thought better of it. Instead he slunk away, taking a chair off to the side.

Proving she was as quick as he, Beth said, "Do you think—"

"I don't think, I know. That explains his lunch with Cassie."

"What a jerk." Beth crossed her arms and shot a look at Mohler that could scare a great white.

"He's a jerk, but he's also not the brightest bulb in the lighthouse, if you know what I mean. Cassie's good at finding the weak ones." Too late he realized what he'd said and saw the question in Beth's eyes. "I'd better get up front so we can get this thing started."

An hour later, Beth sat in the back corner of the room crossing and uncrossing her legs, wanting nothing more than to scratch Phil Mohler's eyes out. The man had attempted to lobby for the Wheeler deal, cutting Joe off every chance he could. Not that his arguments were effective. As Joe pointed out, Phil had one of the few businesses that would benefit from Wheeler bringing in a higher clientele.

The comeback that Joe's business was the same fell flat when Joe reminded the room at large he also had a stake in Dempsey's Restaurant, which would be leveled to make way for Wheeler's resort.

But if the only dissenting voice had been Mohler's, Beth would still be confident that Wheeler didn't stand a chance. Unfortunately, there were at least five others who were considering the developer's offer. Three were rental property owners struggling to keep the cabins fully occupied. Every week or weekend a property sat vacant, the owners lost money.

Though Beth's future tourism predictors showed growth over the next few years, that growth was slow and couldn't be guaranteed. The economy was anything but predictable, and though Anchor was less expensive as vacation destinations went, it was still remote and relatively unknown. A fact Beth knew well since she'd never heard of it before meeting Lucas.

"Are you sure you should be here?" Lola asked for the fourth time since Beth arrived with the Dempseys. "I don't like the idea that you could lose your job over this."

Beth appreciated her new friend's concern. "No one outside the initial group knows I put that document together. And no one but you knows my law firm represents Wheeler's interests. So long as it stays that way, I won't lose my job."

"But you could." Lola pinched her lips, enhancing the wrinkles surrounding them. "What if you do?"

The question took her by surprise. What if she did? She imagined hearing the words "We're letting you go" and waited for the feelings to come. The disappointment. The loss. The anger.

She got nothing. Which seemed odd, since Beth had worked her butt off to gain a position with such a prestigious firm.

Unprepared or maybe unwilling to consider her future, she focused on allaying Lola's fears. "I'm not going to lose my job, and you people are not going to lose this island. Everything will work out the way it should. I'm sure of it."

The woman didn't look convinced, but then her eyes moved past Beth, and Lola smiled.

"What is it?" Beth asked, turning to see Joe talking to a group that included Randy Navarro and two men she didn't know.

Lola took Beth's hand in hers and patted the back as if soothing a lost child. "You're right. Everything is going to work out just like it should."

Beth glanced back to the group. Joe seemed engrossed in whatever Randy was saying. Turning her attention back to Lola, she asked, "What about that conversation has you suddenly convinced?"

Instead of answering, the older woman excused herself with another pat on Beth's hand and moved off to talk with Helga Stepanovich.

What a confusing woman. Beth looked for Joe again, thinking maybe one of the two strangers with whom he'd been speaking was someone who could help them fend off Wheeler. But he wasn't where she'd last seen him, forcing her to scan the room to find him again. Their earlier conversation came back to her.

Cassie's good at finding the weak ones.

The offhand remark gave away more than he'd probably intended.

She'd never have guessed it based on their encounters so far, but Joe was carrying around more baggage than a skycap at JFK. In the last twenty-four hours she'd learned two surprising facts about Joe Dempsey. One, he felt guilty, which meant he also felt responsible for putting Anchor Island in the crosshairs of Tad Wheeler. Second, he considered himself weak for falling for the Wheeler spawn.

Granted, the last made her question his taste level and maybe his sanity, but from everything she'd witnessed, Joe was anything but weak. Stubborn, obstinate, and uncomfortably (for her) sexy, but never weak.

"You can stop your searching, darling. What you're looking for is right here." The words were accompanied by the smell of sweat and fish, forcing Beth to cover her nose. Turning to locate the source, she found it several inches below her chin.

"Excuse me?"

A small man grinned up at her, one missing tooth creating the hole through which the foul odor assailed her. A receding hairline fronted greasy, slicked-back, dirty-blond hair that practically advertised the man didn't believe showering before a professional meeting was necessary.

"The name's Buddy Wilson. How about we get out of here and get to know each other over a few beers?" The cretin winked, and Beth's stomach turned.

"Thanks, but I'll have to pass." Desperate to put distance between herself and the stench, Beth took a step away. A calloused hand clamped around her wrist.

"Come on, honey. I'll make it worth your while."

Beth would have inhaled to fortify her patience, but breathing deep in this idiot's airspace was not a good idea. "I'm sorry, Mr. Wilson, but I'm not interested in your offer." Unwilling to make a scene in front of the entire town, she kept her voice calm. "Now if you'd kindly release my arm."

"No need to run away so fast," he said, maintaining his grip on her. "You haven't even told me your name."

Patience gone, Beth opened her mouth to reply but a menacing voice cut her off.

"She said let her go, Wilson. I suggest you do it. Now." Though the threat wasn't spoken, it was there all the same.

Her admirer's eyes grew wide and he quickly dropped her wrist. "I was just talking to her. You need to mind your own business, Dempsey."

"She is my business. I told you once already, she's off-limits."

His words reminded her of the first thing Randy Navarro had said to her, about Joe warning him she was off-limits. As if she couldn't be trusted to make her status clear.

Joe took a step forward, forcing Wilson to take a step back. When did she become the damsel in distress? And more important, when did being rescued by a white knight in flannel sporting a five o'clock shadow become such a turn-on?

The little man's eyes darted from Joe to Beth and back to Joe, looking like a child trying to solve a puzzle. Beth understood the feeling since she was trying to solve one herself.

"This is that waitress chick?" Bloodshot eyes traveled the length of her body, giving Beth the sudden urge to shower. Then the eyes moved back to Joe. With a smirk, Wilson said, "I see now. You keeping her warm for your brother?"

Joe growled and took another step forward. Still unwilling to cause a scene, Beth put herself between the two. "This has gone far enough. As flattering as this is probably supposed to be, I'm not interested in watching anyone fight over my honor. Besides, we all three know how this would turn out, and I doubt you," she said to the little Napoleon before her, "want to deal with the broken bones."

Joe's warm breath on her neck and coiled body pressed against her back made it difficult to focus on her goal of deflating the situation. She hoped her face looked as impassive and unimpressed as she was trying to make it.

Wilson finally walked away with little more than a grunt. For the first time Beth realized she'd been holding her breath.

"You okay?" Joe asked, turning her to face him. His eyes burned with a combination of protectiveness and possession.

Beth's temperature spiked and her head went a little fuzzy. "Yeah," she said. "I'm fine."

"You don't look fine."

"It was the smell," she said, unable to think of another excuse. Telling him the truth wasn't an option. "Does that man ever bathe?"

"Only if he falls off the boat." Joe took her gently by the elbow. "Come on, let's get out of here."

The offer was the same as Wilson's, but Beth's reaction couldn't have been more different. A puppet under Joe's control, she followed his lead, moving through the crowd as if steered by his touch alone. He must have been really good with a boat.

They found Patty and Tom near the kitchenette at the back of the room. Joe snagged a bottle of water off the tiny counter and handed it to Beth. "I'm taking her back to the house. Do you need me at the restaurant after I drop her off?"

She wasn't sure which bothered her more: the disappointment of him dropping her off and leaving or the desire to give him a reason to stay.

Patty and Tom spoke at the same time.

"We don't need you," from Patty.

"We definitely need you," from Tom.

Patty looked up at Tom. "We're fine. We already have three waitresses and two bussers, and the dinner crowd should have thinned out by now." Turning to Beth and Joe she said, "You kids go on. I'm going to help clean up here and then we'll be home shortly after midnight."

Tom gave Joe a hard look Beth couldn't have interpreted even if her wits hadn't suddenly taken the night off. Joe just nodded. "Fine. We're out of here."

The steering began again, this time with his hand on the small of her back. She heard Tom cough, a noise that sounded more like a bark, and Joe's hand fell away.

"Is something going on between you and your dad?" she asked as Joe pushed through the exit.

"Nothing I can't ignore," he said, closing the door and leaving the hum of the crowd behind them.

CHAPTER FIFTEEN

Joe spent the drive to his parents' house trying not to rip his steering wheel off the column. The moment he saw Wilson grab Beth, a primal instinct took over. The instinct to break the creep's arm just for touching her.

His reaction to the "keeping her warm" comment bordered on homicidal.

The anger should have been aimed at himself since Joe wanted nothing more than to keep Beth warm. More than warm. He wanted her hot and moaning in his bed or wherever he could get her out of that damn skirt. To hell with his brother.

The growl escaped before he could catch it, breaking the silence in the vehicle. Neither of them had spoken since leaving the library, and the few times he threw a glance her way, Beth looked to be processing her own thoughts. Probably trying to get the stench of Buddy Wilson out of her brain.

"Are you okay?" she asked as he pulled into the drive and cut the engine.

He hadn't been okay since he'd found her scared to death on that ferry, but he'd never tell her so. "I'm good."

Resisting the urge to take her arm and check for himself, he said, "I should be asking you that question. Did he hurt you?"

She rubbed her wrist absently. When she didn't answer, he looked to her face and saw green eyes staring back with the same sexual heat currently coursing through his veins.

Son of a bitch.

"You'd better get inside." He rolled out of the Jeep, desperate for distance.

"I don't have a key." She remained in the Jeep as if intending to stay there. "I didn't think to ask Patty for one. If you don't have one, I'll have to wait for them at your place."

Oh, hell no. "I have a key. Come on." Joe crossed in front of the vehicle and headed up the porch steps. By the time he'd opened the door, Beth stood close behind him, her arms crossed, giving him a glimpse of cleavage in the soft porch light.

A cold shower wouldn't be enough tonight.

"You'd better go in." *Before I carry you in and we find out how sturdy that kitchen island is.* "Thanks for coming to the meeting." He kept his eyes focused on a moth hovering around the spiral bulb. "I guess this vacation isn't turning out the way you thought it would."

"No, it isn't," she said, her voice little more than a whisper. "Nothing seems to be what I thought it was."

His eyes caught hers then dropped to her mouth. Sweet vanilla filled his senses and every nerve in his body vibrated with need. Her tongue darted out, leaving a sheen of moisture along her bottom lip, and he was lost. Leaning in, Joe felt her breath mix with his own. So close now he could almost taste her.

But before he could breach the last centimeter between them, a shrill ring cut through the thick night air.

Beth jerked away, the screen door straining on its hinges as Joe jumped back in the opposite direction. A finger against her lips, Beth stepped into the house, looked at the ID on the phone, then turned her back as she answered. "Hello, Lucas."

Joe let the screen door slam behind him. He'd thought the day Cassie's engagement ring showed up in the mail had been the lowest he'd ever feel.

Not even close.

~

If the ringing of the phone had felt like a bucket of cold water, the slamming of the screen was a punch in the chest. A punch of guilt. She could still feel Joe's breath on her lips. Her body still hummed with anticipation. For her fiancé's brother. How had things gotten so out of control?

"Beth? Are you there?"

"Yes," she said, working to keep her voice level. "I'm sorry. What did you say?"

"I asked how your week has been. I didn't realize what day it was until our usual Friday night dinner reminder popped up on my calendar." The fact Lucas kept reminders about her in his calendar had seemed endearing once upon a time. But not tonight. "How is the Cassandra situation?"

Beth shrugged, then remembered Lucas couldn't see her. "I haven't seen her for a few days, but we know she has eyes and ears on the inside."

What sounded like a sporting event blasted over the line, then faded. "Sorry. Just turned on the television. What do you mean 'on the inside'? You make this sound like some undercover assignment."

His words were meant as a joke, but Beth wasn't in the mood for joking. "We had a small meeting last night to get the initial group on the same page and somehow Wheeler found out. By the time the Merchants meeting started tonight, they'd doubled their offers to several business owners."

"Doubled the offers? You mean she really is there trying to buy the island?"

Nice to know he hadn't believed her the first time. "Yes, Lucas. This threat is real." *And you should be here helping your family.*

"What does Joe say about it? I can't believe he'd let this happen."

"What do you expect him to do, Lucas? Chase Cassandra away? Buy up the property himself? He spent an hour at that meeting tonight doing everything he could to persuade the others not to sell. It kills me to see him so worried."

The words were out before she could stop them. She heard as much as felt Lucas's tension traveling through the wires.

"You must be spending a lot of time together." Beth held her breath, thinking of how she'd spent the last few moments before the phone rang. "I should have known if anyone could get him to come around, it would be you.

Even Joe's pain-in-the-ass attitude can't stand up to my sweet Elizabeth."

The sensual lull in his voice was like a jagged stick poking at her conscience. "How is your case going? If you make it back down this weekend we'll still have one more week." Even as she spoke the words, Beth had no idea how she would handle being in the same room with both Lucas and Joe.

"The case isn't good. Prosecution found an eyewitness that puts our client at the scene. We'll be here all weekend trying to figure out how to discredit the testimony." Part of her was relieved, which shot the guilt up another notch. "I might make the last few days. I'm trying my best. I promise."

Beth sighed. "I know you are."

The voice of reason told her to go back to Richmond. Pack her things and drive off first thing in the morning. But she'd made a promise to Sid. And there was the Wheeler issue. Somehow the people on this island felt more important than anything in her life before she'd landed on Anchor.

"Good luck with the case," she said. "Call me when you can."

"Hey," he said. "Keep working on Joe. You might turn him into a decent human being before you leave there. The whole island will raise a statue in your honor."

After what had almost happened, she was pretty sure neither of them felt like decent human beings at the moment.

"I'll do my best," she replied, then ended the call. Glancing out the window, she saw a dim light coming from Joe's place.

Maybe she should go over. They were adults, after all. This attraction, or whatever it was, meant nothing. Bring it into the light, deal with it, and move on. That's what they needed to do.

She took one step away from the kitchen island when her conscience woke up.

Why are you really going over there? What if what almost happened happens again and this time there isn't a well-timed interruption? Are you sure you can touch that flame and not catch fire?

Stupid brain. There was no fire between her and Joe. There couldn't be. Lucas was her future husband, and she would not betray him. Ever.

Which is why she and Joe needed to deal with this now. Beth straightened her shoulders and headed for the door, ignoring the increase in her heart rate. She reached the bottom porch step when Joe's house went dark.

"Well, hell."

Maybe now wasn't the time. Maybe there was nothing to talk about anyway. If Joe wasn't going to lose sleep over a close encounter that amounted to nothing, neither was she.

Her heart slowed.

As she made her way back up the stairs, her rational side assured her irrational side that she had nothing to feel guilty about.

Regardless, all sides continued to feel guilty.

~

Less than an hour before Joe's morning charter, the client called to say they'd gotten in late and would like to reschedule. Hanging around the house increased his chances of running into Beth, something he'd prefer not to do. In fact, if he could avoid her completely for the rest of her time on the island, that would be fine with him.

So Joe headed to the gym. Physical exertion would do him good. If nothing else, he could burn off the frustration that had kept him up most of the night. Pumping iron wasn't what his body wanted, but what his body wanted he couldn't have. Ever.

The punching bag would be his first stop. Every time he thought of Buddy Wilson putting a hand on Beth, he wanted to punch something. Better to work out his anger on a bag than Buddy's face. Not that the anger was for Buddy alone.

After what had happened on his parents' porch, he should be kicking his own ass. What kind of a man tries to kiss his brother's fiancée? A week ago he'd have said only an asshole, but today *he* was the asshole.

"Abby told me you were here," Randy said, reaching out to help Joe wrap his right hand. "You scared the girl half to death."

Joe passed the gauze and looked up. "I didn't do anything to her."

"I'm guessing it was the growl and that demon look in your eye. What's up with you, man?" Randy cut the material and grabbed the tape off the bench.

"Client canceled last-minute, that's all." Joe tested the grip on his right hand as Randy moved to the left. "Tell the kid I'm sorry."

"Tell her yourself on the way out. I'm not your messenger." Silence fell between the men while Randy finished wrapping Joe's other hand. Then the big man stepped back and crossed his arms. "Now let's talk about what's really going on. I saw your run-in with Wilson last night."

Joe's hands balled into fists, stretching the newly applied tape. "He was being an ass. Nothing new."

"He was being an ass with your future sister-in-law, and what should have been a simple heads-up for him to step back looked more like you wanted to rip his head off. You're dancing close to a bad line, my friend."

Joe turned his back on Randy, unwilling to lie to his friend's face. "I don't know what you're talking about."

"Yes, you do."

Joe turned back around, thinking if the man weren't so damn big, he'd forget the bag and start throwing punches now. "I don't want to talk about it."

"I can see that." Randy relaxed, taking a seat on the bench. Clearly he wasn't worried about a punch coming his way. "When you first told me about this Miss Chandler, you warned me she was off-limits. I assumed that meant she belonged to you. And I think you knew that."

Joe paced along the lockers. "I never said she belonged to me."

"But you never said she belonged to Lucas either." Randy sighed. "This is complicated shit, bro."

"Complicated" didn't begin to describe the mess he was in. And if his head weren't halfway up his ass, he might be able to figure it out. "I came here to work out. That's what I'm going to do. I just need to let off some steam." Swiping a towel from a shelf at the end of the lockers, Joe headed for the door.

Before he reached the exit, Randy's words stopped him. "You can beat the hell out of that bag. You can try beating the hell out of me if you don't straighten your ass out. But she'll still be there when you're done."

Randy had seen Joe at his worst, being the one who'd scraped him off the pavement when the Cassie situation blew up in his face. Joe owed him. "I'm not moving in on my brother's girl. I wouldn't do that." He tried running a hand through his hair and remembered the tape. "I just have to make it one more week, right? Then she'll be gone and everything can get back to normal."

Randy joined him near the exit. "Not the best plan you've ever had, but it's a start. Can I give you a piece of advice?"

"Can I stop you?" Joe asked.

"Don't be a martyr."

"What does that mean?"

"Exactly what it says. If the look on her face last night meant anything, you're not the only one hunting for solid ground." Grabbing a basket full of used towels, Randy moved into the doorway, shoulders filling the frame. "Maybe she isn't as off-limits as you think."

~

Beth pulled into the drive of the last house on Tuttles Lane, hoping she had the right place. She'd wanted to verify Sid's address and the directions with Joe, but he'd disappeared before she poured her first cup of coffee. Which was probably for the best, since she had no idea how to act around him.

Should she mention the almost kiss? What if it was her imagination and there was no almost anything? Then she'd not only feel guilty about wanting to kiss Joe, she'd feel like a moron if Joe never intended to kiss her. Though his intention had seemed pretty obvious on the porch in the dark with nothing but crickets and moths for company.

In the light of day, lack of sleep made the entire situation unclear, and the dream that had jarred her upright in bed took guilt to new levels. She'd been walking down an aisle to the wedding march, the tulle of the veil blurring her surroundings. Shapes hovered on both sides, faces and details obscured.

When she reached the end and turned to the man on her right, the veil lifted. Blue eyes danced before her, and a sexy smile, revealing that unmistakable dimple, turned her brain to butter.

Beth had bolted awake, covered in sweat. A long hot shower took care of the sweat, but couldn't wash away the memory of how right she'd felt in the dream. How, in the moment before her brain thrust back to reality, she'd felt a wave of happiness like she'd never known.

"You getting out or what?" Sid's voice jarred Beth out of dreamland.

"For future reference, if I help you catch the eye of this guy you're lusting after, promise me you won't greet him that way on the first date."

"I'll try not to reveal my true self until date three or four." As Sid walked away, she mumbled something under her breath that Beth couldn't hear. Probably for the best.

She followed Sid into a large garage that looked more like a hardware store that had been tossed by burglars. Workbenches, covered in piles of trash and what Beth assumed to be engine parts, lined three walls. Several small paths ran between various tools she couldn't begin to identify. Her grandfather spent a great deal of time in his work shed when Beth was little, but he'd never welcomed her into his little man cave, nor taught her any skill that involved power tools.

"You know how to use all this stuff?" she asked. Crossing into the darker interior, she blinked several times, waiting for her eyes to adjust.

"Why would I own all this shit if I didn't know how to use it?"

Beth shrugged. Sid's belligerent expression grew clearer. "I don't know. Maybe you inherited it from your dad?"

Sid had been wiping her hands on a greasy rag that didn't look up to the task of cleaning anything. The rag flew past Beth's nose, landing on one of the cluttered counter-tops. "Let's get something straight. This is my house and my garage and my shit. Knowing a drill bit from a buzz saw does not make me any less of a woman."

First nerve hit. Beth tilted her head to one side, debating how to approach her subject. Straightforward had worked the night before, and sticking to what worked was always the best choice.

"You've clearly dealt with some real assholes in your time, and I'm sure they've all regretted whatever insult they dealt you. Some probably still bear the scars. But any intelligent human being can look at you and know there's a woman under all that grease and...is that camouflage?"

Sid looked ready to defend her fashion choice, but Beth waved the words away. "Forget I asked. Today is just a simple makeover where we find you a few more...feminine looks and let your natural beauty shine through."

What Sid did next took Beth completely by surprise. She smiled. The change was like watching the sun burst through a thundercloud. Beth could have sworn the birds chirped in celebration as if Cinderella had just emerged from the ashes with a broom and a team of dancing mice.

This scenario put Beth in the position of fairy god-mother, which should have felt overwhelming, especially with such a large task looming before her. Oddly enough, she found it kind of fun.

As if the smile wasn't enough, Sid's next question had Beth looking around for hidden cameras. "You think I'm beautiful?" When Beth didn't answer, as that would require once again picking her jaw up off the floor, Sid added, "We're not back to that lesbian shit again, are we?"

"No," Beth said, shaking her head once, then a second time to clear it. "Don't you own a mirror?"

Sid turned to a fridge on her right and pulled out two bot-tles of beer. "Of course I own a mirror. Doesn't mean I have to spend all day staring at it. I'm not out to impress anybody."

As it was barely noon, Beth declined the offered beer with a quiet "No, thank you."

"Suit yourself." Sid put the beer back in the fridge and Beth realized what she'd said. Their little makeover was happening because Sid supposedly did have someone to impress.

"I'm a little confused here."

"About what?" Sid twisted off the beer cap, hurling it across the room to ding off some invisible metal can.

"You just said you're not out to impress anyone, but isn't that why I'm here? To help you impress someone?"

Sid took a large swallow of the beer. If Beth didn't know better, she'd swear the minidynamo was stalling. "I meant up until now. I wasn't out to impress anybody until now."

"Right." The answer was less than believable, but then Beth couldn't think of any other reason Sid would willingly spend a day with her. Or allow herself to be dressed in anything other than work boots and grease-stained T-shirts. "Why don't we start with your closet then? You must have something in there we can build on."

Sid went from looking nervous to doubtful. "You can look. I have some of my mom's old stuff, but I don't think it'll fit since she was several inches taller than I am."

Beth followed Sid to a side door that led into the house, stopping when she spotted the calendar next to the door frame. A bare-chested man with bright blue eyes and a wicked bad-boy smile stared back at her. One black lock curled over his forehead as if encouraging her to reach up and smooth it back.

If the eyes were hazel, the shoulders slightly broader, Mr. May would bear a striking resemblance to Lucas. Clearly Sid had a type.

"Isn't this guy an actor?"

Sid followed Beth's gaze and shared a less innocent-looking smile. "Good eye. British. It's a whole calendar full of them." A flip of her wrist revealed several other lanky men smiling from the pages, not a shirt in the bunch.

"Don't take this the wrong way, but I expected you to be more the blue-collar type," Beth said.

The scowl returned briefly, but then Sid glanced back at the garage and nodded. "I can see where you'd think that, but no. I like my men lanky and charming with that touch of intensity and passion. The Brits fit the bill perfectly." She shrugged. "The accent is a bonus."

Crossing into the house, Beth was once again surprised. They'd stepped into an immaculately clean kitchen, which stood in stark contrast to the chaos that was the garage. "Does that description fit this crush of yours? Lanky and charming?"

The look on Sid's face told Beth there was definitely a man, and not just on the calendar. "That describes him." Setting her beer on the counter and leaning down to untie her boots, Sid pointed toward the doorway. "Bedroom is the second door on the right. I'll be there as soon as I get these off."

Ignoring the fact that "lanky and charming" described Lucas, Beth did as ordered, exploring Sid's home on her way to the bedroom. Whitewashed paneling gave the perfect beach cottage look to the living room. A large well-worn area rug enveloped the plank wood floor and brought warmth to the cool interior. Picture frames of varying sizes occupied the few surfaces available with more mounted on the wall behind the couch.

There was no mistaking this little house belonged to a woman. A very feminine woman. Sidney Ann Navarro was turning out to be a walking conundrum.

CHAPTER SIXTEEN

By the time Beth reached the hallway, Sid caught up and followed her into the bedroom.

In contrast to the living room, Sid's sleeping quarters sported soft lavender walls and solid sky-blue bedding. A white wrought-iron headboard stood between two matching white wicker nightstands, each of which held a simple yet feminine lamp in a shape reminiscent of the Anchor Lighthouse.

Beth wondered where she could find herself a pair. "Did you get those lamps here on the island?"

"Nah. Brought those with me from Florida. They were my mom's, but I don't know where she got them."

Maybe if she described them to Lola, she'd know where to find something similar.

Sid's bedroom held no frills, but contained several feminine accents. It was clean like the rest of the house. Beth felt a twinge of guilt that she'd expected the room to resemble something she'd seen in a frat house during college.

"Nice room." Trying not to sound doubtful, she asked, "Did you decorate this yourself?"

"It's all me. Don't bother trying to hide your surprise. You'd make a terrible poker player." Sid crossed the room and opened a set of levered doors. "I'm tough. I dig through engines for a living and know my way around a tackle box. But I also like soft colors, pretty undies, and the occasional romance novel." Legs apart and arms crossed, she warned, "If you ever blab that last bit to the guys, I'll turn you into fish food faster than a shark hits chum."

Beth smiled. "I prefer historicals, mostly medievals. Nothing like a Highland warrior to keep a girl warm at night."

Sid's smile returned. "A kilt is always good, but hot FBI agents are my first choice."

Common ground achieved, mission makeover got underway.

~

Joe struggled to dismiss Randy's words long after leaving the gym. Standing on the fueling dock, he replayed the night before. Beth had played as much of a role as he had. She'd stared up at him with those green eyes, dark with need. Though the smell of diesel surrounded him, the memory of her scent, vanilla and sugar and soft woman, sent a jolt through his system.

She wanted him as much as he wanted her.

But what they wanted didn't matter. Changing Beth from off-limits to available didn't change the facts. She was engaged to his brother. Joe was a lot of things, but a man who would steal his brother's girl wasn't one of them.

"I hear things got interesting after I left the meeting last night."

Joe tensed. Today was not the day for Mohler to fuck with him. Not bothering to turn around, he said, "Helga brought out a really good cheesecake, but that's about it."

Phil snorted. "I'm talking about your run-in with Buddy and you know it."

This day just kept getting better. Joe sighed. "I wouldn't call it a run-in."

"That's what Buddy called it. Said you acted like he'd grabbed your best rod. Or maybe you've been dipping your rod in illegal waters."

Mohler had no idea how lucky he was Joe spent the morning beating the shit out of a punching bag. Otherwise, he'd be a bleeding stump by now.

"You can tell a lot about a man by the friends he keeps." Taking his time, Joe secured his gas caps before turning around. "But then I figure you'd be a dumb-ass whether you hung around with Wilson or not."

"Fuck you, Dempsey."

"No thanks, you're not my type." Joe needed to work out with the bag more often. He hadn't felt this tolerant in weeks. "I've got clients to meet."

"I doubt the high-and-mighty act will work when your brother finds out that you're fucking his woman."

Joe stopped with one foot on the boat. He could take this opportunity to stomp Mohler into the dock, but that wouldn't change the thin line of truth in the accusation. Since Mohler didn't know Lucas well enough to call him up with a gossip report, the man's goal had to be getting Joe to throw the first punch.

As Joe placed both feet back on the dock, Mohler retreated two steps. Ball-less wonder. "I could kick your ass, since that seems to be what you're asking for, but I won't. You and Wilson want to have a tea party and gossip like little girls, have at it. But if I hear one person repeat what you just said, I'll come looking for you. And it won't be pretty."

Mohler visibly tensed, sweat beading on his brow. "I don't hear you denying it."

"You're pushing your luck, Mohler. Consider yourself warned." Joe returned to his boat, firing both engines and reminding himself he hadn't done anything wrong.

∽

Within minutes it was clear the contents of Sid's closet would be useless in this Cinderella endeavor. No amount of fairy dust could turn this wardrobe into anything that would catch a man's eye. Unless the goal was to give him ideas for his own wardrobe.

Hedging her bets, Beth had used input from Patty to create a list of stores for everything from dresses to shoes to undergarments. Since Sid was true to her word, sporting an entire drawer of the sexiest and most delicate lingerie Beth had seen outside a Victoria's Secret catalogue, the last store could be scratched immediately.

"I don't like it," Sid said, for what had to be the fifteenth time. So far she'd found a reason not to like any of the dresses Beth picked out.

"What's wrong with this one?"

"The sleeves."

"What about the sleeves?"

"They're frilly."

Beth mentally chanted the pep talk that had saved her from shoving Sid out of the car before they'd reached the first store. Never had there been a more annoying backseat, or in this case, passenger-seat driver.

"It's called a cap sleeve, and it'll perfectly accentuate your amazing arms." Though Beth was slim, she'd never lifted a weight in her life. She couldn't help but envy the complete lack of fat on Sid's well-defined arms.

"It's frilly."

"Fine." Beth moved around to another rack and spotted the perfect dress. The marble swirls of dark purple, blue, and red, mixed with hints of white, green, and aqua would be gorgeous against Sid's olive skin. Sleeveless, it had wide straps that plunged into a deep V, and a thick black belt that would accentuate Sid's tiny waist.

"You're trying this on." Snatching the dress off the rack, Beth headed for the dressing room before Sid could argue.

"What is it? I have to see it first."

"You're putting this on whether you like it or not." Pulling back an orange curtain, Beth snapped the dress hanger onto a hook in the back wall and motioned Sid into the stall. "And I want to see it this time. No 'I don't like it' then ripping it off before I get a glimpse."

"You're a pushy bitch, Curly." Sid had been calling Beth "Curly" since the night at Dempsey's, and though she'd hated the nickname in her elementary school days, she let it slide now. From Sid the name was practically an endearment.

And since Beth had now nicknamed Sid "Stubborn Ass," at least in her own mind, the exchange seemed fair.

When Sid threw the curtain open two minutes later, Beth grinned. "I knew it. Perfect."

Sid shoved her hands in the pockets Beth hadn't noticed before, and walked over to the three-way mirror. "I kind of like it," Sid said, turning from left to right. Their eyes met in the mirror and Beth knew they were done looking.

"There's just one thing," Beth said, snagging the ponytail holder from Sid's head before she could argue. Long black locks fell around the petite woman's shoulders, framing her face and sending the eye down to the deep V in front. Not that Sid's girls needed the assist. The woman had the boobs of a porn star without the scars and silicone.

"Whoever this crush is, he doesn't stand a chance." Sid blushed and took another turn before the mirror. Beth could get used to playing fairy godmother. "Now we can move on to shoes."

"No, we can't." Sid said, looking obstinate. Beth would hog-tie her if necessary. The woman was getting this dress. "It's your turn," Sid said.

"My turn?" Beth didn't remember the fairy godmother getting to play dress-up, too. "I don't need anything. My yellow sundress will work for tonight. This is about you, not me."

Sid propped her hands on her hips. "If I'm getting one, you're getting one." She looked at the price tag. "This is half what I have to spend, so I'll pay for yours, too."

Now who was playing fairy godmother? "I can't let you do that."

"Then I'm not getting this." Sid headed back to the dressing room, undoing the belt as she went.

"But you have to get it. That dress was made for you."

"I get one, you get one."

The demon spawn could drive a saint to violence. "Fine," Beth mumbled. "I'll look for a dress."

"I'll pick it out."

Not a good idea. "You change while I look for my own."

One hand slapped up on the wall of the dressing room. "I'm not a charity case, Curly. And I'm not completely fashion challenged." Beth felt her right brow float up before she could stop it. "I may not have any idea how to dress myself, but finding something for you should be a piece of cake. Now sit your ass down while I get my camo back on."

The words "camo back on" perfectly illustrated why Sid was the last person Beth wanted picking out her clothes. But she sat down as ordered, mostly because the clerk behind the counter kept glancing in their direction with a worry and maybe a little fear in her eyes.

"I know just the one, Curly. Leave it to me," Sid said from behind the curtain. A second later, a marble dress shot over the curtain rod, followed by its hanger. Beth caught the dress in her lap and the hanger a second before it smacked her in the forehead.

Five hours, two mani-pedis, one blowout (for Beth), and copious amounts of whining (from Sid) later, Beth found herself in the Dempseys' guest bedroom in front of a full-length mirror staring at a woman she hardly recognized.

"I never should have let you talk me into this." She tugged the top of the dress up for the third time, but the material refused to cooperate. Her bathing suit covered more than this.

"Stop screwing with it. You look awesome." Sid edged Beth out of the mirror, leaning forward toward the glass. "I had no idea my boobs could look like this."

Though her little Cinderella owned plenty of frilly bras, she'd never put one on with the right dress before. Not only were Beth's girls more exposed than usual, they were getting an inferiority complex having to share the same reflecting surface as Sid's.

"I'm wearing the sweater," Beth said, grabbing her white three-quarter-sleeve cardigan from the bed where Sid had thrown it. Tugging it over her shoulders, she checked the mirror again. Thankfully, Sid was now sitting in a nearby chair to admire her new shoes. They'd settled for wedges after discovering the transition from work boots to stilettos would not happen in an afternoon.

Beth assessed her appearance. She did love the dress. Not as bold or loud as Sid's, which suited her fine. Spaghetti straps held up what there was of the bodice, which was little more than two dark-green triangles of fabric. The A-line skirt shot out from the empire waist, rolling like a wave when she moved. Emerald green faded into a pattern of swirling ribbons in a dance of chaos. Cuts of white and dark green danced along the bottom hem.

The color did wonders for her eyes, and blowing out her curls revealed her hair to be longer than she'd realized. The curls usually rested on her shoulders, but straightened as they were now, the edges brushed several inches lower, drawing more attention to the amount of pale skin not covered by the dress.

Pulling the sweater tight, she decided to get on with the evening and stop worrying about her appearance. Their mission was to show the Anchor natives, or at least one male native Beth had yet to learn the name of, that a real woman lurked under Sid's usual grubby wardrobe.

Based on the bombshell before her, it would be mission accomplished.

As Beth slipped into a pair of white leather sandals, Sid said, "I need to head over to Joe's place before we leave."

"What for?" Beth asked. She'd been hoping to avoid her future brother-in-law in light of the porch incident.

"Let's just say I'm settling a bet." Sid picked up Beth's body mist and spritzed some behind her ears and down her cleavage. Maybe the new dress was *too* sexy. Sid had shot past Cinderella to Barbarella. "This won't take long."

Beth took the coward's way and lingered on the porch while Sid sashayed across the driveway and charged up Joe's front steps.

∼

Joe was determined to avoid his front windows until certain the girls had left, which made checking every few minutes to see if Sid's truck was gone more difficult than it should have been. Part of him was curious to see the girlified Sid, but another part, the part doing most of his thinking lately, just wanted to see Beth.

He dropped his pizza when Sid yelled through his front door.

"Get your ass out here, Dempsey."

"Keep your pants on, I'm coming." Sliding his plate onto the coffee table, Joe turned down the game and headed for the door. He didn't recognize the woman on the other side of the screen.

A short brunette with some of the best cleavage he'd ever seen stood with her arms crossed, tapping one high-heeled foot. Those heels added several inches to her five-foot-two frame, and the short dress made her legs look twice as long.

Beth was a fucking miracle worker.

Not willing to admit defeat right away, Joe asked, "What the hell happened to you?"

"Nice try, Dempsey, but playing it cool doesn't work when you're talking to my tits instead of my face." Not that her face wasn't nice, too. Free of grease smudges, with thick, sweeping lashes and shiny goop on her lips, his little mechanic cleaned up pretty damn good. "Pay up."

"You haven't even walked into the bar yet." Joe glanced over Sid's shoulder to make sure Beth was out of earshot. He didn't see her anywhere and figured she was still primping. "The bet was that you'd be the hottest thing in the bar. You have to be *in the bar* before you can declare victory."

"You think anybody in that bar is going to look better than this?" At that moment, Joe spotted Beth standing on his parents' porch and his heart stopped. Then her eyes met his across the distance and his heart started racing double time. "Dempsey," Sid said, flicking his nose through the screen.

He answered Sid's question with a lie. "Maybe. We stick to the terms of the bet."

Sid narrowed her eyes and huffed. "Fine. But I'm coming to collect tomorrow." She turned to walk away, and a scent caught in the air.

"Hey," he said, stopping Sid before she reached the first step. "What are you wearing?"

"A dress, dumb-ass. What does it look like?"

"Not that. The perfume."

Sid sniffed her wrist. "Something Beth had in her room. Why?"

He wanted to tell her not to wear it again, but didn't. "No reason. I guess I'm not used to you smelling like anything other than motor oil."

"Go back to wanking off, Dempsey." Sid moved down the steps with more agility than he would expect looking at her shoes. She threw a parting shot over one shoulder. "And stop looking at Beth like that or I'll kick your ass myself."

CHAPTER SEVENTEEN

Joe spent an hour imagining liquored-up tourists drooling over Beth. The idea of sweaty middle-aged men buying her drinks, sliding hairy knuckles over her pale skin, and invading her space made him irritated enough that he knew he had to do something. Since going to the bar and dragging her out wasn't an option, he drove over to Dempsey's, figuring he could either help out bussing tables or snooker Alvie out of a few bucks in pool.

The crowd was thick when he arrived, so bussing tables it was. A group of college kids celebrating the start of summer filled a back corner, keeping Joe busy clearing empty longnecks and wing baskets. On the third clearing, a young thing with dark curly hair glanced his way with encouraging green eyes.

A picture of Beth smiling up at a bartender while he looked down her dress resulted in Joe throwing bottles in the bus tub harder than necessary. Beer splashed on the pretty brunette, removing any trace of encouragement from her expression. Joe found the other busboy and offered to switch sections. When Mitch spotted the college girls, he agreed without argument.

What Joe hadn't realized was that someone much worse than a younger version of Beth occupied a booth in his new section.

"I wondered when you'd make your way over." Cassie flashed him the smile that once upon a time would have put him at her feet. Tonight the effect was a slight tightening in his jaw.

"I didn't see you before." Avoiding eye contact, he asked, "Are you done with those dishes?"

Cassie leaned away from the table. "Yes, you can take them." Then as Joe reached for the empty wineglass, she grasped his wrist. "Why don't you put that mess in the kitchen and come have a seat. We need to talk."

"I don't think—"

"Joe," she said, rubbing her thumb over the back of his hand. "One conversation. You can give me that much."

Ironic words, since their relationship had always been about what he could and couldn't give her. Or maybe what he wouldn't give her.

"Right. I'll be back."

Stalling, Joe cleared two more tables on his way to the kitchen. The only thing they had to talk about was the development deal. Maybe she wanted to negotiate. Him for the island. As soon as the thought entered his mind, he chided himself for the arrogance.

Cassie didn't want him that bad. Even if she did, the answer would still be no.

Once the dishes were loaded into the dishwasher, Joe removed his apron, sliding it over the hook near the back door.

"Where are you going?" asked Tom, exiting the pantry with a large bag of pretzels.

"Cassie wants to talk."

Tom's brows shot up and then he blinked as if Joe had said, "I'm having a baby."

"You're going to talk to her? Here?"

Sitting with the enemy in public wasn't his smartest move, but maybe he could talk her out of this crazy idea. Explain where the islanders stood and how determined they were to hold out. He'd take the blame for whatever had happened between them if it would get Cassie and her father to leave the island alone for good.

Drying his freshly washed hands on his jeans, Joe navigated the tables and slid into the booth, taking the seat across from his former fiancée. She'd grown more beautiful, but, like the smile, her full lips and dark blue eyes had lost the effect they once had on him.

The face remained model perfect, but now he knew the real woman behind it. For the first time in more than two years, the guilt and self-contempt were muted by a feeling of relief. He'd been stupid. That wouldn't change. But he'd dodged a bullet and finally saw the end of their relationship for what it was. A lucky break.

Feeling lighter than he had in a while, Joe asked, "What do you want to talk about?"

Cassie's mouth pinched into a flat line. "I'd think that was obvious."

Knowing never to assume anything in regards to a woman, Joe remained obtuse. "You'll have to enlighten me."

"I've been on this crappy island for more than a week, and we both know I'm not here on vacation." Joe leaned back and crossed his arms, not interested in hearing her true feelings about his home. Again.

Recognizing her error, she tried again. "The resort we have planned could put this island on the map, Joe. You have to see that."

"The way I see it, you and your dad are trying to wipe us *off* the map. We've been here for a few centuries, and so far people have found us just fine."

Cassie snorted. "A dingy lighthouse and a patch of old tombstones isn't cutting it anymore. Anchor may not be dead yet, but it'll be on life support in less than five years."

"We don't think so." If Cassie was in charge of the Wheeler sales team, her tactic would take them under long before Anchor went anywhere. "If we're so bad off, why do you want the place so desperately?"

Cassie looked down, one nail tapping the table. Maybe his instincts weren't so far off after all.

"This isn't how you get revenge, Cass. These people didn't do anything to you. And in the end, neither did I." Saying the words felt good. "We were wrong from the start. I was a way to piss off your daddy, and you were a bird in a cage looking for a way out."

"I guess our memories on the matter differ. If all I'd wanted was a way out of the cage, there were plenty of other men I could have chosen." Pride kept her chin up, but the spoiled little girl still pouted behind the makeup.

"Ivy League boys after your name and your money. That would have meant going from one cage to another. And you knew it." A one-mile piece of dirt at the bottom of a barrier reef must have seemed like a cage, too. "Move on, Cass. We both need to move on."

She stared a long time and something in her face changed. The pouting child replaced by an angry woman. "Your ego needs a reality check, Joe. I'm not here for you. Anything personal between us ended when you made your choice." Reaching into her purse, Cassandra pulled out two twenty-dollar bills and dropped them on the table. "This is a business trip. And I intend to close the deal."

~

"Are you drinking that wine or waiting for it to evaporate?"

Beth set the glass on the bar. "I drank the first two too fast. I already feel like I could fall off this stool." Turning at the sound of new arrivals, she asked for the fourth time, "Is that him?"

The new O'Hagan's patrons were two young women who didn't look old enough to be in a bar.

Sid snorted. "Stop watching the door and drink your wine."

Sid had yet to share the name of her mystery guy, and why he had to remain a mystery was a mystery to Beth. A dizzying thought that confirmed the wisdom of nursing her current drink.

Sid's makeover created even better results than expected. Every male in the place took notice the minute the two women walked through the door. An hour into the night and they had yet to pay for a drink.

Smaller than Dempsey's, O'Hagan's Pub catered more to locals and the college-age crowd. Where Dempsey's sported large windows along two sides, O'Hagan's offered a more cave-like ambiance. The lack of windows left dim sconces and table lamps as the only light sources other than randomly hung neon signs.

According to the bartender, a slender woman named Will who wore bangle bracelets and army boots, the first three rounds were gifts from two different groups of men. Getting a good look at their benefactors was impossible in the shadows and smoke.

"So where are you from, anyway?"

"Me?" Beth asked, surprised by Sid's question. The woman had until now shown little interest in learning anything about her.

"No, the stuffed leprechaun hanging from the bar behind you." Makeup and heels may have changed Sid's appearance, but the mouth would always give her away. "Yes, you. You grow up in Richmond?"

"Just outside," Beth said. "Small town."

Sid sipped her rum and Coke through a small straw, which Beth didn't think was a good idea. "This town have a name?"

Giving the name couldn't hurt. "Louisa."

"A town called Louisa?"

Beth twirled her wineglass. "I told you, it's small."

"Right." Sid spun on her stool, turning her back to the bar. "Your family still there?"

A more difficult question. "I don't have any family."

"Oh." Sid spun back around. "That's tough."

An awkward silence fell between them, so Beth filled it. "What about you? Any family other than your brother?"

Sid looked over as if surprised by the question, then focused again on her glass, chewing her bottom lip. "Mom died when I was eight. Dad when I was fourteen. By then, Randy was twenty and had been bouncing around the globe for two years, diving into whatever adventures he could find."

"That explains the pictures on his office wall."

"I think he was determined to climb up or jump off every cliff he could find." A smile softened her face. "He was here on Anchor with some surfing buddies when the doctors called to say Dad was dying. Brought me back with him after Dad passed, and we've been here ever since."

The sting of being an only child surfaced, as it often did when anyone talked about family. "You're lucky to have a brother like that."

Sid wrinkled her nose, swirling the ice in her glass. "He can be a pain in the ass, but what guy can't, right?"

"Pain in the ass" was a good way to describe Joe. He'd definitely been a pain in her head all day. She knew he'd seen her on the porch before they left for the evening. The least he could have done was come over and thank her for doing this. Not that she wanted him to see her in the revealing dress. That wasn't it at all.

She really did suck at lying. Even to herself.

"Here's another one from the two old guys in the corner," Will said, sliding a fresh rum and Coke in front of Sid. "You ready for your next one, hon?" she asked Beth.

"Not yet, thanks." Will nodded and made her way to another customer. "Are you sure this mystery guy is supposed to be here tonight?"

Sid licked the straw from her finished drink, slid the glass back, and pulled the new one forward. "These things are going down easy tonight."

"Shouldn't you slow down? You're our designated driver, you know."

After a long draw on the straw, Sid said, "The drinks are a gift. I can't be rude and not drink 'em."

"Then who is going to drive us out of here?"

Sid slapped her hands on the bar. "Good Lord, woman, unclench your sphincter and have another drink."

"You're already too far gone to drive." Beth pushed her glass away. "I'd better stop now."

Sid pulled the glass back. "This is a girls' night out. We're going to drink and have a good time, and if we can't drive, then Randy will come and get us. When was the last time you cut loose and had a good time?"

Beth searched her memory. There was that party sophomore year of college. "A long time ago," she said, avoiding the specifics. "I guess I could have one or two more."

"There you go," Sid said, waving for Will to bring another glass of wine. "So how did you end up in Richmond? Wait." Dark brows drew together. "Probably not a lot of lawyers in Louisa."

"Howard Maplethorn."

"Howard who?"

"Maplethorn. He's been the only lawyer in Louisa for as long as I can remember." Beth finished her wine in two gulps. "Gosh, he must be pushing seventy by now. Thanks, Will," she said as another drink appeared before her.

"You two look like you need some food to go with this liquor." Will glanced at the Miller Lite clock behind the bar. "Kitchen is open for another hour. How about an appetizer?"

Beth caught the sound of the front door opening again. Spinning her stool to look, her head went fuzzy and one foot slipped off the bar rail.

"Whoa there." Sid steadied her, stifling what sounded like a giggle. "If you fall off that stool, I'm pretending I don't know you."

"Chicken wings and french fries coming up." Will walked away, presumably to put in their order.

"You didn't answer my question," Sid said.

"What question?"

"How did you end up living in Richmond?"

"Oh, that question." Beth shrugged. "My grandparents sent me to law school at UVA. They wanted me to have a better life than what Louisa had to offer. Pap died before I graduated, and I didn't want to be far from Granny, so I settled in Richmond."

Sid blinked, as if trying to focus. "So you were raised by your grandparents?"

"Yeah." She'd already said more than she should have. "When is your mystery guy going to get here? I'd hate to think we did all this for nothing."

"Maybe later. How did you meet Lucas?"

Beth hadn't thought about Lucas all day. She'd been too busy thinking about Joe and the alleged almost kiss. "We met at work. Lucas is a popular guy in the office. Confident. Perfectly dressed. Ambitious." She tipped back her glass and let the red slide down her throat. Her head and the guilt felt a little lighter. "It's a wonder he ever asked me out."

Sid's glass hit the bar hard. "So he asked you out?"

"Well, I never would have had the nerve to ask him out."

"Of course not." Sid's mouth flattened, and Beth remembered Randy's words. *Sid's been half in love with Lucas since high school.* She felt as if she'd just kicked a puppy.

"Lucas has his drawbacks," Beth said. Sid needed to know what her crush was really like.

"What do you mean 'drawbacks'?" Sid stared at Beth, waiting for an answer, sucking down her drink.

Beth set an elbow on the bar and rested her chin in her hand. "I'd only dated a couple guys before Lucas, and they always seemed to need mothering. Someone to take care of them. Cook and clean and organize and herd them around."

"Sound like winners," Sid murmured. "But what do they have to do with Lucas?"

"They were nothing like Lucas." She shook her head as if to clear the tangling threads of her story. "I mean, he's nothing like them. Lucas doesn't need mothering of any kind. In fact, he's more likely to do the mothering." Staring into her wine, Beth added, "When he's around."

Sid sipped from her straw until the glass was once again empty. "What do you mean 'when he's around'? Don't you guys work together? You must see him all the time."

"You'd think so, wouldn't you? But nope. Lucas is very dedicated to his work, so the job always comes first. Which

I know is a good thing, since he's trying to give us a secure future, but sometimes, like now," she said, waving her free hand around to indicate their current location, "it would be nice if a little of that focus could be on me."

"Let me get this straight." Sid signaled for Will to bring her another drink. "You're going to marry Lucas even though you don't like how much time he spends at work? I've never been married, but that sounds like a bad idea to me."

Hearing the fact aloud, it sounded like a bad idea to Beth, too. But she loved Lucas. Didn't she? Of course she did.

"Lucas is so kind and generous. The sweetest guy I've ever met, if a little distracted from time to time. He's exactly the kind of guy my grandparents wanted for me. Smart, stable, not a criminal."

Sid choked on her drink. "Did you just say 'not a criminal'? Wow. Your grandparents had high standards."

"They wanted me to do better than my mom. The bar wasn't set real high." Beth leaned her elbow on the bar and missed, nearly falling off the stool. Again. After righting herself she said, "I shouldn't be complaining. He's only working this much to move up in the firm and make partner."

"Then what?" Sid asked.

"'Then what' what?"

"Once he makes partner, is he going to stop working so much? Won't he still be working cases, and don't those partner guys spend their weekends on the golf course?"

The partners did play a lot of golf. And not just on the weekends. In fact, Lucas was taking lessons so he could have another "in" with the big guys. Beth hated golf.

"I'm sure it'll all work out," Beth said, sure of nothing of the kind. Looking down she noticed her glass was empty again. "Did I drink that wine already?"

Their food arrived and Sid ordered Beth another drink, but then changed her mind. "I think we need some shots."

"Some what?" Beth had never done shots before, but if the wine was making her this loopy, moving on to shots did not sound like a good idea. "I don't think so."

"Girls' night out, Curly. Can't have a girls' night out without shots."

~

Joe had just dropped the last load of dishes to be washed when the sous chef, Chip, let him know he had a call. He couldn't think of anyone who would hunt him down at the restaurant. "Hello?" he said, hanging his apron up by the back door.

"You need to get over here."

"Over where? Randy?"

"O'Hagan's."

Shit. Knowing Sid, some asshole grabbed her ass and she started a bar brawl.

"What's going on? Is Beth okay?" His sweet-natured future sister-in-law didn't seem like the bar-brawl type.

"Let me put it this way, neither of these ladies, and I use that term loosely where Sid is concerned, are feeling any pain. At the moment. But they're going to feel like shit in the morning."

Joe couldn't believe it. "Beth is drunk?"

"Plastered. The bartender says they started doing shots a couple hours ago." Randy didn't sound amused. "Beth says she doesn't have a key, and I doubt you want me to drop her at Dempsey's. Not in this condition."

First thing in the morning he was getting Beth her own damn key. "I'm on my way."

Joe let his dad know where he was going, then hit the road. Five minutes later he pulled into O'Hagan's parking lot and saw Randy hovering behind a bench outside the pub door, looking like a handler trying to keep two rambunctious pups in place. The girls were giggling and snorting. Whatever the joke, Randy didn't find it funny.

"All right, girls, time to go," he said, lifting them each by an elbow. Sid jerked her arm away and nearly fell over the end of the bench. Randy moved to catch his sister, throwing Beth flat against Joe's chest. The scent of sweetened vanilla filled his head.

Regaining her footing, Beth looked up with big green eyes, then breathed out a "Heeeeeyyyyyy."

Her breath could fuel a flamethrower.

"Looks like you had a good time," he said, putting some distance between them but continuing to help her balance. She carried a small purse in one hand and a sweater in the other. One thin strap slid off her shoulder, threatening to take what little material covered her breast down with it.

"I had the best time," Beth said. Then turning to Sid, she yelled, "Hey!"

An unsteady Sid answered back, "Yeah!"

Their volumes seemed to correlate to their elevated alcohol levels.

Beth pumped her fist in the air and together they yelled, "BEST. BAR. EVER!" A fit of giggles followed and Randy seemed to hit his limit.

He tucked Sid under his right arm like a loosely packed sack of flour. "I'm taking her home. Good luck with that one." Randy stalked into the parking lot while Sid squirmed and spewed profanities.

"Did he just say you should get lucky?" Beth asked between a wheeze and a grunt. "Who does he want you to get lucky with?" She searched the tiny porch, looking for the answer to her own question. This was not what he had in mind when he suggested Sid get her a little tipsy.

"Nobody's getting lucky tonight. Especially not me," he said, helping Beth navigate the large rocks covering the parking lot.

"Aw," she said. "Me neither. Though right now it sounds like a good idea." Stopping and turning to Joe, she asked, "Are you sure we can't get lucky?"

CHAPTER EIGHTEEN

Joe experienced a sudden directional change in blood flow. His brain knew all the reasons the answer had to be no. Not the least of which was the fact he made a point of not having sex with a woman who could barely stand up.

But his dick didn't seem interested in what his brain was communicating.

"You need coffee. That gourmet stuff Patty keeps around should do the trick." While the coffee brewed, he could have a tall glass of ice water. Or two.

"Did you know that Sid is, like, an orphan?"

"Sid's kind of old to be an orphan, isn't she?" Joe asked, lifting Beth into the Jeep after her first three attempts to find the step failed. She reached for the seat belt and missed again, so he buckled her in. As he leaned across her, Beth brushed his neck with her lips. All remaining blood headed south in a hurry.

"Hmmmm…" she moaned. "You taste good. Better than I imagined."

Maybe it wasn't too late to switch with Randy. Sid as an angry drunk would be less dangerous than the sex-kitten version of Beth now sitting in his Jeep.

"What about Sid and this orphan thing?" he asked, his voice an octave higher than usual. Keeping her talking would keep her mouth from other things. Three "other" things she could do with that mouth sprung to mind.

Not helping.

"Sid's an orphan, just like me." Joe climbed into his own seat, and Beth's hand landed on his thigh. "Did you know I was an orphan, too?"

"Didn't know that," he said, moving her hand onto her own thigh, which was bare thanks to her dress being shoved up under the lap belt. Trying to touch as little skin as possible, Joe pulled the dress back down.

"You're such a nice guy. I don't think people know that about you." Beth tucked his hair behind his ear then ran one finger over his shoulder and down his arm, leaving a trail of fire in its wake. "I love your arms. Have I ever told you that?"

"Nope." If he'd known what liquor would do to her, he never would have sent Sid on this stupid mission. "Maybe you should close your eyes for a while."

"And your eyes," she said, smacking him in the chest. "My God. You could melt a girl's panties right off with those eyes. Such a pretty blue." Her head lolled to the side, and she shot him a smile somewhere between sexy and goofy.

"What were you two drinking?"

"Tequila!" she yelled, throwing her hands in the air. Then she started a musical number. "Badum badubadu bum bum…"

"So much for stopping at tipsy." Joe made a note to kick Sid's ass as soon as she was sober. "You make a habit of throwing back tequila?"

"Never had it," she slurred between hums. "Burned my nose hairs on that first one, but Sid said I'd get better with practice. And I did." From the corner of his eye, Joe noticed Beth tapping her chin. "I can't feel my lips."

"They're still there," he said, returning his eyes to the road. "What's this orphan stuff?"

"Sid and me are both orphans. Our parents are dead." She flicked her bottom lip and said, "Ouch."

In case whatever information Sid did learn was lost in the swill of tequila, Joe pushed for more answers. "Your parents are dead?"

"Yep." Another flick of her lip and she gasped, clamping her hand around his bicep. "Oh my God!"

Joe slammed on the brakes, skidding the Jeep to a halt in the gravel along Middle Road. "What?" he said, searching the road for a dog or cat that might have run out in front of them. Nothing moved in the headlight beams.

An ear-splitting sound echoed from the passenger seat, sending his stopped heart into action again. His drunk and happy sex kitten was now a sobbing mess, rocking forward and back in her seat.

"Hey," he said, throwing the Jeep in neutral and releasing his seat belt. "What happened?" Her hands covered her face, her head shaking violently from side to side. "Did something hit you?"

"Yes," she cried, dropping her hands. "It just hit me that I've turned into my mother!"

Joe had heard women didn't like to be compared to their mothers, but had no idea the concept would send them into tears. "I'm sure your mom was great."

"No, she wasn't," Beth growled. The transitions from happy to sad to angry happened faster than Joe could process. "She was wild and rebellious and drank herself into an early grave."

He wanted information, and he got it. Not what he was expecting.

The tears returned. "Granny was right. She said if I ever drank I'd be just like her." Beth blew her nose on her sweater. "What am I going to do now?"

The situation had spiraled into dangerous waters and Joe didn't have a clue how to get his bearings. Dealing with a sobbing woman was bad enough. Dealing with a drunk sobbing woman felt akin to facing down a cat-three hurricane.

At least with a hurricane, he'd have warning. He could be prepared.

Unable to answer her question, Joe drove the final block in silence while Beth continued to cry. He wanted to hold her. Tell her she was nothing like her mother. He also wanted to find this Granny person and point out how fucked up it was to tell a child who'd lost her mother how awful that mother was and not to be like her.

Who would do that?

Joe knew how it felt to lose a mother. He'd been ten when he lost his. How old had Beth been?

Pulling into the drive, Joe cut the engine and stared at the steering wheel. Beth's sobs faded into sniffles, then the occasional hiccup.

"I'm sorry," he said. Mediocre words atoning for more than a lost mother. He'd been an ass to set this scheme up. "How old were you?"

"What?" she asked, using her sweater as a handkerchief again. "How old was I when?"

"When your mom died."

Beth waved his words away. "I wasn't even two. I don't remember her at all." The crying jag apparently over, she looked around. "Do you have anything to drink at your place?"

"I'm not giving you anything but coffee." Joe expected Beth to need help getting out but she was dancing in the driveway before he got a foot on the ground. "What are you doing?"

"Don't you hear that?"

Joe listened. The ting of steel drums floated in the air. "That's Buddy Trousseau. He's playing over at the park tonight."

Dropping her purse and sweater on his parents' steps, Beth moved to the music, lifting her swaying skirt higher with every swing of her hips. Joe's mouth went dry.

"The coffee," he said, searching for the house key as he moved by her. Before he made the bottom step, she grabbed his arm, pulling him into the dance.

He put up a fight. "Oh no we don't."

"Come on, Joe, dance with me. The night is young. The stars are out." She buried her hands in her hair. "And I'm feeling alive." Crooking her finger, she whispered, "Come feel alive with me, Joe."

His brain said no, but his feet said yes. She smiled, took his arm, and twirled beneath it. The move threw her off balance and she ended up pressed against him, her ass cradled against his groin. Without missing a beat, she started moving again.

Joe's brain gave the order to push her away, but his body ignored the command same as his feet. "This isn't a good idea," he said. An understatement if he'd ever heard one.

Beth purred, leaning back and throwing her head on his shoulder. The music ended, but their bodies continued the conversation. A conversation Joe's body wanted to explore further.

The moment before he nuzzled into her neck, Dozer barked. Beth's head shot up, just missing Joe's nose. "Is that Dozer? I want to see Dozer."

"Damn it, Dozer," Joe said, chasing Beth across the yard. He needed to get her into bed. A thought that brought him up short. "I need to *put* her to bed. Put. Not get."

The mental delay gave Beth time to reach his porch. She knocked on the door as if Dozer could let her in. The mutt barked louder. "Give it a rest, Doze!" he yelled through the door. The dog went silent.

To Beth he said, "No coffee over here. Back to Patty's, let's go." He tugged on her arm but she slid from his grasp.

"But I want to see Dozer," she whined, her lip pushed out like a toddler begging for a cookie. At least acting childish was better than using him for a stripper pole.

"You can see Dozer tomorrow. Come on."

"Nuh-uh." She crossed her arms, providing Joe an extensive view of perfect cleavage.

"Fine." She could give Dozer a pat on the head, then it was over to the coffee. Any notion of going near a bed was out of the question. He could tuck her in on the couch.

No sooner had he turned the key than Beth went charging into his house. A paper plate and empty pizza box covered the coffee table, while a basket of dirty clothes sagged in the corner to the right of the entrance. He'd planned on doing his laundry next door, but had put the chore off another day.

The smell filling his living room proved that to be a stupid move. But then he hadn't been expecting company.

Beth didn't seem to notice the mess or the smell. She was too busy playing peekaboo with his dog. When had the mutt learned that trick?

"You've seen him. Time to go."

Dodging his grasp, Beth floated farther into the house. When she reached the doorway to the kitchen, she turned and took in his living room. "There's nothing here."

Joe looked around. Since when did a couch, end table, coffee table, floor lamp, and television qualify as nothing?

"Does drinking always make you blind?" he asked. "There's plenty here." Dozer spread out on the couch as if to prove Joe's comment.

"You have nothing but furniture." Beth threw her hands on her hips, missed one hip, and tried again. She had to look down to do it, but succeeded on the third try.

Someday he might look back on this scene and laugh, but the sight of Beth looking soft and sexy and steps away from his bedroom made it difficult to see the humor. "I'd park the Jeep in here, but the tires would be hell on the floors."

"I'll have to do something about this." With that ominous statement, she moved into the kitchen. "This could be a cute little place," she said, opening cupboards and testing the faucet. Maybe she harbored dreams of being a real estate agent. Spinning away from the counter, Beth peeked down the hallway, then threw a come-hither look over her shoulder. "What's down here?"

The woman needed a leash. Determined to get her out of his house, even if he had to carry her over his shoulder, Joe followed her to his bedroom. He'd have caught her if Dozer hadn't cut him off.

"You're pushing it, buddy."

Joe rounded the corner and found Beth spread-eagle on his bed. The hem of her dress hovering at navel level revealed white cotton panties. He'd never considered plain white panties a turn-on, but his body reacted as if she were wearing red lace and garters.

Definitely time to carry her out.

"Time to go." Before he reached the bed, she rolled off the other side and headed for his bathroom. Maybe she'd be grossed out enough to run out of the house and spare him the back strain. "What is wrong with you?"

"Aha!" she yelled, making him wonder if she'd finally become aware of her surroundings. "This is why you smell so good."

That didn't make sense. He smelled good because he left all the funk in his bathroom? "You're a real pain in the ass, you know that?"

Ignoring his question, she turned her back to the sink, holding up his cologne like a trophy. Sending a spritz into the air, she took a deep breath. "It doesn't smell as good in the air as it does on you." Pulling him by the front of his shirt, she sprayed the cologne on his neck and breathed deep again.

"What are you doing?"

"God, that's good. Wonder what it would smell like on me." Pulling out the front of her dress, she shot the mist into her cleavage. "Wanna sniff?"

Joe's mouth watered and his hands shot to her hips. "You don't know what you're doing," he said, his voice strained, control ready to snap.

"I know what I'm doing," she whispered before taking his mouth.

A tidal wave of raw desire took Joe by surprise. She tasted of lime and liquor and a heat to match the fire burning between them. A fire he couldn't help but stoke. He lifted her feet off the floor and Beth threw her arms around his neck. When he dropped her bottom on the countertop, her legs shot around his waist, pressing him tighter against those white panties.

She licked his bottom lip then nipped it, while his hands drew the straps of the dress down her arms. Rubbing a thumb over a tight nipple, Joe reveled in the moan deep in her throat and pressed harder, mentally cursing the material blocking his way. Beth climbed his body, lifting herself off the counter, giving his hands access to her ass.

He could take her right here. Sweet Jesus, he wanted her. To hell with Lucas.

His brother's name in his head was like a punch to the gut. Joe dragged his lips from Beth's, panting and fighting for air. She moaned again, this time in protest. He laid his forehead on her chest. "I can't do this."

"Oh no." Beth's hands flew to her mouth, forcing Joe to raise his head. He didn't want to see the guilt in her eyes. This was his fault. He'd been the sober one.

"I'm sorry," he said, pulling the skirt down over her thighs.

Beth shook her head. Then turned to the side and puked in his sink.

～

Surrounded by darkness, Beth assumed she was dead. Nothing short of impact with a Mack truck could cause this much pain. Her head vibrated like a giant tuning fork, her mouth tasted as if her last meal had been roadkill, and her stomach felt empty and pissed.

However she'd died, it must have been ugly.

And left behind no memories. That was probably a good thing. No one wanted to remember the moment they were smooshed like a bug on a windshield.

The dim light visible through her eyelids was both encouraging and intrusive. The light indicated she'd ended up in heaven, or was at least on the way, but the muted glow enhanced the pounding in her head. How was she supposed to go toward the light when her head felt ready to explode before she'd even found the end of the tunnel?

Screw the light, she thought, throwing an arm over her eyes. Eternity in limbo land would have to do. And then a wet tongue slid over her lips, letting her know she wasn't in this limbo land alone.

"Good God. What the…" Jerking upright brought three things clearly into the light. One, she wore nothing but her sensible white undies and strapless bra. Two, she was very much alive. Three, she was about to throw up all over Patty's good quilt.

Spotting her dress flung over the back of a chair, she used the flimsy garment to cover her front and bolted for the door, one hand firm against her mouth. Thank the wee baby Jesus her room sat directly across from the bathroom. Once whatever had ticked off her system had been purged, Beth dropped to the side of the tub, waiting for the ringing in her ears to subside.

She must have caught some kind of virus. Or maybe she'd eaten something bad. What did she eat the night before? The answer eluded her. The last Beth remembered was throwing back another glass of wine and Sid saying something about shots.

She moaned into her hands. She'd done this to herself. There had to be a less painful way to kill yourself. Like stepping in front of a flamethrower or enduring ancient Chinese water torture.

Dozer whined and nudged her head with his. "Thanks for the kiss, Doze. But if I'm Sleeping Beauty and you're my Prince Charming..." Beth thought about the rest of the statement. "To be honest, I've been kissed by worse."

A memory poked somewhere around her left temple. Something about kissing. She tried concentrating, but nothing came through. "This tub is cold." Getting to her feet, she tested her legs. They held steady, but her head didn't like the change in altitude.

Latching on to the counter, she waited for the fog to clear. Shaking it clear was out of the question. Ready to move, Beth looked both ways down the hall before crossing back to her room. With luck, no one had seen her mad dash a few minutes before. Sliding back under the covers, she wadded up the dress and realized she couldn't have gotten out of it alone. She'd struggled to get into it until Sid showed up to handle the zipper.

So who handled the zipper at the end of the night? How did she get home? Did she talk to Patty and Tom? If she did, they must not think much of her this morning.

"Did you see me last night, Dozer?" The dog tilted his head, tongue lolling to the side. "Maybe rolling around with you is why I smell like this." Beth sniffed her dress. The bottom was stiff and smelled like liquor-soaked chicken wings. "Good Lord." She moved to throw the material on the floor, but another, more familiar scent hit her nose. Joe's cologne.

She sniffed the blankets. Nothing. Lowering her head to the sheet, she realized the scent was strongest between her boobs.

"Oh my God."

She pulled the sheet higher and tighter. Why would Joe's cologne be between her boobs? Did that mean Joe had been between her boobs? Beth frantically searched her memory banks, willing the events of her night of debauchery to rise to the surface.

Pinching her eyes shut, she concentrated. "It's all black." She opened her eyes, and Dozer barked, sending a tearing pain through her skull. "I'll give you anything you want, dog, just don't do that again."

"Dozer, don't wake up—" Patty stopped in the doorway, wringing her hands. "I'm so sorry. I didn't notice he'd wondered off."

If Beth had done anything to offend Patty the night before, she might as well know now. "About last night."

"I heard you had a good time. Maybe too good." Patty chuckled. "That's why I was letting you sleep."

"Did you, uh, talk to me when I got home?"

"You were already in bed by the time Tom and I came in." Crossing her arms, the older woman leaned against the doorjamb. "Word from O'Hagan's is you and Sid were the life of the party."

Beth cringed. Great. "Do you know how I got home?"

Patty's brows drew together. "I don't know. Randy took Sid, so I'm sure he dropped you off, too."

Beth knew she didn't have a key. She'd meant to grab one on her way out but realized she'd forgotten when they reached the bar. If Tom and Patty didn't let her into the house, that left one other person. "Do you know if Joe came over to the bar?"

"You really don't remember anything, do you? Joe worked at the restaurant until late, but I didn't see him leave, so I'm not sure. Is something wrong?"

"No," Beth said, remembering she was practically naked. Joe's scent wafted up from her cleavage, and Beth tried not to think about what she might have done. "I think I need to take a shower."

"Of course," Patty said, rising off the wall. "Come on, Dozer. I'm sorry he woke you up."

"Don't worry about it," Beth said, trying to sound relaxed. "Is there coffee?"

"I'll make a fresh pot while you're in the shower. I'd make you eggs, but from the color of your face, I think we better stick with toast."

"Thanks." Patty's kindness made Beth feel worse. "I'll be down in twenty minutes."

"Take your time." Patty and the mutt left the room, leaving Beth to her thoughts. She tried again to remember how she'd gotten home, or even how she'd gotten undressed. Her mind remained blank.

Rubbing her jaw raised prickles of pain along her skin. Leaning up to see her reflection in the dresser mirror, Beth looked for a scrape from a fall. If her head was any indication, she'd qualified as fall-down drunk. Her reflection revealed something had definitely scraped her chin, but from the pink tint along her jawline, it hadn't been rocks.

"Elizabeth Marie Chandler, what the hell did you do last night? And please let it not have been with Joe."

CHAPTER NINETEEN

No man should be tested the way Joe had been the night before. The schizophrenic mood swings would have sent any man running, but the sex-kitten seduction in the bathroom fried several of his brain cells. Getting Beth undressed and into bed threatened to fry his body.

He couldn't let her sleep in the dress after she'd tossed what looked to be an appetizer sampler over a large part of it. At least she'd passed out cold before they reached her bedroom. His luck she'd have tried to strip him while he got the dress off her, and that was a test he would not have passed.

After scrubbing flammable food chunks out of his sink, followed by an arctic shower, Joe spent the rest of the night trying not to think about his future sister-in-law. Thinking of her by that title was supposed to keep reality front and center.

Reality sucked.

They'd have to deal with what had happened, but he needed her sober and focused when they stared down whatever the hell was going on between them. Based on her condition the night before, Beth might be sober but definitely not able to focus on anything this morning. Better to let her recover and face the issue with a clear head. To that end, Joe headed for the boat as soon as he heard she was up and about.

"Thought I'd find you here," said a voice from the dock. Joe turned from the reel he was stringing to see Derek Paige looking uptight and out of place in his suit and tie. "Mind if I come aboard?"

Dozer gave a low growl. Joe considered doing the same, but curiosity won out.

"Hop on. But watch your step. Hate to see you ruin that suit." Letting the guy talk didn't mean Joe couldn't be a smart-ass.

Paige strolled onto the boat like he'd been doing it all his life. "I've spent enough time on Mr. Wheeler's yacht to handle your little fishing boat."

If this was Paige's selling approach, Wheeler would never get the island. "Why don't we get to why you're here," Joe asked, turning his attention back to the line.

"I'm here to talk about Cassandra."

"What about her?"

"She's spoken for."

Joe returned his attention to the man standing five feet away. If Paige was trying to look relaxed, he was doing a shitty job of it. "She's spoken for?"

"That's right." Tough guy shifted from one foot to the other. "I saw you talking to her last night."

"Yeah," Joe said, leaning the rod against the cabin wall and turning in his chair. "We talked. Not sure what that has to do with you."

"I just told you what that has to do with me."

Joe chuckled. Maybe Paige's tie was cutting off blood flow to his brain. "Are you claiming Cassie as your territory?"

"Her name is Cassandra, and, yes, I am."

"Have you met Cassandra Wheeler? She's not the type to be claimed. Especially not by one of her daddy's ass kissers."

Paige tensed, red crawling out of his collar and up his neck. "I don't give a shit what you think of me, Dempsey. Just stay away from her."

Joe leaned back, crossing his arms over his chest. "She didn't mention you during our talk." Though he had no intention of competing with Paige for Cassie's affections, he couldn't resist pissing him off. "In fact, talking was her idea. She's been trying to get me alone for a week."

Paige took a step forward but Dozer's growl sent him back two. "You had your chance, Dempsey. You dropped the brass ring, and now you want it back."

"Brass ring?"

"Don't act like you weren't after the money. Cassandra is Wheeler's only child and the heir to the empire. Why else would you have tried for a woman so far out of your league?"

Joe tensed, fighting to keep his voice controlled. "Cassie isn't a prize and she sure as hell isn't a piece of property. Now get your ass off my boat before I let Dozer take a bite out of it."

"I'm not afraid of you or your mutt." Dozer moved forward, the hair on the back of his neck standing on end. Paige was back on the dock in one leap. "You're right, she's not a piece of property. But she is a prize. If you loved her like I do, you'd know that."

Joe stared, not sure if he'd heard right. "Did you say you love her?"

Paige crossed his arms. "You heard me. Stay away from her, Dempsey. You hurt her once. I won't let you do it again."

Dozer barked as the weasel stomped back up the pier. How about that. The idiot was in love. Though he'd never like the prissy little shit, Joe couldn't help but respect him in that moment. "Good luck, Paige. Hope she doesn't rip your heart out and make you eat it."

~

Beth needed answers, which led her to the evil person who'd loaded her up on tequila. She'd pounded on Sid's front door for two minutes before running out of patience. The truck in the driveway meant the pint-size monster was still sleeping it off.

Not for long.

If there was any justice in the world, Sid would feel worse than Beth did. Since Beth felt like she'd been hit by a box of hammers, Sid better feel as if she'd taken a wrecking ball upside the head.

"Open the door, Sid. I need to talk to you." Beth squeezed her head at the temples, holding down the pain caused by raising her voice. Still no answer. Contemplating her options, Beth closed the screen door softly—no need to antagonize the little men chiseling through her skull—and moved around the back of the house.

Sid's bedroom window was easy to find. And open. "Sid," she called through the opening, as loud as the pain in her head would permit. A snore came back in response. "Fine. I'm coming in."

Crawling through headfirst, Beth caught her top half on the dresser below the window, sending a small box and two picture frames to the floor. The noise broke through the snoring.

Sid sat straight up in the bed. "What the..." Before the words were out, she was holding her head while squeezing her eyes tightly shut. As Beth hovered, half in and half out of the window, Sid opened her eyes, seemingly struggling to focus.

"Curly?"

"Yes, it's me."

"What the fuck are you doing?"

"Right now I'm stuck in this window trying not to puke on your carpet. Get over here and help me."

"I'm coming, I'm coming," she said, sliding her feet slowly to the floor. "God, this room is spinning like a son of a bitch."

"Why are you still in your dress?" Beth asked. If she had to endure the mystery of waking up wearing almost nothing, Sid should at least be in the same state. "And you have mascara down to your chin."

"I was sleeping, not getting ready for a freaking beauty contest." Grabbing Beth under the arms, Sid pulled until they both hit the floor, moaning for several minutes.

"If I survive long enough to get off this floor, I'm kicking the shit out of you for waking me up."

"I had to wake you up. I need to know what happened last night." Beth rolled over, holding her head with one hand as she pushed herself into a sitting position with the other. Leaning against the foot of the bed, she checked the picture frames. "I don't think they're broken."

One frame held a picture of Sid with a woman who had to be her mother. They looked more like sisters. "Is this your mom?" she asked.

Sid glanced over, still flat on her back. "Yeah, that's her."

"What was her name?" Beth slid a finger over the image, wishing she had a picture of her mother.

"Angelita Pilar Navarro. Beautiful, delicate, and graceful. Everything I'm not."

The admission took Beth by surprise. In the short time she'd known her, Sid had never taken the self-deprecating route. "That's crazy. The resemblance is unmistakable. She'd be proud to see what you've become."

Sid sighed. "I didn't drag your scrawny ass through that window to discuss my mother. What's this shit about answers?"

"I can't remember last night."

Sid peeled herself off the floor, taking a seat next to Beth. "What do you mean you can't remember?"

"The last thing I recall is you announcing we should do tequila shots. The rest is a blank." Tamping down the panic, she added, "I don't even know how I got home."

"That's easy, we..." Sid blinked. "There was..."

"What?" Beth asked, squeezing her knees to her chest. "We what?"

"Shit."

"We shit?!"

"Give me a second, all right?"

Beth swallowed hard. "You don't remember either."

"It'll come back to me. I just woke up. My brain is still foggy."

"I've been up for over an hour and everything is still foggy." Beth's heart sunk. "This isn't good."

"So we partied a little too hard and don't remember. What's the big deal?"

"The big deal is—" Beth stopped before admitting the possibility she might have done something entirely inappropriate with Joe. "What if we did something stupid in that bar?"

"You mean besides the tequila?" Sid asked, massaging her temples. "My head feels like it was used for batting practice."

"Welcome to my world. I thought I was dead until Dozer woke me up this morning."

"Dozer woke you up?" Beth had Sid's full attention. "You woke up at Joe's?"

"Don't be crazy." Waking up mostly naked covered in Joe's cologne was bad enough. She didn't want to think about the implications of waking up in his bed. "I was at Tom and Patty's. Dozer was visiting, I guess. Patty said Joe took Dozer with him to the dock while I was in the shower."

"We didn't have a charter this morning. What's he doing at the dock?"

"I don't know. Right now I don't seem to know anything." Unwilling to reveal her suspicions, Beth kept things vague. "But I have this nagging feeling I did something I shouldn't have last night. If there's something I need to fix, I'd like to know now so I can fix it."

"No matter how drunk I got, I wouldn't have let you do anything stupid." Sid sounded almost protective. An interesting development. At some point in the last twenty-four hours, the women had become friends. "If you were with me, you were fine."

But what if I wasn't with you?

Beth couldn't ask the question, but still needed the answer. "Who could tell us what happened? Patty said Randy took you home. She assumes he took me home, too." The unlikelihood of Randy getting Beth out of her dress made her doubt Patty's assumption. "Should we ask him what happened?"

Sid shrugged. "I could call him, but he's probably out on the water. Can't reach him out there. Besides, he wasn't with us in the bar. I don't think. So he wouldn't know anything."

The idea of asking Joe made Beth's stomach churn. Again. "There has to be someone else." Tapping a finger against her knee, she tried to remember anyone else from the bar. "What about that bartender?"

"Will?"

"Was that her name?" Beth turned and folded her legs Indian style. "She was serving us the drinks, so she was there the whole time. We need to talk to her."

"This is Sunday, right?" Sid asked, getting slowly to her feet.

"Yeah, why?"

"She works at Hava Java on Sundays. Which is good because I need coffee. Bad." Sid moved to the closet and pulled out a pair of work boots.

"What are you doing?" Beth reached her feet, relieved her stomach remained calm.

"You said you wanted to talk to Will."

Black streaks traced down Sid's cheeks while her hair stuck out in all directions. Beth tried not to laugh. "No self-respecting fairy godmother would let her Cinderella go anywhere looking like that."

Sid looked down then back up, throwing a hand into the tangled mess protruding from her head. "Did you just call me Cinderella?"

Beth shrugged. "Better than Greaserella. Bippity bop your butt into the shower so we can go. I'll be on the couch trying to shut off these jackhammers in my head."

Thirty minutes later, Beth and Sid walked into the Hava Java coffee shop in search of Will the bartender and a soothing hit of caffeine. Looking neither surprised nor put out by their request to talk, Will informed her coworker she was taking a break, and the three women took a seat on the deck, cups in hand.

"Surprised you two are upright," said Will, sliding into a black wrought-iron chair. "You must feel like crap."

Sid snorted. "Crap would be an improvement." She nodded toward Beth. "Curly here has a bug up her ass because we can't remember much of last night. We're hoping you can let her know she didn't do anything stupid."

"You mean other than dancing on the bar and flashing the room?"

Beth pressed a hand to her stomach. "Oh my gosh."

"Relax," Will said, leaning back and swirling the liquid in her cup. "I'm kidding. You didn't do anything. Not that I saw, anyway."

What was with the women on this island? "Are you trying to give me a heart attack?"

"It was a joke. You had a better sense of humor when you were tanked."

Sid laughed then grabbed her head. Served her right. After taking a drink, she asked, "So Little Miss Nervous here didn't rub up on a tourist or stick her tongue down anyone's throat?"

The last part of the question put an image in Beth's mind. An image that included Joe and a bathroom she didn't recognize. Her imagination was not helping the situation.

"Like I said, not that I saw. But I don't know what happened after your mountain of a brother took you both outside." Will visibly tensed when she mentioned Randy, making Beth wonder if he'd blamed the bartender for getting them drunk.

"How did he know to come and get us?" Beth asked, desperate to fill in the blanks.

"After a couple rounds of Meatloaf karaoke, which wasn't bad considering how far gone you both were, Beth flipped from happy to tears, crying about being an orphan and something about being a work widow for the rest of her life. The line between happy party girl and sloppy drunk crossed, I suggested you two call someone, and Sid called her brother."

"What was that?" Sid asked.

"What?" Beth and Will said together.

"I'm talking to Will." Sid sat up, resting her elbows on the table. "Every time you mention my brother, you get that weird look on your face."

Will kept her eyes on her cup. "I don't know what you're talking about."

"Did Randy yell at you about letting us get drunk?" Beth asked, prepared to stick up for Will if necessary. No one poured those drinks down her throat, and she'd be sure to tell Randy that.

"Randy was pissed, but not at me."

"Then what is it?" Sid pushed. Will squirmed, her eyes darting between Sid and something in the distance.

"I don't like big guys, that's all."

"Big guys?" Beth said.

"Yeah, big guys." Will shrugged. "I've had some not-nice run-ins with muscle-bound dudes like that."

Sid relaxed, leaning back in her seat. "You know Randy's a big teddy bear, right?"

"If you say so." Will didn't look convinced. "Anyway, Randy showed up and took you both out of the bar. I don't know what happened after that."

Beth hadn't considered the possibility she'd put the moves on Randy instead of Joe. Randy seemed like the type to laugh it off, but that didn't explain Joe's cologne in her cleavage. Or how she got in the house.

"I don't remember any of this," Sid said, tapping her cup on the table. "Randy's never going to let me live this down."

Beth ignored her. "I still feel like there's something missing."

Will rose from the table. "Like I said, once you were outside the bar, anything could have happened. Sid got belligerent as soon as she saw her brother, but you were a ball of charm. When not crying, you were the friendliest drunk I've ever seen. And I've worked in a lot of bars up and down the coast."

Sid lowered her sunglasses as she moved out from under the umbrella. "Thanks for your time, Will. Sorry if we ruined your night."

"No reason to apologize." Will grabbed two empty cups from the next table over and threw them in the trash. "The guys buying your drinks were good tippers. Gave me enough to buy that necklace I've had my eye on up at Lola's."

"What men bought us drinks?" Beth asked, hoping the beard burn didn't come from a total stranger.

"What men didn't? I don't think either of you paid for a drink all night long."

"Great," Beth mumbled, throwing her own cup away. "At least I didn't pay money for this headache."

"I expected you to have way more than a headache," Will said, pushing in chairs around the deck. "You mixed a lot more alcohol than Sid. If I did that, I'd have puked my guts out before I made it home."

The image of Joe in the bathroom returned, clearer this time. Beth closed her eyes and remembered her legs wrapped around Joe's hips. Heat scorched her skin as images flashed before her eyes. The memories came rushing back. Where he'd touched her. How he'd touched her.

And what happened when he stopped touching her.

Beth dropped to the ground, bouncing off a chair on her way down. Palms pressed to her eyes, she rocked, chanting, "No no no no no."

"What happened?" Sid said, taking Beth by the shoulders.

Heat of a different kind raced up her neck and burned to the tips of her ears. Mortification covered her like a heavy blanket, suffocating her as her worst fears were confirmed.

Will's voice sounded far away. "If she's going to be sick, get her to the edge of the deck."

"You're not blowing chunks on me, Curly. Come on." Sid tugged on her arms. "You're heavier than you look."

"I'm not sick," Beth said, finding her voice again. She couldn't let them know what had happened. No one could know. "I thought I was, but I'm okay now."

She focused on breathing, running affirmations in her mind.

I can fix this. I can make this right. I have *to make this right.*

Just as on the ferry, the words were no help. "I need to go home," she said, meaning back to Richmond, where she could hide. Where she could pretend none of this had happened. Pretend she hadn't betrayed her fiancé with his own brother.

"I'll get you home," Sid said, lifting Beth to her feet with Will's help. They tried to carry her to the truck, but Beth pushed them off.

"I'm fine. I can walk on my own."

Oblivious to the world around her, Beth climbed into Sid's truck and stared out the window. She'd spent the morning struggling to remember the night before. Now she longed to forget, but the memories came like body blows one after another.

Joe's forehead pressed to her chest.

His words playing over and over.

I can't do this.

What had she done?

CHAPTER TWENTY

Relaxing on his back deck, sipping a cold beer, Joe pondered the serious predicament of having feelings for his brother's girl. He'd been telling himself for days the sparks between them were nothing but a meaningless attraction. Lust that would go away once she went back to Richmond. Back to her life with Lucas.

But his conversation with Cassie had done more than close an old wound: he'd gained perspective. What had seemed complicated turned out to be simple. And what should have been simple could be really fucking complicated.

The sun sank low in the distance, shades of orange and red setting the horizon ablaze. Joe watched the colors shift and change, accepting what he had to do.

"Got a sec?"

Joe looked back to see his dad coming through his screen door. "Sure. Want a beer?"

"I'm good, thanks." Tom took a seat and remained silent for nearly a minute. Enough time for Joe to know exactly why he was there.

"Nothing happened," he said, in answer to the unasked question. He couldn't blame his dad for being concerned.

One wrong move on Joe's part could implode their entire family. But he also didn't intend to embarrass Beth by sharing any details.

"Patty said Elizabeth looked pretty rough this morning. Said she didn't remember how she got home last night."

Joe hadn't counted on Beth not remembering. That would solve a lot of his problems. "Did you enlighten Patty?"

"Nope. Didn't see the point," Tom said, staring out at the darkening sky. "No need to get her worried about what might or might not be going on between you and Lucas's fiancée."

"There's nothing going on," Joe said. At least there wouldn't be after last night. "She was drunk. I brought her home."

He wanted to be angry with his dad for doubting him. Believing he could actually hurt Lucas that way. But it wasn't as if Joe hadn't considered it. Considered what would happen. If the family would survive.

The answer had come like a mainsail to the back of the skull. Another reason he knew what had to happen next.

Tom rose from his chair. "I trust you to do the right thing."

Before his dad could say more, the small plastic table holding Joe's beer rattled as Dozer hopped to his feet, tail wagging with excitement. "What's with you?" he asked.

The dog hopped off the deck and charged around the right side of the house, returning seconds later with Beth in tow. She kept her focus on the bouncing fur ball, reaching the bottom step before looking up.

The blush on her cheeks brought out the green of her eyes, and he answered the hesitant smile with a reassuring grin of his own.

"Hi there," he said, fighting the urge to reach out to her.

"Hi," she replied, crossing and uncrossing her arms, finally settling on tucking her hands in her pockets and looking at Tom. "I didn't mean to intrude on a private conversation. I'll go back to the house."

"Stay," Tom said, descending the stairs. "I was just leaving." He turned to Joe at the bottom, looked ready to speak again, then closed his mouth. A pat on Beth's shoulder and he was gone.

Once Tom faded from sight, Beth asked, "Is he okay?"

"You'd never know to look at him," Joe said, "but he's a bit of a worrier."

"What's he worried about?"

"Nothing important." Joe took a sip of his beer, waiting for Beth to make the next move.

She rocked on her heels, petted Dozer, then crossed her arms again and finally met his eye. "How are you?" she asked.

"Probably better than you are. Have a seat."

Pursing her lips, she nodded. "Okay."

Joe held his tongue as she folded into the rocker, sliding one leg beneath her bottom then switching it out for the other. Once she settled for more than a few seconds, he asked, "You want something to drink?"

Beth shook her head. "No, thanks." Staring out to the sunset, she said, "I owe you an apology."

"For what?" he asked. He was the one who needed to apologize.

Her eyes flew to his, wide with a mixture of hope and fear. "For what I did last night. Or what I think I did." Pinching the bridge of her nose, she spoke more to herself than to him. "I feel like such an idiot."

So the memories had come back. "I'm as much to blame as you are. More so since I was the sober one."

Covering her face with her hands, she asked, "Did I really throw up in your sink?"

Joe chuckled. "You did. I'm used to people getting sick off the side of my boat. In my bathroom, not so much."

"I'm never touching another drop of alcohol as long as I live."

"I wouldn't go that far, but avoiding tequila might be a good idea."

Beth moaned, bringing Dozer to his feet. His large head landed in her lap. "Thanks for the sympathy, Doze."

Joe exhaled. "We need to talk about what happened before you got sick."

"I know." Beth leaned back in the chair, scratching Dozer behind an ear. "The details are sketchy at best, but I remember enough. I don't know what I was thinking."

"The tequila was thinking for you. I should have controlled the situation better."

Beth's snort took him by surprise. "I realize it's more manly to fall on your sword and take all the blame, but as you said, *we* took part in what happened. I downed that tequila all by myself, and I instigated the kiss. That part I remember."

"In case you haven't noticed, I'm a big boy."

"That part I remember as well." A pink hue crept up her cheeks as if the words had come out before she could stop them.

Joe tried to ignore the compliment but his ego won out. "Right." How long had it been since he'd blushed? "But that's not what I meant. Pretending there isn't something between us won't make it go away."

"There can't be anything between us," Beth insisted, though the statement sounded more like a plea. She ran a hand through her hair. "How did this get so complicated?"

He didn't have an answer, but he had a plan. Make it simple again.

"There's only one thing to do."

"I know. I need to leave."

"What would that solve?"

"Don't you think distance would be a good thing right now?"

If he hadn't spent the day working out their problem, he might have agreed with her. "Then what happens the next time? What happens when you're here for Christmas and we're next to each other at the dinner table?"

"I didn't think of that." She stared at her feet. "What do you suggest?"

"We become friends."

"Now you're the one on tequila. Haven't we tried that already?"

Joe leaned forward, determined to convince her. "What we've tried is dancing around each other ignoring the whale in the back of the boat."

"Is that the fisherman's version of the elephant in the room?" Beth's smile hit him in the chest. This would not be easy.

"Something like that." He turned his eyes to the distance. Pastel shades of blue, yellow, and pink painted the horizon. "If you're going to become a Dempsey, we can't avoid each other. So we become friends. Or family really. You'll come to see me as a brother and I'll eventually see you as a sister. In-law." Meeting her eyes again, he played his trump card. "For Lucas."

Beth bit her lip. Regardless of the hesitation, he could see he'd pushed the right button. With a stiff nod, she agreed. "For Lucas." Relaxing into the chair as if a weight had been lifted, she closed her eyes. "I've tried to call him three times. No answer. I hate keeping this a secret, but confessing would hurt him so much."

"We're not going to hurt Lucas. If you'd been sober we never would have kissed." Another lie to add to the pile. "It's never going to happen again, so there's no reason to tell him."

"Never again," Beth whispered, staring out to the now sunless sky.

Joe lifted the bottle to his lips, ignoring the hint of disappointment in her voice. "Problem solved."

~

The chimes attached to the front door of Island Arts & Crafts made a violent sound thanks to Beth pushing the door open harder than intended. The last twenty-four hours had frayed her nerves to the point of breaking, making her skin prickle as if she were carrying a live grenade.

Lola glanced up from her worktable, pinning Beth over the reading glasses perched on the end of her nose. "Hey there, sugar. What's got you so riled up?"

"Nothing," Beth replied, struggling to stand still. "Do you have any of that calming herbal tea around?"

Lola's brows shot up. She removed the glasses, letting them dangle from a purple tether around her neck. "You better sit down and tell old Lola what has you so lit up. You're as jumpy as a juniper bug dancing along a berry patch."

The mention of a bug made Beth itchy, increasing her fidgeting. "It's been a rough couple days and I'm a bit nervous about this afternoon."

Lola pressed Beth into her favorite chair, a tall-backed armchair upholstered in a light blue material covered in white mums. Beth tried to relax into the soft cushion but failed.

"Close your eyes and try to breathe while I get that tea. Looks like we're going to need the whole pot."

Beth attempted to follow Lola's instructions. Leaning her head back, she closed her eyes and focused on her breathing. Steady breathing always helped with the panic. Three deep breaths later, her left foot slowed its tapping. Three more and her hands unclenched.

"Here's the water now."

The mention of water sent the foot tapping double time. "There's no way I can do this. I thought I could and Joe says I can, but I can't. I'll just tell him I changed my mind."

"Whoa, child. You're about to crawl out of your skin. What's Joe say you can do?"

"Get on a boat."

Lola blinked. "That's it? Get on a boat?"

Beth recognized her shallow breathing as a bad sign. "To think, this was my idea." Leaning forward, she flattened a hand over her heart. "I might need a paper bag."

"Don't go having a heart attack else you'll give me one, and I'm not about to die before Marcus gets here."

Beth was not having a heart attack, though sometimes she thought cardiac arrest might be easier to deal with than the panic attacks. "Marcus is coming here?" she asked, rubbing above her left breast. "Why didn't you tell me?"

"I didn't know myself until last night. Tried to talk him out of it, but he's determined. Hard to argue with a determined man."

"When will he be here?" Beth asked. "I'd love to meet him."

"He's sailing down on his boat." Lola paused and watched Beth for a reaction.

Beth waved a hand in the air. "Keep going. I'm good." Snagging a magazine off the table beside her, she used it as a fan. "I'm so excited for you."

"If this is you excited, I'd hate to see you on a bad day."

Beth shook her head. "Panic attack. This happens every time I even think about getting on a boat." The quick breathing made talking difficult. "It's a phobia."

"How in the world did you get on this island if you don't like boats?" Lola asked, handing her an oversized coffee cup filled with the herbal concoction.

"With Joe."

"I thought you didn't know Joe before you got here?"

"I didn't."

"It's not nice to tease an old lady," Lola said, crossing her legs and kicking one foot in impatience. "How did Joe help you make the ferry crossing if you didn't know him?"

A good-size gulp of tea made talking easier. "I didn't know it was Joe. We were on the same crossing and he found me in the throes of an attack." He'd made her laugh that day. Stopped to help a total stranger. Joe Dempsey was a nice guy under all the gruff. "He talked to me until we reached the other side."

"That sounds like Joe. Never can pass up a creature in distress."

"That's Joe?"

Lola smiled the same knowing smile she'd flashed the night of the Merchants meeting. "Whether it's a bird with a broken wing or a cat stuck in a tree, everyone on the island knows to call Joe."

Beth thought of Joe as many things. Grumpy. Cranky. Bossy. Sexy. Knight in shining armor did not make the list. But there was that time with her blisters.

"You look surprised," Lola said. "You just said yourself he helped you before he even knew who you were."

"He did. But then he insulted me before we reached the island."

Lola scoffed. "I don't believe it."

"Well," Beth hedged, "he didn't know he was insulting me at the time."

"You're talking in riddles again."

Beth searched for the indignation she'd felt that day, but found it strangely absent. "During our talk, he said he was meeting his brother's fiancée that weekend. He'd never seen her but knew she'd be some long-legged blonde bimbo after Lucas for his earning potential."

The snort of laughter took Beth by surprise. Lola's eyes twinkled. "That does sound like Joe. What did he say when you told him who you were?"

Avoiding Lola's gaze, Beth admitted, "I didn't."

"What do you mean, you didn't? Girl, you let him go on like that without knowing he was talking to the woman he was insulting?" The older woman pursed her lips, shaking her head. "That's just wrong."

"I wanted to make a good impression with Lucas's family," Beth defended. "I was warned Joe would be the hardest sell, and embarrassing him right out of the gate didn't seem like a good way to start."

"He must have been fit to be tied when he found out."

Beth exhaled. Fit to be tied for sure. "Let's just say it made for a rocky start."

"You two seem to be getting along well enough now."

"Maybe too well," Beth said, before catching herself.

Lola sat up straighter. "Do tell."

She had to tell someone, and Lola was the one person on the island she could trust not to judge or spread gossip. Beth looked around for prying ears. "I did the worst thing."

"You didn't..." Lola wiggled her brows.

"No!" she answered, cringing at the thought. "I wouldn't still be on this island if we did that."

"But you did something. Throw an old woman a bone."

Beth stared at her knees and blurted, "I kissed him."

Lola remained silent, forcing Beth to glance her way. The woman looked as if someone spit in her tea. "That's it?"

"I'm engaged to his brother, for heaven's sake. That's enough."

"Honey child, you got me all excited over nothing."

"Nothing? That kiss wasn't nothing. I practically climbed him like a...a spider monkey."

"When you put it that way, it does get more interesting."

Beth shook her head. "I was so drunk I didn't even remember what happened until several hours into the next day. Then it all came screaming back in vivid detail. If Joe hadn't stopped, I don't know how far we would have gone."

"Was Joe drunk?" Lola asked, running a gnarled finger around the rim of her mug.

"No," Beth said. "Sid's brother, Randy, called him from the bar to come pick me up. He was trying to get me home safe, and I threw myself at him."

"But he hadn't been drinking?"

"No." There was that grin again. "I know what that look is. Lola, I'm engaged to Lucas, and I'm going to marry Lucas, so you just get those ideas out of your head."

"You promised me."

"I promised you what?" Even contemplating what Lola was insinuating made Beth ache, knowing the pain it would cause Lucas.

Lola stopped smiling. "Don't ever let the real thing get away. That's what I told you. And you promised you wouldn't."

Pain shot through Beth's chest. But not from panic. "Joe isn't the real thing. Lucas is the real thing."

"Take it from a wise old woman," Lola whispered. "We both know that's not what your heart is telling you. The sooner you face the truth, the easier this will be."

Beth leaned close, taking Lola's hand in hers. "I am following my heart. I won't hurt Lucas. I can't. And I won't destroy this family. They mean too much to me now."

Brown eyes stared into green ones. A dark hand reached up to slide a curl across Beth's forehead. "Just think about it. For me. I don't want to see you make the same mistake I did."

The care in her eyes moved Beth to tears. She repeated the words Lola had once said to her. "Everything is going to work out."

"I hope you're right," Lola said, shaking her head. "Back to this boat thing. Did you say this was your idea?"

The shaking returned. "I don't know what I was thinking. Patty and I were talking, and she said Lucas loves to go out sailing when he comes home and she hoped he'd come home more often, which requires riding the ferry, of course. And I realized I'd be the one holding Lucas back."

Beth scooted to the edge of her seat. "I'd be afraid to ride the ferry, and I'd never go out sailing with him. Sometimes I feel like I'm not as ambitious as Lucas would like, and I thought maybe if I could overcome this fear, that would be a good start in being more like Lucas wants me to be."

Now Lola sat forward. "You're doing this to become what some man wants you to be?"

"Well, yeah," she said, the concept sounding less positive when Lola said it. "That's what you do when you care about someone."

"Honey, when you care about someone you accept them for who they are. You don't try to change them. Would you try to change Lucas?"

"This is about me, Lola." And it was. Deep down, Beth was doing this for herself, too. "As freaked out as I am, I want to do this. I need to face my fears head-on."

"Then you'll do it," Lola said.

Just then the store phone rang, jarring Beth back to the present. The older woman rose to answer the phone and after a quick hello, Lola went silent for several moments. Then she turned toward Beth and said, "I think I have someone who can help. Let me send her over."

Beth didn't like the sound of that. What was she being volunteered for? Once Lola had ended the call, Beth asked, "What was that?"

"You need a distraction to get your mind off this boating thing. Helga has too many babies, and her helper is out sick. Go hold some babies." Grabbing their mugs and heading for the break room, Lola said over her shoulder, "Ain't a soul alive can worry about anything when they're staring into the sweet face of a child."

"But I want to hear more about Marcus."

Lola turned but continued walking away. "He'll be here by the end of the week. I'll tell you all about him before then." Waving the mugs toward the door, she added, "Go on now. Those babies are waiting."

CHAPTER TWENTY-ONE

Joe could hear the screams from the parking lot, which should have been a warning. The second he stepped inside, high-pitched wailing made his ears ring. Four round tables took up the four corners of a large room, surrounded by tiny, bright-colored chairs. Foam squares covered the floor, and the walls were decorated with ladybugs, bumblebees, and butterflies.

Messy, finger-painted mobiles hung from the ceiling, forcing Joe to bob and weave while simultaneously avoiding the little people spinning around his knees. He'd never have believed four munchkins would be enough to send his balls into hiding.

How the hell did Helga stay sane dealing with these creatures every day?

One pudgy little person attacked from the right, wrapping his arms around Joe's calf and plopping a mushy-feeling bottom onto his foot. Joe's first instinct was to shake the kid off, but his brain kicked in before his leg took action.

"Spencer, let go of Joe's leg," yelled Helga from the far corner, where she was wrestling a large chunk of her hair from another toddler's grip. To Joe she said, "He thinks every adult is a ride for his enjoyment. I'm guessing his dad does that with him at home."

Spencer looked up at Joe and made his demands clear. "I wanna wide."

At that same moment, something slammed into the heel of Joe's left boot. The new assailant sported black curls and big brown eyes, which grew round as quarters when he looked up and spotted Joe staring down at him. "You're in da way," he said, defiantly slamming the yellow dump truck into Joe's heel for a second time.

Helga peeled off the pudgy one first, then turned to the reckless driver. "Take the trucks back to the highway rug. We've talked about this. Trucks drive on the highway, not on people."

Shooting Joe the evil eye, the boy picked up his Tonka and stormed off. Joe made a mental note to pick up a new box of condoms. Not that he was having much sex lately, but better safe than pudgy munchkins.

"Sorry about that." Helga collected four small cups from a nearby table. "The weather was so nice, I let them go outside. They were supposed to wear themselves out, but I think they came back in with even more energy."

"You've got my vote for Merchant of the Year, Helga. Beth around here somewhere?" She wasn't in the main room. Maybe the rug rats had sent her screaming into the sound.

"You mean Elizabeth? She's in the baby room. Thankfully, I'm down to one baby, and these little ones' parents should be here soon." Helga walked away and Joe followed, afraid she might leave him alone with the wild ones. Pointing to a door to her left, she said, "You'll find her in there. That girl was a lifesaver today."

Helga continued her way back to a kitchen area while Joe peered over the closed half door. What he saw set off something in his chest. Beth was swaying along a narrow space surrounded by empty cribs and playpens. A little box step up then over and back. Her own humming accompanying the dance, her eyes locked on the infant in her arms. She was oblivious to his presence.

Joe smiled and leaned against the wall to watch, unwilling to disturb the dancing pair. A thought floated through his mind. Beth would make a great mom someday. He imagined a headstrong little boy with her green eyes and his dimple. Then reality punched him in the gut.

Beth's children would be his nieces and nephews, not his own. A fact he couldn't and wouldn't change. No matter how much he wanted things to be different.

Beth belonged to Lucas. End of story.

Another twirl to her right and Beth spotted him. "Oh." She jumped then checked the baby, whose eyes had popped open at the sudden movement. "Fudge. I'd just gotten her to sleep."

"I didn't mean to scare you," Joe said, sliding by the half door then closing it behind him. "You look like a natural with one of those."

"To tell you the truth, I was scared to death when Lola volunteered me for this. I can't remember the last time I held a baby." She looked down at the infant waving its fists in the air. "This is Cecelia. She's been very tolerant throughout my crash course in baby care."

Joe ignored the tightening in his chest. "Guess you're a quick learner. The ones in the other room tried to take me down." Feeling like a marlin in a school of minnows, he decided to move things along. "The boat is fueled and waiting. You ready to go?"

Beth visibly tensed. "Ready?" she asked, her voice rising an octave. She cleared her throat. "Ready. Sure. I just…" Green eyes darted around the room. If Joe didn't know better, he'd swear she was looking for an escape hatch. "I need to clean up a bit. You know," she said, passing the now-fidgeting baby into his arms, "help Helga out before I go. She has her hands full and all."

Before he could blink or argue, Joe found himself staring into deep blue eyes that looked as surprised as he felt. Cecelia's bottom lip began to quiver, sending warning bells off in his brain.

"You'd better take her back," he said, but Beth was already lifting a bag out of a garbage can sitting next to a high table. The smell smacked him between the eyes. "That smell came out of this?"

"Her and two others I had earlier."

"But…" Joe looked down again and one tiny hand latched onto his bottom lip. He tugged on her arm, but Cecelia held tight. "She's got me," he said, the words sounding more like "Shegobbie."

Beth stopped on her way to the door, dropping the bag to pry tiny fingers out of his mouth. "Sorry. She's done that to me twice today."

"I'm going to drop her," he said, looking around for a place to put her.

"Haven't you ever played football?" Beth asked.

"What does that have to do with Miss Grip of Steel here?"

"Act like she's a football. Tuck her against your body and you'll be fine."

The analogy made sense, and when he applied the concept, Cecelia calmed in his arms. What did you know? Remembering how Beth had danced her to sleep, Joe tried swaying from side to side. He interpreted the gurgle to mean she liked it. When he added a soft bounce, her eyes closed and dark lashes settled on chubby cheeks.

"This isn't so hard," he said under his breath. Maintaining the motion, he looked up to find Beth watching him. Somehow they'd reversed roles.

A corner of her mouth quirked up and her eyes sparkled. "Looks like I'm not the only fast learner around here." Covering the distance between them, she tucked a dark curl behind the baby's ear. When she met his eyes again, her smile was gone. "You're going to make a good dad someday."

Lost in Beth's green eyes and lulled by the weight of peace in his arms, he said the first thing that came to mind. "I thought the same thing about you earlier."

Beth picked up the motion of his body and the three swayed together. He could have these few seconds. Pretend the complications didn't exist. Pretend nothing stood between them.

Cecelia snorted and Joe felt something press against the hand holding her bottom. A smell similar to the one that had lofted from the recently removed garbage bag filled the air.

Beth stepped back and flashed an evil smile. "You know the rule."

Unless she could read his mind and meant the rule about not stealing your brother's girl, he had no idea what she was referring to. "What rule?"

"The one holding the child is the one who changes the diaper."

He'd handled some raunchy situations in his life. Cleaned more fish than he could count. Bathed a filthy dog on more than one occasion. Even found six-month-old gym socks in his duffel bag once. But there was no way Joe was changing this diaper.

"Not happening," he said, passing the baby back fast enough to give Beth no choice. "I'll wait outside."

∼

Cecelia's timing was excellent. She'd saved Beth from making another stupid mistake. Not that she wanted to change one more hazardous-waste diaper. What *did* they put in baby food these days? But that whole happy family scene had sent impossible images floating through her mind. Images of a life with Joe. Of watching the sunset with Dozer sleeping at their feet. Of blue-eyed, dimpled babies tugging on Dozer's ears.

Guilt-inducing images that further strengthened her doubts.

How could she have these thoughts about Joe and be in love with Lucas?

She did love Lucas. His kindness and generosity. His ambition and how he embraced every day with enthusiasm and determination. But she wasn't in love with him. Not the way a woman should be with the man she was going to marry.

The realization had solidified an hour into her baby-room duties. Babies didn't talk back, which gave Beth plenty of time to talk to herself. Not that Cecelia wasn't a good listener. The poor thing had heard all of Beth's woes and concerns. Listened to her argue with herself, toss around solutions, and, in general, talk herself in circles.

She could walk away. Let Lucas down easy and give him the chance to find a woman who would fall madly in love with him. But she'd made a promise. Agreed to be his wife and wear his ring. Just because that ring was back in Richmond being sized didn't mean the commitment wasn't made.

Call her antiquated, but Beth took her promises seriously. She couldn't just call him up and say, "Sorry, I've changed my mind." Lucas deserved better. His family, whom she now thought of as her own, deserved better. And she could do better.

She would just have to fall in love with him. They hadn't set a date, so it wasn't as if she had to walk down the aisle next week. When this trip was over, they'd spend more time together. He'd been pushing her to branch out at work. Try practicing law instead of hiding in the library writing briefs and hunting down precedents for the real attorneys in the office.

She could work on Lucas's team, giving them more time together without cutting into his work. And her decision to come out of the stacks would make him happy. So what if the thought of speaking to a jury gave her heart palpitations. With Lucas as a mentor, she'd be winning cases during the week and acting as the perfect dinner-party hostess on the weekends.

Everything Lucas wanted her to be. And after today she'd be able to enjoy time away from work with him as well.

With that thought, Beth walked out of the day care to find Joe sitting sideways in his driver's seat, playing tug-of-war with Dozer. Her heart skipped a beat and again the images of a simple life with the dog and the babies and the little island cottage clouded her vision.

Shoving them aside, she closed her eyes, stirring up the courage not to run away when Joe wasn't looking. The future didn't seem so important when she was about to step onto a boat in the present. Running her affirmations on a loop in her mind, Beth forced herself to cross the parking lot and climb into the Jeep.

"Let's do this," she said, buckling her seat belt and staring straight ahead.

Joe clicked his own belt then brought the engine to life. "Nice Bruce Willis impersonation."

"In case you didn't notice, I'm barely breathing over here. Not in the mood for jokes."

The Jeep gained speed and Joe shifted to a higher gear. "This was your idea. We don't have to do it. But remember what I told you. Going on a boat is no big deal."

A pain shot through her jaw and Beth realized she was clenching her teeth like a vise grip. Rolling her head from left to right, she forced her shoulders and jaw to relax. "I know what you told me, but my brain is used to running this show, and this show stays on land."

"Hey," he said, going silent until she made eye contact. "You trust me?"

Narrowing her eyes, Beth contemplated the question. The answer surprised her. "Yes."

Joe grinned, flashing one bristly dimple her way. "Then we're all good."

Fifteen minutes later, Beth stood on the dock, squeezed into a bright-orange life jacket, watching Dozer bounce around on a boat roughly the size of a city block. Okay, it wasn't that big. But the term *fishing boat* didn't come close to describing the monstrosity bobbing before her. The word *yacht* came to mind.

Albeit a yacht covered in extra-long fishing poles.

When Dozer realized she wasn't on the boat with him, he threw his paws up on the side and stared at her expectantly, tongue lolling and tail wagging. She wanted to believe that if the dog could do it, she could do it, but then remembered the dog wasn't smart enough to realize death loomed beneath him.

"Think of it like getting in a car," Joe said, coming up behind her. "Just another mode of transportation." He took a step toward the boat, nudging her by the elbow.

"No way could I compare that...thing to a car. I'm just not ready yet." She took two steps back. "This is a bad idea."

"You can't let fear run your life. Take charge. Tell the fear to go to hell."

"Funny. The fear wants me to tell you the same thing." If her heart beat any faster, it was going to shoot through the life jacket. A boat that big probably wouldn't go down easy, she thought.

But hadn't they said that about the *Titanic?*

Joe moved to stand directly in front of her, close enough to block out her view of the death trap bobbing behind him. "Keep your eyes on me," he said, his voice calm and coaxing. He took her hands in his. "Look at me and follow my lead."

His touch did nothing to slow her heart rate, but her feet obeyed his orders.

The intensity of his azure eyes held her mesmerized. His full lips encouraged her. "That's it now. Stay with me. We're almost there." The words took on a sensual lilt. His breath mingled with hers. "Lift for me. Nice. One more time. Now come with me. A little more."

Her brain turned to mush. She wouldn't have been surprised if it oozed out her ears. Other parts were feeling a bit liquefied as well. Joe stopped and she took one more step, crushing their hands between them. The backs of his hands would have been pressed against her breasts if the life jacket hadn't been in the way.

The life jacket needed to come off. And maybe his shirt. Joe smiled down at her and she wondered if he was thinking the same thing she was.

"Beth?"

"Uh-huh."

"You did it."

"Did what?" Why wasn't he unbuttoning his shirt?

"You're on the boat."

The words took several seconds to register. When they did, she latched on to his signature red flannel as if it were the only thing standing between her and the pearly gates. "Oh my God."

"Holy shit," he said, prying her hands away from his chest. "Take it easy now."

"You have to get me off this boat." Her lungs kicked into double time. Breathing was always the first to go. "I can't feel my legs."

"Your legs are under you and working fine." He removed one hand, but it latched right back on. "Watch the chest hair."

She would have helped him if she'd had any control over her limbs.

"Listen to me," he said, loud enough to turn her brain back to a solid. "There's nothing to be afraid of. Look." He bounced, and she screamed. Joe placed a hand over her mouth. "Knock that off before someone thinks I'm kidnapping you. You're a smart woman. You know this fear is irrational, right?"

Beth nodded, his hand still covering her mouth.

"Then fight back. Don't let the fear win. You're stronger than the fear."

Her grip on his shirt loosened, but she wasn't ready to let go. He was right. This fear stemmed from one stupid accident that happened twenty years ago. Twenty years was long enough.

She nodded again, pulling back from his hand. "I'm good. I got this." Control of her extremities returned. Bouncing the way Joe had, she was surprised to find the boat didn't move beneath her. In fact, standing on the boat didn't feel that different from standing on solid ground.

"See? Nothing to be afraid of," he said, looking relieved.

She bounced again, then shifted from one foot to the other. "I'm standing on a boat." Dropping one hand from

Joe's shirt, she turned to look back at the dock. "I'm really standing on a boat. And I can breathe."

"I told you you could do it. The boat will move more when we're out on the water, but the *Mary Ann* is as solid as they come."

Beth blinked. "Your boat is called the *Mary Ann*? As in *Gilligan's Island*?" Before he could answer, she added, "I would have pegged you for a Ginger man."

"Cute." Joe turned serious. "Mary Ann was my mother's name."

No one in the family ever talked about Joe's mother. Beth hadn't even seen a picture. She knew Joe had been young when she died, but no other details. "I'm sorry," she said, needing to say something but not sure what.

He shrugged, being strong as usual. But she could see the sad boy still living in the man.

"I lost my mom, too." Beth had never said those words to anyone. She wasn't sure why she was saying them now.

"I know," Joe said. "You told me Saturday night on the way home from the bar."

"I did?" Tequila should be renamed truth serum. "I was too young to remember her. Not even three when she passed."

"But you still grew up without her. So you get it."

"Yeah. I get it."

They stood there, staring at each other, sharing something few people understood. Though Lucas had lost his father, he never seemed affected by it. Which said a great deal about Tom Dempsey.

"We'd better get going. You want to sit up top with me or inside?"

Beth looked around, taking in details she'd been too distracted to notice before. Such as the missing dog. She spotted him sitting in a doorway to her left. "There's an inside?"

"Full cabin. A/C, heat, microwave. Good for large parties, especially when the men bring their wives." Dozer hopped up as Joe headed for the narrow entrance. "Wouldn't want to mess up their hair with a little sea spray."

Beth ran after him, panic setting in at the idea of Joe being more than arm's length away. His chauvinistic comment raised her hackles, but the defense of her gender died on her tongue the moment she entered the cabin. "Good heavens, this is huge."

CHAPTER TWENTY-TWO

Joe's chest swelled with pride when Beth marveled at the cabin as if they'd walked into a museum. Her opinion shouldn't matter so much. But it did.

He cleared his throat, not sure what to say. "You want a drink? I've got bottled water in the fridge."

"There's a fridge?" Beth looked as if he'd told her the boat had wings. "This is almost as big as my kitchen back in Richmond. Or should I say, kitchenette. I could live in here."

"You remember we're on a boat, right?"

Beth paused, bending at the knees as if bracing against an impending wave. "Right. I'd better sit down." Stretching out on the white bench seat to the right, encased in a bright orange life jacket, she stared at the ceiling. "I can't get over how big it is. You should warn a girl next time." A hand slapped her forehead. "That sounds way dirtier than it did in my head."

Unable to resist, he said, "It *is* fifty-seven feet long."

Beth shook her head. "I made that too easy." Leaning up on an elbow, she asked, "Isn't something like this really expensive?"

"It wasn't cheap, but this one was a repo, so I got a good deal." He'd never felt the need to advertise his income the way Lucas did, but that didn't mean he couldn't measure up in the bank account either. "Some blow their money on high-dollar foreign cars. I'd rather invest in this."

The second the words were out he felt like a moron. As if he needed to compete with Lucas.

"I didn't mean to offend you," Beth said, moving to the counter and sliding a hand over smooth mahogany. He imagined her fingers sliding up his spine. "She's so beautiful." Shooting a smile over her shoulder, she added, "Better than a BMW."

"I didn't mean—"

"I know what you meant. He who dies with the most shit, right? That's Lucas."

"Nothing wrong with having nice things." Too bad Lucas had the nicest thing Joe had ever found. And it wasn't his car.

"True. Not if you understand the value of what you have." Beth sighed as she opened and closed the microwave. "Not all men do." Changing the subject, she asked, "You ever sleep here?"

"Not often. Hard to let Dozer out to do his business without a yard around."

Nice, asshole. Perfect time to bring up dog shit.

"What's down there?" she asked, pointing to the steps dropping down between the two counters.

Joe crossed his arms, then uncrossed them and slid his hands in his pockets. He felt like a teenager talking to the hottest girl in school. Even in bright orange she made his mouth go dry. "That's the head."

"The head?"

"The bathroom on a boat is called the head."

"Oh." Beth made the full circle, ending her exploration standing between him and the bench that turned into a bed with one flip of the wrist.

He could probably undo that button on her jeans just as easily.

"We need to set out," he said, heading for the exit. Leaping into the water to cool off would probably be hard to explain.

"Where are you going?" she asked, catching him before he'd taken two steps.

"Up to the cockpit. I can't drive the boat from here."

He took another step and she moved with him. "I'm coming with you."

Getting her on the boat had been one thing. Getting her another six feet up would not be as easy. "You sure you don't want to start in here and work your way out?"

Rubbing a hand over her heart, she started to wheeze. "No. No. I'd better stick with you." Leaning forward, she braced her hands on her knees.

"You're losing it again," he said, crossing his arms to save his chest hair. "Sit down and let me get us out on the water. Then you can come out and enjoy the view."

"No!" she yelled, wrapping pale hands around his forearm, digging her nails into his flesh. "You're my lifeline. If I don't stay with you, I'll never make it."

"I'm your lifeline?" This development would not help his need to cool off. "I thought that's what the vest was for."

He removed the nails, but one hand clutched the sleeve of his flannel.

"The life jacket isn't working. Not that I'm taking it off, but the panic only subsides so long as I'm next to you."

Looked like he'd have a copilot for the day. "Okay then. Let's head up."

~

Cassandra felt the phone vibrate from inside her Coach clutch. Checking the ID, she let the wave of revulsion run its course before answering.

"What do you want, Mr. Mohler?" Calling the cretin "Mr. Mohler" made a muscle tick in her jaw, but men were more cooperative when she feigned courtesy.

"You said you wanted anything you could use against Dempsey."

Cassie didn't know what Joe had ever done to Mohler to make the man hate him so, but in all honesty, she didn't care either. So long as Mohler served his purpose.

"You have something?"

"I do. Something that will put more than a ding in Dempsey family relations."

Cassie rolled her eyes. "Get to the point, Mr. Mohler. I'm a busy woman."

"Let's just say Dempsey is dipping his rod where he shouldn't be."

"The point, Mr. Mohler. And I don't appreciate the vulgarity." If this was about Joe dropping his standards to that little shopgirl, Mohler was wasting her time.

"He's boffing his brother's fiancée. They're together all the time, and they just set out on his boat. Alone." His voice grew muffled, as if he were holding his mouth too close to the phone. "I know I'd be pissed to find out my brother was fucking my woman."

Cassie cringed. She'd dealt with her share of sycophants, but this association was turning out to be outright repugnant. "I didn't know Lucas's fiancée was on the island. Seeing them together is not proof. I can't make this kind of accusation unless I'm certain."

"See for yourself," Mohler said, a loud air horn sounding behind him. "Meet me at the marina restaurant in two hours. I'd bet my best rod they'll be gone at least that long. That brunette has wild written all over her. If she wasn't so snooty, I'd take a crack at her myself."

The woman from the shop was a brunette. But why would Lucas's fiancée be working at a shop on Anchor? "Describe the woman."

"Little thing. Curly hair. Tight ass. Always looks like she's just smelled something bad."

Every woman who found herself in Mohler's vicinity probably looked as if she'd smelled something bad. But the rest of the description fit. Though she'd never met the woman, Cassie heard enough gossip to know Lucas's fiancée worked at the same law firm Lucas did.

The firm that worked for Wheeler Development. Good thing the woman displayed a knack for retail, since she'd need that job before long.

"I'll be there, Mr. Mohler. Make sure we have a seat near the window."

~

The lifeline thing was no joke. Having only one seat in the cockpit meant Joe had to drive the boat while standing behind the chair and reaching around Beth and her bright-orange life jacket to steer. Joe wouldn't have minded so much if Beth's scent hadn't tortured his senses. She'd pulled her hair to one side so it wouldn't flutter in his face, but that left her pale neck bare, tempting him to drop a kiss just below her ear.

At least the life jacket blocked the view down her shirt.

But distance from Joe wasn't the only factor. Distance from the shore mattered as well. They'd found a comfortable spot about half a mile out where he'd coaxed her to sit on the floor of the cockpit, letting their feet dangle above the lower deck. From there Beth could keep an eye on the island, which allowed him to put a few feet between them.

"Can I ask you a question?" she said, breaking the comfortable silence.

"You just did."

"That's a lawyerlike response. Maybe you should have gone to law school."

The thought of studying law made his asshole pucker. "I'll stick with fishing. What do you want to know?"

"Why do you call Patty by her name? I know Lucas calls Tom Dad."

Joe sighed. "I love Patty, but I had a mom. Giving Patty the title felt like saying my mom never existed." He snorted, recalling the early years of their blended family. "I was a real pain in the ass when Dad married her. Mom hadn't been

gone two years, and I was mad as hell. It's a wonder Patty
didn't sell me or peddle me off to some boarding school."

"You, difficult? I don't believe it."

He glanced over and caught the smile on her face.
"Funny, smart-ass. How about you?"

"Me?" she asked. "I'm the complete opposite. Never gave
anyone a hard time. I was taught at an early age to behave
and never rebel. Nod and smile and make everyone happy."

She stared over the water as she spoke and he couldn't
help but ask the obvious question. "You don't sound happy
about that. Why do you keep it up?"

"What do you mean?" She leaned back on her hands,
brows drawn.

"Why don't you stop trying to make everyone else happy
and do something to make yourself happy?"

Beth blinked, looking as if he'd just asked her to solve
all the mysteries of the universe. "But making people happy
does make me happy."

"Really?"

"Really."

"I don't believe it."

"Well, I don't care what you believe." She crossed her
arms and huffed at the sky. He waited, knowing she'd cave.
"Why don't you believe it?"

"You spend a lot of time at Lola's place. You like hanging out up there?"

"Of course, but what does that have to do with anything?"

"What do you do when you're there?" he pushed.

"We talk and I make things. Like this bracelet." She held
out her left wrist.

He turned to face her, raising one knee and leaning on the wall behind him. "How often do you make stuff like this when you're back home?"

She opened her mouth, then closed it again. Pursing her lips, she stared at the shoreline again. "I don't. I haven't made anything in ten years."

"Why not?"

Scooting back against the opposite wall, she crossed her arms. "I don't have time is all. There was school—law school isn't easy—and then work, and now I spend time with Lucas whenever I can." Playing with a loose thread hanging from the cuff of her jeans, she repeated, "I don't have time."

Changing direction, Joe asked, "Did your grandmother really warn you not to be like your mom?"

Her eyes went wide. "How do you know that?"

"Cuervo again. You cried that night, saying you'd turned into your mother and that was the worst thing you could ever do. At least according to your grandmother. Made me want to shake the shit out of anyone who'd tell that to a kid, especially one who'd lost her mother."

"You don't know what my mother was like." Beth curled into herself.

"No, I don't. But I know that's a lot of weight to put on a little girl."

Beth tilted her head back and closed her eyes, holding silent.

"Where was your dad?" he asked.

Her eyes remained closed as her head rolled from side to side. He didn't think she was going to answer, but then she looked up, her green eyes staring into his. "Jail. At least when my mother died. Armed robbery. He was released when I was in elementary school, but never came to see me. I found out in high school he'd been shot to death in a robbery gone bad out in California."

The words were delivered with no emotion. No feeling. She stared another few seconds, then her head dropped back again, as if saying the words had worn her out. He guessed she'd never said them before.

"Lucas doesn't know, does he?"

"No."

"Why not?" Joe suspected he knew the answer, and it made him want to kick the shit out of his baby brother.

Beth sighed and her shoulders dropped. "Lucas is climbing a steep ladder built on dinner parties, expensive suits, and people ready to stab you in the back before you reach the next rung. His career means everything to him. A wife from backwoods Louisa County with a drunk for a mother and a thief for a father wouldn't reflect well on a man aiming for partner at a law firm."

Joe tapped the boat floor with his fist. "Do you think he'd break it off if he knew?"

"No. Well, probably not. But appearances are so important to Lucas, to everyone at the firm. I guess I figured if it ever did get around the office and he didn't know about it, then there wouldn't be any guilt by association. He could claim ignorance, and my past wouldn't damage his future." She looked down. "Anyway, if no one knows, including Lucas, then no one gets hurt."

"Except you."

~

Beth ignored the statement. She'd spent too many years running from the past to let it hurt her now. Or anyone else. Scanning the coast of the island that had filled a tiny hole in her heart she hadn't known was there, a ray of light caught her eye.

"Is that the lighthouse?" Rising to her feet, she held tight to the rail.

"That's it. Hold on and I'll cut over so you can see it straight on."

Joe fired up the engine and Beth's heart raced in her chest. Instead of the panic she expected, the increase stemmed from anticipation. This boating thing wasn't so bad. Granted, she wasn't ready to live on the water, but the paralyzing fear felt less…paralyzing. Lucas would have a seafaring wife yet.

The *Mary Ann* rounded a bend to draw level with a strand of tall pines, and the air flew out of her lungs. Small boats bobbed against a short pier with two large cabins looming behind them. Gold light glowed from the cabin windows and danced across the surface of the sound. Between the two cabins, proud and solid, stood the Anchor Lighthouse.

The image could have been taken right from a postcard. A quaint village with its fishermen and quirky characters, slow pace, and protective beam of light. One word looped through her mind.

Home.

"This is the best time to see it," Joe said, joining her at the rail. "The island won't look so sleepy when the tourists arrive in full force."

"It's perfect," she whispered, feeling a sadness seep into her bones, knowing she'd be leaving this heaven on earth in less than a week. When Joe brushed her arm, a different sense of loss slid in beside the first. She fought to ignore the wedge in her chest.

"We need to head back before it gets too dark." He returned to the wheel and Beth felt an emptiness edge its way into her heart. "You good over there or you want back in the chair?"

She wanted to feel his arms around her again. To take his warmth with her. Beth reminded herself this trip was about Lucas. "I'm good over here, thanks."

They reached the dock in a matter of minutes, Beth relieved that she'd made the trip without falling overboard or tossing her lunch. Once he'd secured the boat, Joe helped her disembark. "We've probably missed dinner at Dad and Patty's. Want to grab something up at the restaurant?"

Her hand felt right in his. If she thought she could be just friends with Joe, she'd been fooling herself. "Not sure I should eat right after being on the water."

Joe chuckled. "I think that rule pertains to swimming. We weren't in the water, remember?"

Maybe not, but Beth felt the distinct sensation of drowning. "Right. Sure. We can eat, I guess."

Removing her life jacket, she passed it off to Joe, who flung it onto the boat. "Shouldn't be a problem to get a table on a Monday night," he said, motioning Beth up the dock. "So what do you think?"

"About what?" she asked, not about to confess her true thoughts.

"The boat. You seemed to relax into it. This is when I say I told you so." Joe smiled, dazzling her with the dimple of doom. "Not that I'd do that."

Being "just friends" didn't seem to be a problem for Joe. She tried not to resent him for it. Maybe she could convince herself she was falling for the island and not the man walking beside her.

Would he have the same pull for her if they'd met in a coffee shop in Richmond? Maybe it was the water or the salty air. The peaceful, almost romantic ambiance of Anchor.

She tried for the same casual tone. "You can say it. I doubt I'll be buying a houseboat any time soon, but an afternoon on the water with Lucas won't be so bad. And the ferry ride home should be easier, too." Mentioning the ferry ride brought back the melancholy of her imminent departure. At least her time at Lola's had guaranteed she'd take pieces of the island home with her.

They'd have to make up for the piece of herself she'd be leaving behind.

Joe had been right about the table situation. The row along the windows, which provided a stellar view of the harbor, was occupied, but most others remained open. As they followed the waiter toward the back corner, Beth noticed Cassandra Wheeler sitting at a table with Phil Mohler.

Two things were instantly clear. Cassie had terrible taste in dinner companions and an issue of some kind with Beth. If looks could kill, they'd be arranging her funeral.

"Hello, Joe," Cassie said, as they approached the table. "And your little shopgirl. How cute." The title was meant to insult, but Beth refused to take the bait and gave little more than a nod.

"Shopgirl?" Joe asked, looking from Cassie to Beth and back again. All of her nonexistent telepathic powers went into the look Beth gave him. By some miracle, he got the message. "Beth is visiting from Richmond. She's…a friend of the family."

"Really?" Cassie asked, feigning surprise or interest, Beth wasn't sure which. Mohler snorted.

"Don't let us intrude on your meal," Beth said, moving toward the server waiting for them two tables down.

"Don't be silly," the conniving blonde said, lifting her leather bag from the chair beside her. "You two must join us. I insist." Two snaps from Miss Bossy and the waiter placed their menus at the open settings.

Joe's response to another pleading look was a raised brow and quick nod indicating she should have a seat. After pulling the empty chair from beside Mohler, he placed it around the end of the table, putting himself out in the aisle. Beth assumed he intended to find out once and for all how Mohler fit into Cassie's plan.

Either Mohler had inhaled pepper or suffered from a cold, but Cassie's dinner partner couldn't seem to control the odd noises coming through his nose.

Beth had no choice but to take the seat beside Joe's ex, entering a cloud of Chanel. "I feel bad, infringing on your date this way," she said, deciding to score the first hit. Not her usual style, but watching the woman's face pucker was worth the effort.

Instead of correcting her, Cassie kept to her mission, which was clearly to torture Beth. "How do you know the Dempseys, Beth? I don't remember Joe mentioning you when we were engaged."

A lawyer recognized a leading question when she heard one. Cassie knew.

CHAPTER TWENTY-THREE

"I'm engaged to Joe's brother, Lucas." Now to see how many details she could avoid. "During your brief time with Joe, Lucas and I hadn't met yet."

Cassie gave a weak smile, and Beth knew she'd disarmed her. Somewhat.

"Well, congratulations. I'd heard Lucas was engaged, but you're not quite what I expected."

Score a point for the blonde. Beth glanced at Joe, who stared back, brows raised. The man was smiling. He wouldn't find this funny if he knew what she'd put on the line for him and his island.

"You're not what I'd expect for Joe either, so I guess we're all full of surprises." Engaging in a battle with Mean Barbie was probably a bad idea, but Beth found she couldn't help herself. "How do you and Mr. Mohler know each other? You seem like an unlikely pair as well."

"What's that supposed to mean?" Mohler asked. "I'm just as good as Dempsey."

"Shut up, Mohler," Joe said, keeping his eyes on Beth and Cassie. "What are you doing here with Phil? It can't be to talk business, since he doesn't own more than a dinky cabin that, based on the plans I've seen, isn't anywhere near the area you want."

Cassie stalled by sipping her wine. Wearing the fakest smile Beth had ever seen, she said, "Mr. Mohler was kind enough to invite me here to discuss the island. Anchor is going to be an important business holding for Wheeler Development, and we like to know the people we'll be dealing with."

"Anchor is never going to be a business holding for anyone," Joe said. "The sooner you realize that, the sooner you can catch the next ferry out. It's time to move on, Cassie."

The two stared like cats in a contest to see who would blink first. Beth felt the two were carrying on the conversation without saying a word. And she didn't like it. "I've lost my appetite," she said, pushing her chair back.

Cassie broke eye contact and turned on Beth. "Before you go, I was wondering. Is it true you work for the same firm as Lucas?"

Beth froze. Hoping her face remained expressionless, she answered, "Yes. I work in the research department of Bracken, Franks, and Holcomb."

A smile spread across Cassandra Wheeler's face, twisting Beth's stomach into knots. Lucas had warned her, but she didn't listen. Why hadn't she listened?

"Well then, maybe we'll run into each other again sometime. I'll look you up when I'm in the office. On business."

Beth didn't have to respond. Cassie's meaning was loud and clear. There was no doubt Cruella knew she'd won the battle.

And maybe the war.

"Can we go?" Beth asked Joe, rising though her limbs were numb.

Joe looked to his ex then back at Beth. "Yeah, sure. After you."

∼

Beth remained quiet on the ride home. Though he'd witnessed the entire conversation, Joe had no idea what had happened. Far as he could tell, Beth was getting in as many digs as Cassie was throwing back. But in the end, Cassie seemed to throw the winning punch.

If only he knew what the hell that was.

When he pulled into the drive and cut the engine, neither moved to get out. After a minute of silence, he couldn't take it anymore. "I get the feeling I missed something back there?"

"She knows," Beth said, staring straight ahead.

"Knows what?"

"That I work at the law firm."

"And that's a problem?"

She turned his way. With attitude. "Did you hear what she said? When she's in the office? Doesn't that mean anything to you?"

He hadn't expected a fight. Feeling his way, Joe replied, "I wondered about that. Why would she be in your law office?"

"Because my firm works for her daddy. We're retained by Wheeler Development to handle all legal matters for the company."

"Okay." The more questions he asked, the more agitated Beth grew. Which meant asking another question would be stupid, so he tried a question in the form of a statement. "And that's a bad thing."

"She knows I helped the Merchants. That means I worked against Wheeler Development. Don't you get it?"

He didn't get it but saying so was clearly going to lead to trouble. So he kept his mouth shut. Beth huffed, undid her seat belt, and bolted out of the Jeep. "How could you not get it?"

"You need to calm down and tell me what I'm missing here," he said, hopping out and catching her at the base of his parents' porch steps. "Why are you so pissed?"

Beth spun around so fast Joe had to stop and pedal backward as she charged. "She's going to get me fired."

That he didn't see coming. "Cassie can be a hard-ass, but why would she get you fired?"

"Because she can. How could you have almost married that hateful, conniving woman?" She crossed her arms, waiting impatiently for a response. "I forgot. You're a man. That explains everything."

"Hey. Wait a minute."

"Wait for what? For my official termination letter? For all my grandparents' dreams to go up in flames? For Lucas to…"

"For Lucas to what?" Joe asked, anger and hope dancing up his spine. "For Lucas to dump you because you lost your job?"

"He wouldn't do that," she said, her eyes locked on the sandy drive at their feet.

Joe took her by the arms. "What's going on here? Last I knew, we had a good day out on the water. I'm no lawyer, but I know you haven't done anything to get yourself fired."

Beth shook her head, one tear sliding down her cheek. "You don't understand. You live on this island utopia, sheltered from the rest of the world. This bucolic scene off a postcard where every day is like a vacation." Jerking her arms away, she stomped back to the porch. "Some of us don't have the luxury of hiding from real life."

Joe's fists clenched and he felt a vein throb in his neck. "You think I'm hiding?"

She turned, one foot on the step. "Aren't you? What are you afraid of, Joe?"

"Try asking yourself that question. All I ever hear is what your grandparents wanted for you. Or what Lucas wants. What about what you want?" He crossed the distance between them. "What do you want, Beth? Do you want to be a lawyer? Because everything you've told me says you don't."

"It doesn't matter what I want."

"God, are you stubborn," he said, running a hand through his hair, then putting several feet between them to keep from shaking some sense into her. "Answer the question, damn it. What do you want?"

She scrubbed her hands over her face, then shoved them back in her hair. "I want...I just..."

"Say it."

Beth closed her eyes and another tear followed the first. "I want to go back to the way things were before I got here. Before I drove onto that ferry and found you with those blue eyes and that damn dimple. Before I fell in love with this island and the people on it." Dropping her hands to her sides, her shoulders dropped. "*All* of the people on it."

The air left his lungs, and a single thought roared through his mind.

She loves me.

"What are we going to do?"

"Nothing," she said, and walked into the house.

∼

Beth gave herself an hour to pull it together before calling Lucas. He needed to know what was going on. If he was called into the HR office to discuss her actions, he should have some idea what they were talking about.

"Hey there," Lucas said, sounding groggy but happy to hear from her. "How are things down there?"

Ignoring his question, she asked, "Did I wake you? I'm sorry, I should let you sleep."

"No, it's fine. I just fell asleep watching SportsCenter." He yawned. "I'm glad you called. Sorry I missed your calls over the weekend."

"That's okay," she said, searching for some reserve of courage. "I need to talk to you about something." Her chest grew tight.

"What is it? Patty trying to talk you into having the wedding down there?" Lucas gave a soft laugh and Beth curled into herself on the bed.

"No. We haven't talked about the wedding." Like ripping off a Band-Aid, she thought. "It's about Cassandra Wheeler."

"Is she still down there? I'd have expected Joe to run her off by now."

"She's here. We saw her at dinner tonight."

"We? You and the family?"

"No," she admitted, squeezing her eyes tight. "Joe and I. Anyway, she knows."

Lucas sounded more alert. "Knows what?"

"That I work for the firm and I helped gather information for the Merchants Society. Information they could use to keep Wheeler from getting the island."

"I told you not to get involved. What were you thinking?"

She was thinking she wanted to help Joe protect the island that meant so much to him. And now to her. But she couldn't tell Lucas that.

"I guess I wasn't thinking. In case this becomes an issue before I get back, I wanted you to know." Fighting the tears, she added, "I'm sorry."

"Let's think about this," he said, and she could tell he'd started pacing. Lucas always paced while trying to solve a problem. "Tell me specifically how you helped."

Beth swiped a wayward tear before it fell off her chin. "I put together a list of merchants with their contact information. Gathered data on the local economy and tourism numbers, then used those to create future predictions."

"Did you find any legal means for the Merchants to hold off Wheeler?"

"I couldn't do that without a law library. I don't know how long it's been since you were here, but the Anchor library isn't exactly overflowing with law books."

"Then you're fine. You put together information anyone could have acquired on the Internet. No legal research. No laws cited or precedents determined. Can they even prove you did it?"

No wonder Lucas had such a high acquittal rating. "I didn't sign my name to anything, but if someone asks me I'm not going to lie and say I didn't do it."

"Doesn't matter," Lucas said, in full defense mode. "Cassandra Wheeler can try pulling whatever strings she wants, but there are no grounds to terminate you based on what you've told me. Is there anything you're not telling me?"

Beth held her breath.

I'm in love with your brother.

"No."

"Good." Lucas exhaled. "If they try anything, we'll handle it. Together. Okay?"

The guilt nearly ripped her apart. "Okay."

"Are you crying? Hon, don't cry. Everything will work out. You made a mistake, but nothing we can't fix."

Her whole life felt like something she couldn't fix. "I'm fine. Really. But I'm tired, so I think I'm going to bed." Sliding to her side and curling a pillow against her stomach, she said, "I'll call you tomorrow night."

"We might be at the office late. The evidentiary hearing is Friday. But I'll keep my cell on me." Silence filled the line for several seconds. "Try not to worry about this, Elizabeth. Things will look better in the morning."

"I know. Night."

"Love you," Lucas said, delivering the fatal blow.

She couldn't say it back. "Night," she said, ending the call and turning to cry into her pillow.

~

Cassandra had been transferred twice by the time she reached Lucas Dempsey's office, at which point a woman informed her he wasn't available. After ordering the secretary to make him available, she sat on hold for several more minutes before he picked up.

"This is Lucas Dempsey," he said, sounding as irritated as she felt.

"Hello, Lucas. This is Cassandra Wheeler." She'd been writing the script for this call since watching that curly-haired bitch walk out of the restaurant with Joe.

Her Joe.

"What do you want, Cassie? I was in an important meeting."

"I have some information for you regarding your fiancée's activities on Anchor Island."

"I know about my fiancée's activities. She told me last night. Was there something else you wanted to discuss?"

Cassandra hesitated. She'd never expected the hussy to confess on her own. "She told you last night?"

"Yes," he said.

"I must admit," she said, "you're taking this better than most men would."

"I'm not most men. Now, if we're finished here..."

Cassandra snorted. "I don't care how evolved you consider yourself, Lucas, but finding out your fiancée is having an affair with your brother would elicit more than this placid response from most of the men I know."

Stunned silence crackled over the line and Cassandra smiled. So, little Beth hadn't confessed after all.

"What did you say?"

"I guess she didn't tell you everything." Pinning the phone between her ear and shoulder, Cassie folded a pair of black slacks, then dropped them in the suitcase. "Your fiancée isn't as innocent as she looks. Though I would expect better from Joe. He is your brother."

Lucas's voice carried a growl. "Why should I believe you? You've had it out for my brother since the day he cut you off. I'm not going to be part of your petty plan for revenge."

"He didn't cut me off," she argued. "I wasn't about to live on this speck of an island for the rest of my life. And if he'd really loved me, he never would have chosen this hellhole over me."

"I think your motives are clear. This conversation is over."

"They're making a fool of you, and everyone on this island can see it. If you don't believe me, come down here and see for yourself. But when you lose your fiancée, don't say I didn't warn you."

With that parting shot, Cassandra ended the call, zipped her suitcase, and headed for home. The sooner she got off this filthy patch of sand, the better.

∾

To Beth's relief, Joe was booked solid for the next two days, which meant she didn't have to see him. She needed the time to think. When she woke Tuesday morning to the most intense sinus headache she'd ever experienced, courtesy of sobbing herself to sleep, Beth remembered Lola's words.

Ain't a soul alive can worry about anything when they're staring into the sweet face of a child.

Thankfully, Helga was happy for the help. The babies were a soothing distraction and made Beth smile when she thought she'd never smile again. And then a wayward thought would creep in. Thoughts of her and Lucas having children. Eyes closed, she attempted to conjure the image of Lucas swaying back and forth with a child in his arms.

The image never came. Instead, the memory of Joe gently bouncing baby Cecelia played on a loop like a movie reel she was being forced to watch over and over. The harder she tried to slide Lucas into the role of father, the brighter Joe smiled, his eyes pulling her into the fantasy.

How had she let this happen? This was supposed to be a relaxing two-week vacation with her fiancé. Time to get to know his family and win their approval. She was never supposed to question whether Lucas should even be her fiancé. Falling in love with his brother was definitely not in the plan.

And she was in love with him. No point in denying her feelings now. Especially since she'd admitted as much to Joe.

Such a stupid thing to do. And the jerk couldn't even call her crazy or tell her he didn't feel the same. *What are we going to do?* What did he think they were going to do? Hop on the boat and ride off into the sunset? Follow their hearts and leave others to deal with the hurt and betrayal?

She couldn't do that. Deep down, she knew Joe couldn't either. But after two days of thinking through all the possible solutions, Beth was no closer to an answer than she'd been before.

"It's about time you got here," Lola said, rushing out to meet Beth in the art shop parking lot.

"I didn't know I was punching a clock." Lola tugged Beth toward the porch. "Why are we in such a hurry?"

"I've got something to show you." For a woman twice Beth's age, Lola moved with remarkable speed. "He's been here less than an hour and I've already run out of things to say."

"Who's been here?" Before Lola could answer, the light went on. "Oh my gosh. Marcus is here?" Beth picked up the pace. "Why didn't you call me?"

"I called Miss Patty and she said you left over a half hour ago. What did you do, take the long way around?" She'd never heard Lola so flustered. It was kind of cute.

"I stopped for coffee and took my time. I am on vacation, you know." Beth pulled the door open. "Not that anyone on this island seems to realize that."

The store was littered with tourists, same as the coffee shop had been. Not an overwhelming crowd. She hoped numbers would be better after Memorial Day. Not that she'd be there to see them.

To her surprise, Will stood behind the register, ringing up a customer. "What's Will doing here?"

"She helps out once the season gets going."

"But I thought she worked at O'Hagan's? And Hava Java?"

Lola maneuvered them both through the shoppers, headed for the pottery classroom at the back. "Hard to make a living on this island if you don't own one of the businesses. Far as I know, Will works for everyone at some point or another."

Talk about a Jack of all trades. "Why does she live here if it's so hard to make a living?"

The older woman stopped next to a table of vases and turned around. "That's something you'd have to ask her." Lola closed her eyes and did what looked like yoga breathing. After three breaths, she opened her eyes. "Okay. I'm ready."

"What are you so nervous about?" Beth asked, following Lola toward a beaded curtain. "You're usually a pillar of calm. I can't believe a man has you this worked up."

Lola turned again, causing Beth to bump into her. "This isn't just any man. This is the man I haven't seen in thirty-five years who is as knicker-meltingly handsome as he ever was." The breathing started again.

The truth of the matter seemed obvious, though Beth had trouble believing it. "You're scared. Lola, if this man has half a brain in his head, he's going to see you're still the most beautiful, most vibrant woman he's ever going to meet. And if he can't see that, then he doesn't deserve you."

Brown eyes went misty. "Good Lord, child. Don't make me cry before I go in there. He's already liable to think I'm a loon for running out of the room like I did."

Beth giggled. "You ran out of the room?"

"I couldn't help it," she said, giving Beth a don't-hassle-me look that felt more like the Lola she knew. "I walked away from him once. What if he can't forgive me?"

"He's here, isn't he?" Beth asked, wiping a tear from Lola's weathered cheek. "He tracked you down after all these years. You have a second chance. Go take it."

At that moment, a tall black man with cropped white hair and bright hazel eyes strolled through the curtain. He had to bend slightly to duck under the doorway, and the hat dangling from his fingers looked as if it had been worried to death. The moment his eyes found Lola, a smile split his face and his shoulders relaxed.

Beth couldn't remember ever seeing a man so smitten. One look at Lola told her the feeling was mutual. For several long moments, the two stared at one another as if they were alone in the world. Beth cleared her throat and Lola jumped.

"Oh," she said, taking Beth's hand. "This is my friend, Beth. The one I told you about. Beth, this is Marcus Granville."

"Nice to meet you, Beth," Marcus said, his deep, rich baritone vibrating over her skin. How had Lola ever let this man get away? "Lola has told me a lot about you. Says you're practically a native of this island now."

A native. The word didn't apply to her and never would. Even if she wanted nothing more. "Not me, I'm just a tourist. I'll be leaving in a few days."

Leaving the island. Leaving Joe.

CHAPTER TWENTY-FOUR

"Beth, hon, are you okay?" Lola lifted her chin with a gentle touch. "You went pale all of a sudden."

Ignoring the pain in her chest, she smiled, though she knew it didn't reach her eyes. "I'm fine." Lola's eyes narrowed. "Really. I'll be fine." Turning to Marcus, Beth asked, "How long will you be on the island? Or are you looking to become a native yourself?"

Focusing on Lola's love life felt less earth-shattering.

Marcus looked to Lola and smiled. "One of the joys of retirement is freedom. Which means I'm here as long as Lola will have me."

Pink tinged Lola's mocha skin. If the woman was smart, she'd grab this man with both hands and never let him leave.

"Excuse me," said Will, walking up between Lola and Beth. "Mail arrived. Top one is from Wheeler Development. Think they're upping the offers again?"

For a non–business owner, Will was well-informed on the Wheeler situation. But then, working at every business in town was probably a good way to stay in the loop.

Lola took the top envelope and let Will hold the rest. "They can offer me a fool's ransom, and I'm still not selling."

While Lola worked the envelope open, Will nudged Beth. "Karaoke at O'Hagan's tonight. You were pretty good when you were tanked on tequila."

Beth rubbed her arm. The woman had a mean left elbow. "That was a one-time performance, but thanks anyway."

Will shrugged. "Suit yourself. Hundred dollars prize money is nothing to sneeze at."

A gasp from Lola grabbed their attention.

"What is it?" Will asked.

"I don't believe it." She grinned. "They've rescinded all offers."

"They've what?" Beth asked, certain she'd heard wrong.

"Look for yourself," Lola said, passing the letter over. Beth scanned the page, finding the pertinent information.

Wheeler Development rescinds all offers for purchase of subject business and any and all accompanying properties. This letter supersedes all previous communications including any verbal agreements made to date.

"They're giving up," Beth whispered in awe. Something wasn't right. "But why would they give up?"

"Who cares?" Lola said. "Wheeler ain't getting our island, and that's all that matters."

It couldn't be that simple. From everything she knew about Wheeler and his business dealings, he wasn't the type to back down. Not because of a few, as he would see it, reluctant islanders. He'd barrel through them and take what he wanted.

Unless he'd never wanted the island to begin with. Cassandra's determined glare flashed through Beth's mind. Joe had been right. Cassie had done all of this out of revenge. If she was giving up, there must be a reason. Getting Beth fired wouldn't hurt Joe. So what would?

"Lola, I need to go."

"But you just got here." Dropping her voice, she added, "You can't leave me now."

Beth threw her arms around the slender woman and whispered in her ear, "He loves you, Lola. Don't let him go." Pulling back, she took the woman's hands and nodded. "I need you to call around and confirm Wheeler has rescinded all the offers. We need to make sure this isn't just a case of changed plans that put you outside the property lines."

"I can make the calls," Will said, drawing everyone's attention. Beth looked her way and Will shrugged. "Lola has company. I know all the numbers anyway."

Beth recognized a kindred soul when she saw one. Will, too, was looking for a place to belong. Another regret of leaving the island. They might be friends if she stayed. "Thank you."

"But where are you going?" Lola asked.

Whatever had happened between Joe and Cassie wasn't anyone else's business, so Beth kept her explanation vague. "I have something to check on. Better to be safe and make sure this really is over." Not giving Lola time to respond, she turned to Marcus. "It was nice to meet you, and I hope we get to visit more before I leave. We share a special friend here."

"That we do."

With a quick kiss on Lola's cheek, Beth headed toward the door. Cassandra Wheeler would never give up without something else tucked up her Kate Spade sleeve. She had to warn Joe before that something else hit the fan.

~

Ribbons of red and orange decorated the horizon, but Beth was too busy pacing to appreciate the sunset. Will had called two hours before to say what Beth had already guessed. Every business on the island that had had any contact with Wheeler Development received the same letter as Lola. The threat of the island being developed into a Vegas-style playground for the rich and famous was gone.

And so was Cassandra Wheeler, according to Will's contact at the property rental office. If the information was correct, Cassie had been gone twenty-four hours by the time the letters arrived, and all letters were dated for Tuesday. Odd, since the barracuda had made it clear Monday night that the island would eventually belong to the Wheelers.

If she knew they were pulling the offers, why didn't she just say so? Then again, Cassie wasn't used to losing. Beth wondered if the spoiled woman had ever not gotten something she wanted. Other than Joe.

There had to have been a clue in that meeting at the marina. Phil Mohler was there, so maybe he was the connection. Could he have given Cassie a way to hurt Joe?

Beth heard a bark behind her and turned to see Joe's Jeep rolling into the drive. Running down the steps, she was at Joe's door before he cut the engine. "We need to talk."

"We probably do, but I don't have the energy to deal with this right now." Grabbing a backpack from the passenger floor, he climbed out and waited for Dozer to do the same. "Right now I want a beer and my couch."

She grabbed the door as he tried to close it. "This isn't about us. It's about the island. Wheeler rescinded all the offers. The fight is over."

Joe dropped the pack on his seat. "Are you serious?"

"I was there when Lola got her letter. Will called around and everyone else got one, too."

"Will?"

"The bartender from O'Hagan's. And the coffee shop. And Lola's place."

"That hippie chick that works everywhere? How do you know her?"

"She served us the night Sid and I went out, but that's not the point." Beth smacked the door in frustration. "Wheeler took all the offers off the table and Cassandra left the island."

"Then we won. That's a good thing."

With narrowed eyes, she asked, "Why would they suddenly give up?"

Joe looked away, removing the sunglasses from the collar of his black T-shirt and sliding them onto his visor. "I don't know and I don't care."

"Bull," she said, waiting for him to meet her eyes again. "You and I both know the real reason Cassie came after this island."

"I don't know what you're talking about."

"Yes, you do. I saw it on your face that night at the Merchants meeting. She came here for revenge on you. What happened to end your engagement?"

Joe crossed his arms. "That's none of your business."

"The hell it isn't. I put my job on the line to help you. What happened?"

With a sigh of resignation, Joe threw the backpack on his shoulder and ran a hand through his dark hair. "If I'm going to do this, I want that beer." Closing the Jeep door, he headed for his house.

~

After dropping his pack on the couch, Joe led Beth through the house, stopping to grab a soda and a beer on the way to the back deck. He took a long draw before setting the bottle on the floor and staring out at the last strips of orange over the sound.

"I met Cassie when she was on the island for a summer internship. I had no idea she came from money until a month or so in, but I didn't care either way. I wanted her, bought a ring, and popped the question by month three."

He glanced to Beth for her reaction. If she thought him reckless and stupid, which he was, the fact didn't show on her face.

"Her internship ended and she went home. I thought she was only going to tell her daddy and then come back. A month went by with one excuse after another for why she wasn't back yet."

"So you went after her," Beth said. "That part Patty told me."

"Right." Joe took another swig from his bottle, then picked at the label. "When I got there and saw where she lived, I knew the chances for us weren't good."

"I've never been to the Wheeler estate, but heard enough to know it's impressive."

"'Impressive' is one way to put it." He'd never seen a house with actual wings before. That monstrosity could never be called a home. It was more like an oversized mausoleum. "During our brief chat in what the butler called the parlor, Cassie let me know she'd never live on Anchor and if I was going to marry her I had to move up there. Needless to say, that didn't work for me."

Beth rocked in the chair beside him. "She gave you an ultimatum. Rookie mistake."

Joe snorted. "I told her it was a package deal. Me, the dog, and the island. You've seen how Dozer feels about her, and she'd already stated she wouldn't live on the island, so I'm sure you can guess how that went over."

They sat in silence for several seconds. Joe had never told anyone what happened when he'd gone to Richmond. Not even Randy, who'd found him in a drunken stupor every night for a month afterward.

"Did you really think a girl like that would live here?" she asked.

"I don't know what I thought. To me, this place is perfect. Why would anyone want to leave?" He turned his head to meet her eyes. "That's the divide between me and Lucas. To him, the world is a thing to be conquered. Out there. To me, the whole world is right here to enjoy."

Beth looked away, setting the rocker in motion with the toe of her sandal. "Do you think Lucas holds it against you that you don't chase life the same way he does?"

Lucas had never pushed him to leave the island. Never talked down about his choices. "No."

"Then why do you hold his choices against him? Not wanting to spend his life on Anchor isn't some human flaw. It's just not his thing."

Joe had never thought of it that way. He was so focused on defending his own choices, pushing his own beliefs, he'd forgotten that Lucas had every right to choose his own path.

"You're right. Further proof I'm a dumb-ass who can't see beyond his own ego."

"I wouldn't go that far," Beth said, smiling. "So in Cassie's mind, you chose this island over her. That explains her need for revenge." Pulling her legs under her, Beth turned in the chair to face him. "But that doesn't explain why she gave up. She set out to hurt you by attacking the thing most important to you. Now she's walked away. Why?"

He considered the talk they'd had at Dempsey's. "Maybe she's moving on. We talked Saturday night. I wasn't sure I got through to her, but maybe I did."

"You talked to Cassie Saturday night?"

"At Dempsey's. I was bussing tables, and she was in for dinner. The bottom line is I was just a means to an end for her. Marrying me was a way to piss off her daddy and save her from the yuppie ass-kissers chasing her for the money." Dozer propped his head on Joe's knee and he gave him a scratch behind the ear. "I could have been any fisherman she met down here and she knew it."

"You told her all this?"

"Sure. Why?"

"Did you tell her you never loved her?"

Joe thought back. "No, but I made it clear I'd moved on and she needed to do the same." Beth made an odd noise and bit her bottom lip. "What?" he asked.

"You told a woman who's used to getting what she wants, who was so mad at you that she was willing to spend millions of her daddy's money to buy an island out from under you, that you were over her and she needed to move on."

When she put it that way…"I wasn't mean about it."

"Does anything you know about Cassandra Wheeler tell you she's the type to let something like this go?" Beth leaned farther over the arm of the chair. "Think about it."

"You're right."

Beth sat back. "The letters were all dated for Tuesday, but at the marina Monday night she was still claiming she'd get the island. Something changed during or right after that encounter."

Joe ran the conversation back through his mind. All he remembered was enjoying watching Beth spar with Cassie and how hot she looked doing it. That probably wasn't what Beth wanted to hear right now.

"I don't know what it could be."

"Phil Mohler was there. Could he have told her something she could use against you?"

"Shit." He should have known. "This isn't good."

Beth's feet hit the deck. "What isn't good?"

Elbows on his knees, Joe leaned forward, dropping his head into his hands. "Mohler caught me at the fuel dock last week. Kept dropping hints about you and me."

"What do you mean about you and me? What about you and me?"

"That we're having an affair."

Beth gasped. "Why would he say that?"

Bolting out of his chair, Joe paced the porch, hands balled at his sides. "I thought he was just trying to get a rise out of me. I warned him if he repeated that bullshit to anyone else I'd kick his ass." Fury burned his gut. "And I will. He must have told Cassie."

"But then why did she leave? That would put a target on me, and I'm here."

Joe stopped pacing. "You don't live here. You live in Richmond. Where your fiancé is."

"What does that have to do with anything? I already know she'll try to get me fired, but that wouldn't hurt you."

"No." He leaned against the porch railing, knowing exactly what Cassie meant to do. "But telling Lucas we're having an affair would."

Beth jumped out of her chair. "He wouldn't believe her."

"Cassie can be convincing when she wants something. She sure as hell put on a good act of loving me and this island for four months."

"Joe," Beth said, grabbing his arm and turning him to face her. Heat sparked at the touch. "We haven't done anything wrong. We can convince him."

"Convince him of what? That I don't want you? How am I supposed to do that when I do?" She wasn't the only one who could spit out surprise declarations. "I've wanted you since that day on the ferry. Maybe it happened when you called me an asshole." He tucked a curl behind her ear. "Sometimes I wish I hadn't been on that damn ferry, but then I realize I'd have fallen for you anyway. Some things are just meant to be, I guess."

She stared up at him, her head shaking back and forth. And then she collapsed into him, grasping his shirt, her forehead against his chest. Nothing had ever felt so right. "I never meant for this to happen. I've made a mess of every-thing."

He pulled her closer, resting his arms around her hips. "*We've* made a mess of everything. But we can't hurt him, Beth. I have to let you go." Doing so would kill him, but there was no other way.

This time she nodded yes, her head still on his chest. "I'll pack my things tonight and leave for Richmond in the morning." Joe's gut clenched and he fought the urge to pull her closer. He'd never let her go if he did that. "I can't stay with Lucas, though. I can't marry him and pretend for the rest of my life."

Guilt added to the pain. Guilt brought on by the relief of knowing she wouldn't marry Lucas.

Dropping a kiss on the top of her head, he gave in and pulled her against him. Her arms slid around his back. "I'm sorry," he said, feeling useless. "I don't know how to fix this."

They stood together, holding on as they let go. Clinging to one last moment together. Too late. Joe heard the foot-steps coming around the house.

"That's my fiancée, you son of a bitch."

CHAPTER TWENTY-FIVE

"Oh my God," Beth said, jerking away from Joe. "Lucas, what are you doing here?"

"I'm the one who gets to ask the questions." Lucas stopped at the base of the stairs, arms crossed, eyes shifting from one to the other. "What the fuck's going on here?"

The words flew out before Beth could stop them. "It's not what you think." Such a cliché thing to say. "I mean, there's nothing going on here."

"That embrace didn't look like nothing. Cassandra Wheeler was right. Goddamn it, how could you do this to me?"

Beth was about to answer when she realized Lucas had directed the question to Joe.

"She's telling you the truth. Nothing's going on here." Lucas made it two steps before Joe's words stopped him. "Don't do it, Lucas. Throwing a punch isn't going to solve anything."

"Maybe not," Lucas said, bracing on the middle step, "but it'll feel damn good."

"You two are not going to fight over this."

"The hell we aren't." Lucas took another step.

"Lucas, look at me," Beth pleaded. "Joe hasn't done anything wrong. He did what you asked him to do. Entertain me. Maybe if you'd been here yourself instead of playing big-time lawyer, he wouldn't have had to."

Spurred by anger and growing confidence, her true feelings poured through. "This was supposed to be our vacation. Yours and mine. Instead you left me here without a second thought. I should have been more important than that case."

He climbed another step, moving toward her. She held her ground in the face of his anger, her own gaining strength. "Elizabeth, you know I'm trying to make partner. We've talked about how important my career is to us."

"Not to us," she said, feeling a weight lift from her shoulders. "To you. And we haven't talked, you talked. I listened, nodding and agreeing because that's what I've always done. You've never asked what's important to me." Looking to Joe, she drew strength from his steady gaze. "Maybe I didn't know myself before, but I know now."

"Beth, calm down," Joe said, taking a step toward her.

Lucas turned on him. "What did you call her?"

"He called me Beth because that's the name I gave him. That's the name that suits me. Short. Simple. Small-town Beth." She switched her attention to Joe. "And don't tell me to calm down. I don't want to calm down. Joe, tell him this isn't what it looks like. Help me make him understand."

He shook his head and kept silent. Why wasn't he helping her?

"I don't understand any of this. Where's Elizabeth? My Elizabeth? The woman I was going to marry?" Lucas made the final step and shoved Joe in the chest. "She was perfect until I left her with you."

Dozer growled. "Easy, boy," Joe said, holding his hand in front of the dog, palm down. "I didn't do anything, Lucas. She figured this all out on her own."

"Don't talk about me like I'm not here!" Beth yelled, tired of being dismissed. "You fell for Elizabeth because she was the dutiful wife who would nod and follow wherever you led. That's my fault, because that's who I was."

"Well, I want her back," Lucas said, more angry than she'd ever seen him. A clear sign of how much he cared about her.

"I'm sorry, Lucas. She's not coming back."

Her words seem to take the wind out of him, but they felt good crossing her lips. Then a muted shade of red crept up Lucas's neck. He turned abruptly, shoving Joe again, who had to jerk to the left to halt Dozer's attack. "I'm not doing this, Lucas."

"Wait a minute," Beth said, remembering Lucas's words. "Cassandra Wheeler was right about what? What did she tell you, Lucas?"

"What do you think she told me? That you two were fucking around behind my back. Making a fool of me," he growled, punching the railing.

"And you believed her? Knowing how she feels about Joe? Knowing she was here trying to buy up the island?" She poked him in the chest. "Something you should have been here fighting with us. Knowing all that, you doubted your fiancée and your brother but believed Cassandra Wheeler?"

Lucas stuttered. "Well…but…what does it matter what I believed? It's true."

"No, it isn't," she said, walking down the steps. "But you're right, it doesn't matter. None of this matters."

Beth kept walking, anger keeping the tears at bay. She didn't want Lucas, but she still couldn't have Joe. Not that he'd done anything just now to show he wanted her. He wouldn't even help her explain to Lucas.

"Where are you going?" Lucas yelled after her.

"To pack my things," she said, never breaking stride. "I'm going home. Tonight."

∿

Lucas watched his fiancée walk away. Though from what had just happened, Joe figured she wasn't his fiancée anymore. Another clusterfuck to add to his growing collection.

Silence loomed, broken by the occasional cricket chirp and Dozer's questioning whine. He knew what Dozer was asking. Is everything all right?

Things wouldn't be all right for a long time.

"Are you going after her?" Joe asked, struggling not to do so himself.

"Go after her? I don't even know her." Lucas turned to face Joe, leaning against the porch post. He may have been shooting for relaxed but his body remained coiled for a fight. Joe couldn't blame him.

"Until tonight, I'm not sure she knew herself," Joe said. She definitely knew now. A flicker of pride filled his chest. His Beth had come alive.

Though she wasn't *his* anything. A muscle twitched along his jaw, and he again fought the urge to go after her. But there was Lucas.

Snagging his beer from the floor, Joe dropped into a rocker. In a voice more controlled than he felt, he said, "Have a seat."

Lucas stood his ground, opening and closing his fists at his sides. Joe ignored him, waiting for the adrenaline to drop. The silent treatment worked, and Lucas sat.

"What happened here?" Lucas asked.

"A woman handed us our asses."

Lucas growled. "I don't mean just now. Ten days ago I had a sweet, mild-mannered fiancée. Something happened to change that." Driving a knuckle into the chair arm, he drilled Joe with a glare. "That something is you."

Joe couldn't take all the credit. The fire had always been in her, she just needed someone to light the fuse. He'd lit the fuse all right.

Maintaining his casual act, Joe said, "The woman was tangled up in knots. I tugged and pushed, with her fighting all the way. I guess tonight she got herself untangled."

"Did you tug her into bed along the way?"

Joe stopped rocking and locked his jaw, reminding himself Lucas had every right to be pissed. He'd feel the same way. "No. And if you think she'd do that, then you really don't know her. Or me."

Lucas leapt from the chair to pace the porch. "What am I supposed to believe? I get a call that you two are screwing around behind my back, drive down here telling myself the whole way that it can't be true, then find you two standing on this porch in each other's arms." He stopped pacing and pointed a finger at Joe's chest. "Say what you want, but that wasn't a brotherly hug you were giving her."

"No, it wasn't." He could still feel the heat where her head had rested on his chest. He had to be the unluckiest son of a bitch he knew. At least when it came to women. "I'm not her brother, I'm yours. That's why we were saying good-bye."

Lucas stopped. "She wasn't supposed to leave until Saturday."

Joe leaned forward in his chair and looked Lucas in the eye. "She decided to leave tomorrow. You want to know why, talk to her." Done talking, Joe rose from his chair. His gut was on fire with more pain than he knew what to do with.

He picked up Beth's soda along with his beer bottle. As tempting as it was to spend the night finishing off the six-pack in his fridge, he'd learned the hard way alcohol didn't do much for getting over a woman. The last time the damage had been to his ego. He knew that now. This time felt like a twenty-aught hook ripping through his chest.

"No one set out to hurt you, little brother. Doesn't mean shit right now, but it's the truth." Joe kept another truth to himself. Like it or not, he was full-force in love with the woman who'd just walked away. And that was never going to change.

~

Beth sent up a prayer of thanks that Patty and Tom were working at the restaurant so she wouldn't have to explain why she was packing to leave. Not that she had an explanation. How could she tell them she was leaving one of their sons because she'd fallen in love with the other?

Not that Joe was the reason she was calling off the engagement. She knew now agreeing to marry Lucas had been a mistake. One more in a long line of mistakes. Breaking it off now was better than five years down the road, when she might snap after the three hundred and twelfth vapid dinner party.

But at least she'd have had a family for those five years. An amazing, caring, generous family. The reality of how much she was losing intensified the ache around Beth's heart.

Pulling into the last drive on Tuttles Lane, she grabbed the overnight bag and her purse, leaving the suitcase in the trunk. Standing on the porch, Beth screwed up the courage to knock. This was going to take an explanation, and she hoped their fragile friendship would keep Sid from decking her upon learning the truth.

The door opened before she had the chance to knock. Sid wore a white tank and purple pajama shorts covered with Jolly Roger flags. A toothbrush stuck in her mouth, she looked down to the overnight bag and back to Beth.

Swinging the screen wide, she mumbled around the toothbrush. "This should be intawesting."

Beth embraced her right to remain silent, followed Sid inside, and sat on the couch while her hostess presumably finished brushing her teeth. When she returned, Sid passed over a glass of red wine, then plopped down on the other end of the couch with a glass of water.

"Spill."

Where to start. Anger and righteous indignation had gotten her this far, but both had faded, and all she could think was, *What have I done?*

"Lucas is here."

"Here where?"

"On the island."

"Your fiancé is here, and you show up at my door with an overnight bag?" Sid was taking this much better than expected. Not that Beth had gotten to the decking-worthy offense yet. "You trying to save it for the wedding night?"

"He's not my fiancé anymore."

One brow shot up. "Because of Joe?"

Beth stared at her wineglass. "Why do you say that?"

"Doesn't take a genius to see you two set the furniture on fire whenever you're in the same room."

"That's not true," Beth argued. Did the entire island think she and Joe were having an affair? "Tell me that's not true."

"Did Lucas catch you?" Sid took a sip of water and set her glass on the table. Probably to free her hands in case she needed to throw a punch.

"There was nothing to catch." Beth remembered what she and Joe had been doing when Lucas showed up. "Mostly nothing. But Joe isn't the reason I'm not marrying Lucas."

"Then why aren't you?"

"Let's just say he's not the man for me. I would have figured that out with or without falling for Joe. Might have taken longer, but reality would have smacked me eventually."

Sid took a turn remaining silent.

"You're taking this better than I expected. With your feelings for Lucas, I thought you might deck me for hurting him."

Narrowed eyes bored through her. "What do you know about my feelings for Lucas?"

Beth pulled a throw pillow from behind her to use as protection. "Your brother told me the first time I met him. Said you'd had a thing for Lucas since high school. I thought that's why you hated me when I first got here."

"My brother has a big mouth. I had a thing for Lucas, but we can see from his taste in women that I'm not his type."

Beth wasn't sure if that was an insult or a compliment and decided not to ask. "Well, I'm not his type either. Though to be fair to him, I acted the part well enough."

"Explain this to me." Sid sat up and Beth pulled the pillow tighter. "Move the damn pillow; I'm not going to hit you."

"Are you sure?"

"Yes, I'm sure." Sid snatched the pillow and threw it onto a chair to her left. "You agreed to marry a man you don't love. True?"

"Yes." Leave it to Sid to make this feel like a root canal. "But I thought I loved him."

Sid scratched her head. "But now you know you don't love Lucas and you're sure you love Joe."

"I didn't say that."

"I'm too tired to pussyfoot around this, Curly. Do you love Joe or not?"

She considered lying, because saying the words out loud would make driving onto that ferry even harder. But as always, she caved. "Yes, I love Joe."

Sid whistled. "You know how to make a mess of shit, don't you?" Snatching her glass off the table, she sat back. "What are you going to do now? And I hope you don't think the answer is live with me. I like you, but not that much."

"We established our boundaries a long time ago, remember? I just need a place to stay tonight so I can head back to Richmond in the morning. I don't know the way well enough to make it in the dark."

"Do they know you're here?"

Beth tapped the glass she had yet to drink from. "I don't think so. The last thing I said when I walked away was that I was leaving tonight."

"Fine. I'll get the extra blankets for the couch then give Joe a call."

"Why?" Beth asked, jumping to her feet. "I don't want to see either of them."

"Don't get your fancy pants in a wad. If either of them decides to be a hero and go after you, they deserve to know you haven't left yet." Holding up a hand to silence Beth's argument, she added, "I'll make it clear neither is to show up at my door unless they want their balls ripped off with a monkey wrench."

The threat sounded painful and sincere. "All right, but if they show up anyway, I'm not talking to them." She wasn't ready to face Lucas again, but she couldn't ignore the glimmer of hope Joe would come for her.

"Fair enough," Sid said, reaching for the phone behind her. "I've got enough wine and chocolate to stay holed up for a week. Since you're leaving in the morning, I think we can make it."

~

The following Monday, Beth returned to work, checking her voice mail while waiting for her computer to load. As expected, there was a message asking that she report to the Human Resources department as soon as possible.

She knew this was coming. If Cassie had the nerve to call Lucas and report an alleged affair, she'd have no qualms about getting Beth fired. Oddly enough, the idea of losing her job didn't bother Beth anymore. Over the weekend, she'd decided several changes were in order.

Buttoning the jacket of her blue business suit, Beth knocked on the door of Rita Ramsey, Human Resource Manager of Bracken, Franks, and Holcomb, LLC. Rita opened the door and smiled, inviting Beth to have a seat. What happened next would be a defining moment in Beth's life. The moment she took control and started basing decisions on what would make *her* happy.

When she left Rita behind, Beth went directly to Lucas's office. She knew he was there because she'd seen his car in his reserved space when she pulled into the garage. Nothing as trivial as losing a fiancée would keep Lucas Dempsey from his work. A bubble of resentment threatened to float to the surface, but Beth pushed it down.

She couldn't blame Lucas for his ambition any more than he could blame her for a lack of it. He hadn't been willing to choose her over the job until he thought she was sleeping with his brother. And then he'd driven all the way back to Anchor to catch them in the act. The lawyer wanting ironclad proof.

Things should have ended differently. Regardless of her intentions, she'd hurt him. For that she would always be sorry. His assistant, Pamela, was on the phone, so Beth tapped on the door, entering when she heard the muffled "Come in" from the other side.

Lucas didn't look up at first, instead saying, "What is it, Pamela?"

"It isn't Pamela."

His head shot up and a muscle twitched in his jaw. Tie perfect. Shirt starched. Chin clean-shaven. Lucas looked as put together as always, but the slight darkening beneath his eyes revealed he'd lost as much sleep as she had in the last few days. She felt bad about that.

He dropped his pen then leaned back in his chair. "You have nerve, I'll give you that."

Beth kept her head up. "I'm sorry." He snorted, but she continued. "I'm sorry you were hurt in all this. I never set out to hurt anyone."

"Funny. Joe said something similar. Did you work out your stories ahead of time?"

Ignoring the taunt, she took a step forward, barreling ahead. "I've been living a lie for a long time. Maybe my whole life. You became a victim of my mess, and though I wish things could be different, they can't. I can't change the past, but I can change the future."

She had to make this right. "Whatever you think of me, know that your brother is innocent in this. He was my friend, and that's all. He never crossed the line. Ever. He loves you, Lucas. Don't punish him for my mistakes."

Lucas moved around the desk, propped on the corner, and crossed his arms. "Valiant defense. Is that it?"

Beth gripped the back of the chair in front of her, struggling to control her temper. "I'm not a criminal, and I won't be treated like one. I came to tell you I won't be working here anymore."

He slapped his hands down on the desk. "They have no grounds to fire you." He moved back to his chair and picked up the phone. "Cassandra Wheeler has done enough damage."

"They didn't fire me. I quit."

His hand froze over the buttons, the receiver halfway to his ear. "You what?"

She let go of the chair and toyed with the buttons on her jacket. "I quit. I don't want to work in law. I never did."

The receiver slid back into place. "What are you going to do?"

Crossing her arms, she said, "I've contacted an old college friend. She runs a crafts supply store and could use some help managing the weekend classes. I'm starting over. In Boston."

Lucas dropped to his chair. "In Boston?"

"Yes. A new start needs a new town." She'd rather her new start happen on a certain tiny island, but that couldn't be.

"I see." He picked up the pen and tapped it absently on the desktop. "When do you leave?"

"There are still some arrangements to make, but I'd like to move as soon as possible. I'm flying up this weekend to look for an apartment."

"That soon?"

"Yes." There was nothing else to say. "You deserve happiness, Lucas. I hope you find it. And I hope you don't give up on your brother. He deserves happiness, too." Beth turned to leave, but Lucas stopped her with one question.

"Do you love him?"

She couldn't answer but she couldn't lie either. So she kept walking.

"I'll take that as a yes" were the last words she heard before the door closed behind her.

CHAPTER TWENTY-SIX

"Dempsey!" Sid yelled, two inches from Joe's ear.
"What the—"

"I've called your name four times, dickweed. What's your problem?"

Stupid question when she knew what his problem was. Or, rather, who. Though he'd appreciated Sid not talking about Beth since she'd left the island.

"We need to get this Beth shit out in the open."

So much for that.

"There is no Beth shit. Hand me those hooks."

Sid crossed her arms, ignoring the order. "You've been walking around like a zombie since she left. Go get her."

Joe cut the line and reached for the next pole, choosing to remain silent.

"I said go get her."

He threw the pole across the deck. "You think I don't want to drive up there and bring her back? You think I haven't had to stop myself from climbing in the Jeep and saying to hell with it all? It's not an option." Turning his back, he added, "I'm taking a break."

As he walked away, Sid threw a dirty shot. "I never pegged you for a coward."

Fucking hell. He spun and charged across the deck.

"How am I a coward, Sid? Explain it to me. Because last I knew, playing the coward meant getting out without getting hurt." Too late for that. "This is a waste of time."

"She's hurting, too, you know. You're both being stubborn about this."

The temptation to ask overruled his common sense. "You've talked to her?"

"Yeah," Sid said, taking a seat on the side of the boat. "Last night. She quit her job."

"What?"

"Cassie tried to get her fired, but the firm wouldn't do it. Told her she was a valuable asset to the research department. Didn't matter, though; she'd already made up her mind." Sid chuckled. "Curly has bigger balls than I gave her credit for."

"But why?" Beth had been furious the day she'd told him Cassie would get her fired. Near panic over losing her job. Why would she walk away?

Sid shrugged. "Said she realized being a lawyer wasn't for her. Something about her time with you helping her see that." She hopped to her feet. "Beth was good for you, and by some bizarre twist, you were good for her. I don't say a lot of sappy shit, so listen close. This kind of love doesn't come along every day. Don't throw it away."

Joe wasn't sure what to make of this softer, gentler Sid. Nor did he know what to do with what she'd just said. "I can't, Sid. I can't do that to Lucas."

Sid shook her head and said, more to the air than to him, "Men." Then she poked him in the chest, the old Sid returning. "This isn't the playground, Dempsey. You don't need to protect your baby brother. He's a grown man, and he screwed up that relationship all by himself. Long before she fell for you."

Joe rubbed his chest. "What are you talking about? She was going to marry him."

"I doubt it," Sid said, crossing her arms. "That night at the bar she was bitching about him never paying attention to her and how he was really married to his work. The fact is, you did them both a favor."

"Stealing my brother's fiancée sounds like the opposite of doing him a favor. Would you do something you knew would tear Randy apart?"

She scrunched up her face. "Me stealing a girl from Randy is too weird to think about, so I don't know how to answer that. I wouldn't hurt him if I could help it." She shrugged. "But sometimes you can't help it. Shit happens, and life gets messy. We're family. We'd deal with it."

Sid didn't have the anatomy necessary to understand the situation. "I'm not doing it. End of discussion." Joe crossed the boat to pick up the pole he'd thrown. "Let's get this done."

"Do you really think Lucas would hate you?" Sid asked, picking up the box of hooks.

Joe didn't hesitate. "I know he would."

≈

Beth had been crying on and off for more than a week, resulting in the worst headache she could ever remember, when Lucas appeared at her door. After their last encounter, she was less than enthusiastic to see him. She felt bad for hurting him, and always would, but seeing him reminded her of what she'd done. And what she'd lost.

Or, rather, who.

"I'm not in any shape for company, Lucas, and I have a lot to do. I know I deserve them, but I can't take another barrage of insults tonight."

Hovering in her hallway, Lucas stood his ground, hands in his pockets. He wore jeans and a red polo shirt. Unusually casual for her former fiancé. "I'm not here to fight. I just want to talk."

Beth sighed. "All right then. Come in." She left Lucas to close the door behind him and headed for the tissue box. She was going to need them before this conversation was over.

"I've been thinking," Lucas began. "And I've realized a few things."

"What have you realized?" she asked, not sure she wanted to hear the answer.

"This wasn't all your fault."

She would have rolled her eyes if they weren't so puffy and swollen. "If you're going to start insulting Joe, I don't want to hear that either. I told you this was my fault."

"Hear me out. I'm saying some of the blame goes to me, too."

Beth dropped into a chair, thankful there was one close enough to keep her from hitting the floor. "What do you mean?"

Lucas moved to sit on the couch, but all three cushions were covered in dishes, linens, and books. She should have gotten up to move them, but couldn't find the energy to be a good hostess at the moment.

He sat on the edge of the coffee table instead. "I wasn't there for you. And I don't mean on Anchor, but before that. You said I never asked what was important to you." He leapt up and began pacing. "I've driven myself crazy trying to remember a time I asked what you wanted or where you wanted to go. I never did, did I?"

Beth shrugged. "You let me pick the restaurant the night we got engaged."

Lucas sat again, this time on the arm of couch. "Why did you say yes?"

How could she answer without hurting him more? "I'd like to think because that's what I wanted. Because I loved you and wanted to be your wife."

"But you didn't, did you?" He asked the question with no anger or recrimination. Beth's heart broke a little more.

"No, I didn't." She closed her eyes, unable to look at him. "I wish I could tell you I was madly in love with you or that being with you made me happy. But I can't." Opening her eyes, she kept them focused on her knees. "I've spent my entire life doing whatever would make other people happy. Marrying you would have made you happy. So I said yes."

Lucas kneeled down beside her chair and lifted her chin until their eyes met. "It would have made me happy. I'd be the luckiest guy in the world. If you loved me."

A tear slid down her cheek. "I wanted to. Whoever you do marry is going to be a lucky girl, Lucas Dempsey."

He gave a crooked grin. "Not if I don't get my priorities straight." Standing up, he glanced around the room. "So you're really going, huh?"

"Yeah, I'm going," Beth said, wiping her nose with a tissue. "Not for good yet, but soon enough." Waving a hand toward the sofa, she said, "I needed something to keep me busy. Packing seemed like a good distraction."

"A distraction from thinking about Joe?" he asked, picking up a piece of newspaper and wrapping it around a glass.

Beth tried not to flinch at the mention of his name. Like trying not to blink when poked in the eye. "There's nothing to think about. We both agreed there couldn't be anything between us."

"You agreed," he said. "How's that working for you?"

"Not well," she admitted, blowing her nose in earnest. "Have you talked to him? Please don't hold this against him. Patty said you two were close once. I know Joe wants that back again."

"I haven't talked to Joe, not since the night I made an ass of myself." Lucas looked to Beth as if waiting for an argument. She remained silent. "Right. I've talked to Mom though. She says he's a mess. Working himself to death and ripping the head off of anybody stupid enough to try talking to him."

"I'm sorry to hear that." Though *sorry* wasn't the right word. Relieved to know he was hurting, too. Guilty for being the cause of that hurt. Tempted to race back to Anchor and throw her arms around him.

"I hear you were good for him. Brought back some of the old Joe." Another sheet of newspaper, another glass wrapped. "The way he was before Cassie chewed him up and spit him out."

Beth froze, tissue midway to her nose. "We need to change the subject."

Lucas added the new glass to the box. "We need to stop dancing around this. You love Joe. He loves you. I'd be an idiot to stand in the way of that."

Shaking her head, she pushed the temptation away. "We wouldn't do that to you. We couldn't. I'm leaving for Boston tomorrow, and I'll be settled there permanently in a few weeks." Beth jumped from the chair and grabbed the piece of newspaper from Lucas's hand. "Joe will get over this, and he'll move on. Besides, he has all he needs. His island, his boat, and his dog. He doesn't need me."

"You're being stubborn about this," he said. "I admit, it's not going to be easy to see you two together, but I'll get over it. Eventually. Don't be a martyr on my account."

Why was he making this so hard? She'd spent a week convincing herself she and Joe could never be together. Rationalized every argument. Every but-maybe-if desperate thought. Didn't he know he was making this harder?

"You need to leave," she said, walking to the door. "I appreciate you coming over here and giving me the chance to explain. I really do. But I can't talk about Joe. That's over."

"I see," he said, joining her in the front hall. "What time is your flight tomorrow?"

"Why?"

"I can take you to the airport."

She knew Lucas well enough to know he'd use any chance to argue his case. She couldn't give him another opportunity. "My flight isn't until seven tomorrow night, so you'll be at work when I'd have to leave. I can take a cab; it's no problem."

"You're sure? I can leave early." Lucas had never left early in all the time she'd known him. Maybe he *was* trying to get his priorities straight.

"I'll be fine, thanks."

He stepped into the hall, then turned back. "Think about what I said. You both being miserable isn't going to make anyone happy. Especially not me."

With that he was gone, leaving Beth standing with her door open, blinking into an empty hall. Once her wits returned, she slammed the door. "I am going to Boston, damn it," she said into the mirror hanging on the wall. The red-nose woman staring back did not look convinced.

～

With Memorial Day weekend at the end of the week, the charter schedule was booked solid, which kept Joe running nonstop. Staying busy should have kept his mind off Beth, but it didn't. He saw her standing at the rail or spread out on a bench in the cabin, crooking a finger in his direction, inviting him to join her. The woman was even haunting his dreams, making what little sleep he did get another form of torture.

By Thursday night he was exhausted, sore, and willing to book a lobotomy if that would get her out of his head. Dropping onto the couch, he ate half a slice of pizza with a can of soda and passed out in the middle of the game.

When the phone rang before dawn the next morning, he nearly rolled off the couch before figuring out where he was. "Do you know what fucking time it is?" he asked in greeting once he found the talk button.

"It's four thirty in the morning, and you need to start packing."

"What?" The voice sounded like Lucas, but that couldn't be. "Lucas?"

"She's leaving for Boston at seven tonight. If you don't stop her, you'll lose her for good."

Maybe he was dreaming. Joe smacked the phone against his head to wake himself up. That hurt. Putting the phone back to his ear, he heard, "Are you listening to me? She's leaving."

"Who is leaving?"

"Beth, you idiot."

Joe sat up and tried to clear his head. "Leaving for where? Did you just tell me to stop her?"

An exasperated breath came through the line. "Do you love her or not?"

If this was some kind of test, he didn't have the brain function to pass. "Yes. But you—"

"Then come and get her before it's too late."

This didn't make any sense. "Not a week ago you wanted to kick my ass. Now you're telling me to go after her. If this is some stupid game, I'm not playing."

"I was a moron. Not the first time, probably not the last," Lucas said. "I know you two didn't have an affair. Or at least you never hopped into bed together. I never should have believed Cassandra, but something did happen between you, didn't it?"

"Yeah, it did."

"Is she the one?"

Joe ran a hand through his hair. "She is. But I can't."

"Bullshit. Pack a bag, throw that mutt in the Jeep, and get your ass up here."

Joe felt as if his life had capsized and he was being thrown a lifeline. "Why are you doing this?"

"Because Beth was right. You deserve happiness. And so does she."

∼

After sleeping for twelve hours, Beth awoke feeling almost human again, and toyed with the idea that Lucas's visit had been a dream. But the glasses he'd packed proved he'd really been there. With less snot on the brain, she replayed the encounter over and over all afternoon, coming to some interesting conclusions.

Conclusion one was that Lucas would be fine. He was still the sweetest guy she'd ever met, and she looked forward to the day he'd find the right girl. Not that she'd be around to meet her.

Conclusion two took longer to process. Joe was as miserable as she was. But Beth rationalized that most of his misery, if not all, had to be over the widening chasm between himself and Lucas. He couldn't be miserable because of Beth. After all, he hadn't come after her. Even after he knew she was still on the island. He didn't come pounding on Sid's door.

Like she'd hoped.

He hadn't fought for her. Didn't even defend them against Cassandra's sordid accusations. He'd let her speak for herself. Stand up for herself. Tell Lucas how she felt.

Then the truth hit like a head butt from Dozer.

Joe hadn't defended her because he knew she could defend herself. He'd given her that. Joe taught her to think for herself and, when the real test came, stood silent while she passed with flying colors. Stayed behind while she found her wings and soared off without him.

Beth's head hit the kitchen table then lolled from side to side. Stupid, stupid, stupid. She hadn't found herself. Joe had pointed her out with big neon signs and a freaking road map. And she hadn't even thanked him.

"I'm such an idiot," she said, the words echoing off the empty walls. "And now it's too late."

As her head hit the table again, a knock sounded at her front door. If this was her cab to the airport, he was an hour early. Kicking newspapers out of her path, she charged to the door and ripped it open. "I'm not ready yet," she said, the words dying on her lips when Dozer stepped back and whimpered. "What the…" she trailed off, looking into intense blue eyes. "Joe?"

CHAPTER TWENTY-SEVEN

"Hi," he said, as if him showing up on her doorstep was a natural thing. "We were in the neighborhood. Are you busy?"

"No...I..." She pulled the door wide, indicating for them to come in. Thirty million thoughts raced through her mind at once. She wanted to throw her arms around him and punch him at the same time. She wanted to cry and laugh, scream and dance. Instead, she swept the bathroom towels and stack of picture frames onto the floor so Joe could sit on the couch. He followed her, but remained standing.

"I've been an idiot," he said, then held up a hand when she tried to speak. "Let me get this out, and we'll be on our way."

On his way? The man was six hours from home.

"I've been an idiot, expecting life to always go my way. Expecting others to follow my choices, live on my terms. But I've learned something. Sometimes you have to give something up to get what really matters."

He took a deep breath while Beth held hers. She watched his mouth as he talked, longing to run her tongue along his full lips. A heat started in her belly. Lower actually.

"You're what matters, Beth. Not an island or a boat or anything else. As long as I have you, I have everything I need."

Why was he still talking? Why wasn't he touching her?

"I know you're moving to Boston, and I'm good with that. I'll sell the boat and rent out the cabin. Boston has a harbor, right? They should have boats in the harbor. I'll find work up there."

"Wait." His words broke through her fog of lust. "What? Leave the island? You can't leave the island."

Joe stepped closer, cupping her cheeks. "Yes, I can. For you, I can do anything."

He tilted his head, lowering his mouth to hers, but Beth stepped away. "You're not listening to me. I don't want to live anywhere but the island. I want you and Dozer and Anchor. Why would we live anywhere else?"

Blue eyes blinked before her. "You want to live on the island?"

She punched him in the chest. "Of course I do. I love that island. Almost as much as I love you."

Joe looked stunned, and Dozer barked. Bending to rub beneath his chin, she cooed, "I love you, too, Dozer."

Standing, she slipped her hands over Joe's shoulders. "I don't want you to leave the island for me. I want to live there with you. For the rest of my life. If you'll have me."

A grin spread across his face, revealing one sexy dimple. "How did I get so lucky as to find you?" he asked.

Beth couldn't resist the poke. "Technically, Lucas found me." One eyebrow shot up and she quickly added, "But you were smart enough to see the real me." She grew serious. "How can I ever thank you for that?"

Sliding his arms around her and pulling her against his chest, he whispered in her ear. "I have some ideas. And now seems like a good time to start." Joe drew his head back, and the look in his eyes made her breath hitch. Long lashes lowered over dark blue eyes as his focus shifted to her mouth. Beth's heart swelled. This man was really hers.

Joe leaned in, and Beth's own eyes slid closed. What came next was sensory overload. Wet tongue sliding between parted lips. Hot breath mingling with her own. Hard edges fitting against her softer curves. The kiss started as something gentle, and Beth knew this is what she'd been searching for her whole life. This was coming home.

But her body grew impatient, and with a tug on his sleeve and a moan of pleading from somewhere deep and desperate, Beth made Joe understand she wanted more.

So much more.

Joe's hands slid up to cup her face, a calloused thumb sliding over heated cheeks. God he tasted so good. Minty and crisp. Hot and heady. He burned like tequila and soothed like whiskey, making her feel drunk with desire and raw lust. When he broke the kiss, they were both panting, clinging to each other as if neither could stand alone. His tongue slid along her jawline to suckle her earlobe. Beth shivered.

One hand held firm on the small of her back while the other cupped her bottom. Heat permeated the denim, and she pressed her lips to his neck. "I thought I could never have this," she whispered, savoring the taste of salt and heat and man. "I may never get enough."

"I hope not," he said, lifting her off the ground until her legs circled his waist. "Which way to the bedroom?" He nuzzled her neck and she tilted her head to give him better access. "The doorway to your left. But the bed's a mess."

"We'll clean it off."

As if she weighed no more than a feather, Joe carried her the short distance to the bedroom, stopping long enough to prop her against the doorjamb and take her lips with his once more. Heat coiled in her belly, sensations overloading her system. Breaking the kiss, he started moving again.

Beth glanced over Joe's shoulder and saw Dozer following them into the room. "Joe," she said, tapping him on the shoulder.

He was busy dropping bites along her chin but gave a low growl in response. "It's Dozer." She tapped again.

Lifting his head, he looked behind him. "Sorry, bud, this is a twosome only." Joe kicked the door shut, leaving the orange mutt on the other side.

"Is he going to be all right out there?"

"If you're worried about my dog, I'm not doing a very good job." With that Joe put his work ethic to the task at hand, lowering them both to the daisy-covered comforter. "You're supposed to be showing your gratitude."

The giggle escaped before she could stop it. "Oh, I'm feeling very grateful right now." Running a hand through his hair, she took his mouth, sliding her tongue along the curve of his bottom lip. "I love your mouth."

Panting, he pulled his T-shirt over his head. "You're going to love it more before this night is over."

Beth purred and tangled her fingers in the dark hair sprinkled across solid muscle. His skin burned her fingertips, and she wanted to feel the connection in other places. "You need to get those boots off while I work on other things."

Joe leaned up on one elbow and ran his thumb across her lips. "You're so beautiful. I don't deserve you."

The love in his eyes moved her to tears. Happy ones this time. Desperate to lighten the mood, she said, "Too bad. You're stuck with me now." Joe smiled and her heart did a somersault in her chest. He sat up and started working on his boots, so she seized the opportunity to pull her own shirt over her head.

Sliding her hands over his shoulders and down his chest, she reveled in the feel of his hot skin against her breasts. With every kiss she pressed along his shoulders, the muscles bunched and jumped in response. Like stoking a banked fire, her fingers floated down his abs to the button of his jeans.

"You need to get those boots off faster," she said, biting his earlobe.

With one shift of his weight, he turned around and pinned her to the bed. "I'll go barefoot from now on." Swooping down like an eagle after prey, Joe took her mouth in a vicious, panty-melting kiss, sending her body up in flames.

Alarms went off in her brain, and her only coherent thought was, *What a way to die.*

Nails clawed at his back, willing him closer. Demanding more. She couldn't get enough but feared one more second would be too much. Joe moved down to her breasts, taking a nipple between his teeth, and her hands pushed into his hair. "Oh good God."

Joe tugged, and her hips jerked off the bed. "You like that?" he asked.

What a time for stupid questions. "Mmmmm..." was all she managed.

His deep chuckle vibrated through her body. She moved the leg pinned beneath his, finding the part of him she wanted most. He pressed solid against her thigh and grew harder with each brush across his fly. "We need to get these off," she said, pushing down on his waistband.

To her surprise, Joe climbed off the bed, sending cool air rushing over her skin. Standing tall before her, he reached for his zipper and Beth stopped breathing. Stopped thinking. His shoulders were wide and tapered to a narrow waist. The dark hair she'd run her fingers through narrowed and then disappeared several inches below his navel.

Her mouth went dry. With the zipper down, he slid his hands around to the side, then stopped. "I'll take off mine if you'll take off yours."

Any attempt to look seductive went out the window when she saw the gleam in his eye. She needed those pants off of him, and if removing her own was the way to achieve that, then remove them she would. Fast.

Shimmying the tight denim down her legs, she grabbed the hems and extricated her feet with two tugs. The pants hit the floor. Scooting onto the pillow, she stretched one leg out while pulling the other up and flattened her hands on the bed. "There. Your turn."

He struggled to hold back a laugh but fulfilled his promise. Though she was wearing light purple panties with lace around the top, he wore nothing under his jeans. Kicking the pants to land on top of his boots, he strolled back to the bed and Beth grew light-headed from lack of blood flow. In her brain.

As he leaned over her, one hand pinned on either side of her head, she stared into intense blue eyes dark with desire. She'd never seen anything hotter. "Are you really all mine?" she asked, afraid of waking up and finding this a dream.

"All yours. To do whatever you want." He stretched out next to her, and she understood the true meaning of the phrase *died and gone to heaven*. She trailed a finger from his shoulder to his neck, then up the pulsing vein along his tan skin and the stubble that covered his jawline.

She wanted to explore him. Memorize him. Drive him wild. Taking his mouth once more, she slid a hand down between them until she reached her prize. He gasped against her mouth, his body jolting at her touch. Toying with his tongue, showing him what she wanted, she explored the length of him, enjoying the power she held in her hand.

With gritted teeth, he reached to the nightstand to draw back a small blue packet. When had he put that there? For a second she thought of the arrogance of showing up prepared, but was too thankful he'd thought ahead to mention it.

Sheathed, he tugged the panties down her body, devouring an appreciative nipple as he leaned lower to clear them of her toes. When Joe covered her, she pulled up her knees, straddling him against her center. The kiss went deeper, leaving Beth panting with need, pressing her heels into the mattress.

Breaking the kiss, Joe lifted off the bed and pinned her with his gaze. Reading the question in his eyes, she nodded. "Please. I can't take any more."

Joe didn't have to be told twice. He entered her in one stroke, and the whole world began to fall away. Beth drew her nails down his back, feeling the muscles bunch and give, dancing beneath her touch. When she reached his bottom, she tugged and pulled, urging him on. They fell into a rhythm, and she drew on his tongue. Bit his top lip.

He picked up the pace, dropping his forehead to her shoulder. A high-pitched moan floated around them and Beth realized the sound was coming from her. She'd never made that sound before. When her teeth started to tingle, she hooked her ankles around Joe's hips and met his strong thrusts.

What could have been minutes or hours later, her body sailed over the edge with a triumphant "Oh yes!" and Joe went with her, the growl from low in his chest sounding primal and satisfying. As she drifted back to the bed, a thought danced through her mind.

We have to try this on the water.

And she started to laugh.

∾

Joe couldn't stop staring at her. Facedown on the bed, the sheet barely covering her ass. This woman was the catch of his life.

"Is Dozer happy now?" she asked, her voice groggy but contented. Curls covering her beard-burned cheek. He'd need to shave more often to save her from that.

"He's happy, but not as much as I am." Joe removed the jeans he'd slipped on to take Dozer outside. Then he crawled across the bed and dropped a kiss just above the sheet. She even tasted better than he'd dreamed. "I hope you don't think you're going to sleep."

Looking over her shoulder, she wiggled her bottom below his nose. "I don't know if I can stay awake." On a fake yawn, she added, "You'll have to help me."

Sliding along her body, setting off sparks where skin met skin, Joe settled in beside her. "We're just getting started on the night's activities." She raised her brows, smiling from the pillow, and his chest went tight.

"I love you, Beth." There. He'd said it. After holding the words in for so long, it felt good to let them out. "I know I can be a cranky ass and not good at the romantic stuff, but I'll show you every day how I feel about you."

She shifted onto her side and traced the outline of his bottom lip. "I love you, too, Joe. And I'm going to drive you crazy trying to make everyone happy, but I promise to get better at that. Old habits and all."

"We'll make each other happy and to hell with everyone else." He threw his leg over her hip and pulled her flush against him. "Thank you for loving my island. And my dog."

She flicked his nipple and he grew hard. Or rather, harder. "Thank you for pushing me to stand up for myself. And coming after me." Leaning up on an elbow, she asked, "Isn't this Memorial Day weekend? You must have a ton of clients waiting for you."

Joe rolled to his back, taking her with him until she covered him. "Thoughts of clients went out the window after

Lucas called me at the butt crack of dawn telling me to get my ass up here and catch you before you left. Speaking of that, didn't you have a plane to catch?"

She ignored his question. "Lucas called you?"

"I was shocked, too. Once I woke up and figured out the call wasn't some weird dream."

"I should have known after last night he'd do something like this."

Joe stopped kissing her neck and looked up. "Last night?"

Beth nodded, running a finger along his ear. "He came over and we talked. I think it was closure for us both. Then he started talking about you and me. Said we should be together."

Shit. When Sid heard about this, he'd be hearing "I told you so" for months. Maybe years. But having Beth in his arms was worth a little ribbing now and then.

Beth leaned up on her elbow. "If you're here, who's taking care of the boat?"

"I found some people to cover for me."

One eyebrow shot up. "Who could cover for you on your own fishing boat?"

"That would be Sid and Will."

Beth laughed. "Sid and Will are running your charters?" She toyed with the hair on his chest. "An all-girl crew. I like that."

He rolled again, pinning her beneath him. "Don't get any ideas." He brushed her hair back. "I'm more interested in the girl I'm with right now."

"That's good," she said, wrapping her legs around his hips. "Because the girl you're with is very interested in you."

Joe stared into her dark green eyes for a moment longer, then kissed the base of her neck before dragging his lips down between her breasts. Her skin felt so hot he expected steam to rise into the air around them. Slipping lower, he nuzzled her belly button, lifting one thigh to rest on his shoulder. A sigh, filled with pleasure and anticipation, escaped her lips. He moved lower and her hands pushed into his hair.

"Do I have your attention?" he asked, blowing softly on her most sensitive spot. "Or are you still tired?"

"Not tired," she groaned, gripping the sheet on both sides. "Just don't stop."

"Never," Joe said. And proceeded to send them both back into the waves.

CHAPTER ONE

Sid Navarro considered calling a nurse to remove the stick of righteous indignation from Lucas Dempsey's ass. If he tensed up any more, the thing would snap off and put an eye out. Observing from the back of the hospital room, she watched Lucas linger at the foot of his father's bed, waging what looked to be a battle between shedding a tear, and tearing someone's head off.

Her best guess for the head-ripping victim would be Lucas's brother, Joe.

Joe carried tension of his own as he stood four feet to Lucas's right, holding hands with his girlfriend, Beth Chandler. Beth had been Lucas's fiancée until six weeks before, which justified the tension, but since Lucas had supposedly given his blessing to the new couple, the blatant anger didn't make much sense.

Maybe the fiancée swap wasn't the problem. Since Lucas had bolted off of Anchor Island the moment the tassel on his high school graduation cap switched sides, he and Joe hadn't seen eye to eye on much of anything. That made the rift ten years wide.

Sid worked with Joe on his fishing boat, and couldn't recall him saying anything about a new dustup with his brother. Then again, Joe wasn't exactly a talker, one of the things Sid liked best about him. Some women wanted a man to share his every thought and feeling.

In Sid's opinion, women were just asking for trouble with that nonsense. As a boat mechanic raised mostly by her father and big brother, she had enough experience around testosterone to know the shit going through a man's head at any given moment should never be revealed for public consumption.

Especially not the female public.

"The nurse says five days in here then no less than six weeks recovery at home," said Patty, Lucas and Joe's mom. Technically, Lucas's birth mother and Joe's stepmom. She was talking about the boys' father, who occupied the bed around which they all hovered. Technically Joe's biological dad and Lucas's stepfather.

The Dempseys were a complicated bunch even before the fiancée fiasco.

Tom Dempsey had suffered a near-fatal heart attack while tending bar in the family-owned restaurant during the lunch hour. Eight hours later, he lay prostrate with translucent skin and a mess of tubes sticking out of each arm. Cables looped into the neck of his hospital gown, assumably plugged into stickers glued somewhere around the vicinity of his heart.

For a giant of a man known to be a pillar of strength and good health, Tom was doing a damn accurate imitation of a beached jellyfish. Sid fought a tear of her own, wiping the corner of an eye with the sleeve of her hoodie.

"But after six weeks he'll be good as new, right?" Joe asked. Beth leaned closer, and he tucked her under his arm. Lucas's eyes narrowed, but he otherwise remained stoic.

Patty sighed. "I'm not sure good as new is in the cards, Joe, but he'll be with us, and that's enough for now."

"Is there still a chance he could..." Beth let the question trail off. The group exchanged glances as if daring one another to say the word no one wanted to hear.

"I'm not dying anytime soon," Tom said in a low, gravel-choked voice. His eyes were still closed, making it seem as if they'd all imagined the words.

"Tom? Honey?" Patty lifted his hand to her lips, pressing them against the tape holding an IV needle in place. "Can you hear me?"

"The heart might be on the fritz, but the ears still work." The patient opened first one eye, then the other. He licked his lips, motioned toward a cup sitting on the tray to his right, then took a sip as Patty held the straw to his mouth. Tom's head dropped back, but his eyes stayed on Patty. "Do I look half as bad as that look on your face says I do?"

Patty laughed as a tear slid down her cheek. "Don't you ever scare me like that again, Thomas Dempsey. I thought I was going to lose you."

Tom smiled, ran a finger along Patty's cheek, then looked around. "Now I know what it takes to get everyone in this family in the same room." He bounced a raised-brow look between Joe and Lucas, then addressed the latter. "Thanks for coming all the way down here."

"Not a problem," Lucas said, jaw tight with a smile that didn't reach his eyes. "Though you could have just asked. No need to get this dramatic to call a family meeting."

Noticing Sid in the back of the room, Tom asked, "You think you could modify this bed to power me out of this place?"

Sid stepped up next to Lucas and tried to ignore how good he smelled. "Got my tools in the truck. We can have you doing thirty-five down the highway in no time."

"Don't encourage him, Sid," Patty scolded. "You'll stay here until they say you can come home, and then you're going to do everything the doctor says."

"I've got a restaurant to run, woman." Sid wouldn't put it past the Dempsey patriarch to leap out of the bed and stomp back to the island, ass cheeks shining through the hospital gown all the way.

"You're not running anything for at least six weeks," Patty said, sounding as firm as possible under the circumstances.

"Then tell me who's going to run the place. We can't close the doors. Not in July, for Christ's sake."

"We'll take care of it," Joe said. Leave it to Mr. Responsible to step up.

"If you're going to run the restaurant, who's going to run the charters?" Sid asked. She could run the boat, but not alone. And any break in her income would jeopardize the dream she was so close to getting her hands on.

"I can find someone else to run the boat for a couple months."

Sid pointed out the obvious. "Every fisherman capable of running that boat is already running his own."

Patty interrupted before Joe could argue. "You kids have businesses of your own. We'll find someone to run the restaurant through Labor Day, then we'll reevaluate for fall."

"I'll do it," Lucas said. He might as well have pulled the pin on a live hand grenade and held it over his head. The room fell silent, exaggerating the incessant chirping of the machines monitoring Tom's every heartbeat.

"You'll what?" Joe asked, stepping forward. This was so not the time for a confrontation.

Lucas crossed his arms, looking anything but relaxed. "I said I'll do it. I'll run the restaurant while Dad recovers."

"You heard the part about six weeks, right?" big brother asked. Beth tugged on Joe's belt loop, and he stepped back.

"I may miss a clue now and then, but I got that part."

Sid wasn't sure if Lucas meant to take a shot at Beth, but that's what he'd done. Joe stepped forward again.

"As much as I want out of here, I'm not getting kicked out because of you two." Tom hit a button on the bed rail, sending the mattress into motion. Once he was satisfied with his new position, he released the button and turned on his sons. "Lucas, I appreciate the offer, but are you sure you can get away from the law firm?"

Lucas leaned on the bottom bed rail. "I'm sure. Do you trust me to run your restaurant?"

Tom's eyes narrowed. "I won't dignify that with an answer." He turned to Joe. "If he runs the place while you run the charters, can you cover some nights?"

"I'll be there whenever you need me."

"Nights," Tom said again, as if passing down a final judgment. "Then it's settled. You boys will run it together. I expect the place to still be in one piece when I come back. Understand?"

Both men nodded but neither spoke. Tom's head dropped, the brief exchange taking what little energy he had.

Patty turned to Beth. "You're running the art store, right?"

Beth straightened like a soldier called to attention. "Yes, but only until Lola and Marcus come back from New Orleans."

"How long is that?"

"Another month."

Patty nodded. "Sid?"

Oh shit.

"Yeah?"

"If Joe recruits one of the high school kids to run the charters with him, can you help Lucas during the day? I'm not letting Tom out of my sight, and that puts us two people down instead of one."

"Well…" Sid looked around. Nothing like being put on the spot. "I'll need to be available for mechanic work if a call comes in."

"I'm sure we can work around that. It's all settled then. Beth can work with Joe to cover nights, and Sid will help Lucas during the day." Before Sid could bring up the pay, Patty added, "All tips are yours to keep, and we'll put you on the payroll so you won't be losing money."

How did she do that?

"Then it sounds like I'm in."

Sid had never experienced seasickness, but the thought of working side by side with Lucas made her queasy. Six weeks with the guy for whom she'd secretly pined for more than ten years. Or not so secretly, since Joe knew, and thanks to Sid's brother, Randy, Beth knew.

Not only did Lucas have no idea how she felt, he barely acknowledged her existence. Which should have made her hate him, but for reasons Sid kept to herself, she didn't.

Sid made eye contact with Beth and caught the unspoken question.

This is good, right?

Then she turned to Lucas to catch his reaction. He looked like someone had just shit in his shoe.

Not from where I'm standing.

~

Life was about to become a living hell. Or rather, more of a living hell than it had been since his fiancée had fallen in love with his brother. Lucas didn't regret being the one to convince Beth and Joe not to become martyrs for his sake. He'd loved Beth, or thought he had the night he proposed. And he loved his brother for all they understood each other, which wasn't much.

Something had happened to Beth back in May when he'd left her behind on the island to head back to Richmond for a case. The change could have been caused by Joe, or the island, or maybe the distance from Lucas and the law firm where they'd worked together. Whatever the reason, the Beth he'd left behind was not the woman waiting when he returned.

In fact, she'd been Elizabeth to him. He still struggled to call her Beth. From Richmond he didn't have to call her anything. The gossip in the office had been a pain in the ass, but faded into ancient history as soon as Van Dyke got caught boffing his assistant in the janitor's closet.

According to Beth, she'd never set out to hurt him. She'd been living a lie for a long time, pretending to be someone else to make people happy, and somehow he'd become part of that lie. One more person she'd set out to please. The truth was, whether he'd brought her to Anchor or not, their life together never would have worked out.

Which drove him nuts, but he wasn't about to let Beth know that. Or anyone else. So she'd picked his brother over him. Nothing new there.

Through no effort of his own, and exuding no discernible charm Lucas could see, Joe had always come out on top. People *loved* him. They listened when he talked, cleared a path when he crossed a room.

Being Joe Dempsey's little brother was like playing second fiddle to a set of spoons, which is why Lucas preferred to live elsewhere. In Richmond, he was the star attorney. The up-and-coming counselor. Or he had been until Beth dumped him for Joe.

"Hey there," came a voice from behind him. Speak of the devil. "This is a really nice thing you're doing."

Lucas kept his eyes on the vending machine before him. "Yeah. Well. Mom and Dad need me. I'm here for them."

Beth leaned on the corner of the machine. "And you're sure this won't be a problem? Getting away from the firm?"

He should have known she'd wonder about that. "Not a problem." Lucas pushed the number-letter combination for the barbeque chips, then watched the steel rod turn. And the chips stay where they were. "Damn it."

Beth ignored the expletive. "Leaving in the middle of a case isn't going to cause issues? No one wants you to jeopardize your career."

Lucas smacked the glass between him and the chips. Nothing. "I'm not in the middle of a case." Another smack. The chips didn't budge.

"Oh," Beth said. "Then you just wrapped one up?"

Meeting her eyes for the first time, he blurted. "I'm on leave. I lost three cases in a month, and Holcomb *suggested* I take a leave of absence until I've 'regained my focus,' as he put it." Lucas turned back to the machine to stare at the seemingly unattainable bag of chips. There was a metaphor in there somewhere.

His former fiancée stayed quiet, indicating she might hopefully be ready to drop the subject. No such luck. "I'm sorry. How long have you been off?"

"Two weeks."

"And you didn't tell us?" she asked. "Were you going to come down here?"

He shook his head, filtering through the possible replies. He picked honesty. "If what I need is focus, Anchor is the last place I'm likely to find it." Then before he could stop the words, he said, "That's more like returning to the scene of the crime."

Beth inhaled sharply and his gut churned. He'd sworn he wouldn't do this. "Look. I'm sorry. I didn't mean that."

Beth shook her head. "No, it's all right. We knew this was going to be a transition." She blushed. "That's not the right word. I mean—"

"I know what you mean," he interrupted. Loading his guilt onto her shoulders might make him feel better for a whole five seconds, but Beth wasn't the only person he didn't recognize anymore.

"Don't worry about it. We'll make this work." He tried a grin, but his heart wasn't in it. "Six weeks. We can handle six weeks, right?"

Beth spotted someone behind him and straightened. "Right. Six weeks. I'd better get back in the room."

Lucas turned to see Sid Navarro coming down the hall. The pint-size boat mechanic had been on the fringe of his reality since high school, but he wouldn't say they were friends. Not like she and Joe were. In fact, Lucas couldn't remember ever having an actual conversation with the woman.

Every time he saw her she was either snarling at someone or covered in grease and cursing a blue streak. She had to be the least ladylike chick he'd ever met.

"How's it going?" Sid said, joining him at the machine. He expected an assault of diesel fumes but instead caught the scent of…watermelon?

"Hi."

Chocolate-brown eyes met his for a brief moment then turned to the machine. "You getting something?"

"Trying to." He pulled his eyes from the smooth patch of olive skin exposed under the ponytail. "The machine is holding my chips for ransom, and I'm not paying. Guess I'll go without."

"I wouldn't say that." Sid stepped forward and pressed her ear to the side of the worthless box of bolts.

As she moved to listen at another spot, Lucas asked, "What are you—" but she shushed him with one finger in front of his nose. He was so shocked, he clamped his mouth shut.

Pulling back, Sid smacked the side of the machine with the butt of her hand, causing his chips to drop into the tray. He'd smacked the damn thing twice and gotten nothing.

"How did you do that?"

Sid shrugged. "I've got a way with machines. Are those the right chips?"

"Yeah." Lucas pushed the door to retrieve the snack as Sid pulled a wallet from her back pocket. "You don't carry a purse?"

She looked at him as if he'd asked if she had meth for sale. "Do I look like a purse carrier to you?"

He took in the hoodie, cargo pants, and work boots. "Guess not."

"You good with this working together thing?" she asked, falling into step beside him after retrieving her candy bar from the drawer. Which fell on the first try.

"Fine with me. You probably know the staff better than I do. That should help until I get my bearings and the staff realize I'm in charge."

Sid stopped. "You're in charge?"

Lucas crossed his arms, nearly smashing his chips. "It *is* my family business."

She crossed her arms, mimicking his stance. Her head didn't reach his shoulder, but she still managed to look like a badass. Must have been the boots. "I'm covering for Patty, who is as much in charge, if not more so, than your dad.

So you may be in charge of everyone else, but you're not in charge of me."

Lucas took several deep breaths and debated how to handle the situation. He couldn't tell her to take a flying leap because he needed her. And his mom would kick his ass if he screwed this up before he'd even stepped behind the bar.

"Equals?"

"That's right."

"We'll see." Not the strongest comeback, but for a tiny woman, Sid had a steady gaze.

"For a lawyer, you suck at this." Sid started walking again, then turned his way and walked backward. "I hope you tend bar better than you argue, or I'm going to have to cover the whole damn place."

With that she disappeared into the hospital room, leaving Lucas in the hall with crushed chips and a bruised ego. Six weeks in hell had officially begun.

ACKNOWLEDGMENTS

There is no way I could give proper thanks to every person who helped me get to this point. If I try to name them all, I will inevitably forget someone. And yet, here I go. Romance novels have always been a part of my life, but not until I fell in love with the works of Eloisa James did writing them become part of my future. Stumbling across the Eloisa James Bulletin Board in 2006 was a catalyst event in my life, and I owe a debt of gratitude to Ms. James for creating such an amazing, open, giving community of like-minded readers and writers. The women I met on that board have become some of my best friends, and I cannot imagine my life without them. To the Bon Bons, you changed my life, and I thank you.

Meant to Be is set on the fictitious Anchor Island, but is completely based on the very real Ocracoke, a remote island at the base of the Outer Banks accessible only by ferry. I had the pleasure of visiting several years ago, and have never forgotten the experience. I set out to recreate the charm, joy, and otherworldliness of this lovely little wonder-island inside the pages of this book, and hope to have done it at least a hint of justice. If after reading *Meant to Be* you wish you could visit Anchor Island, book yourself a trip to Ocracoke

Island, NC. I can't promise a hunky fisherman and his loveable mutt will greet you on the ferry, but you never know.

Thank you to Romance Writers of America®, an organization of support, education, and endless resources. This manuscript was named a finalist in the RWA 2012 Golden Heart® contest (go Firebirds!), and from the moment I received the news, my publishing dreams began to come true. Mine is one of many stories that follow this same path. Without hopping on the RWA train, I doubt any of this would be happening.

Thank you to my agent, Nalini Akolekar, who gave me that one "yes" that every author desires, and then made my dream come true. Thank you to my editors, Kelli, Lindsay, and Becky. I am a better writer for having worked with you, and will be forever grateful for the chance you've taken on me and my stories.

Now to my pirates. For half a decade I've been sailing the publishing seas with the best writing pirates on the planet. To Hellie (who spent years convincing me I was a writer), Chance, Marn, Sin, Hal, Scape, Donna, and Lisa. Thank you for swabbing these decks with me, and always being there through calm and stormy seas.

Thank you to my beta readers. This is where I will forget someone so you know who you are. Your feedback, encouragement, and support have been priceless. And to my daughter, to whom this book is dedicated. As I've said before, you will always be my greatest achievement, the love of my life, and the impetus behind everything I do.

ABOUT THE AUTHOR

A Yankee by birth, Terri moved below the Mason-Dixon line in the mid-1990s and has refused to return to the land of snow and sub-freezing temperatures ever since. Introduced to reading at a young age through condensed versions of *Little Women, The Wizard of Oz,* and *The Hound of the Baskervilles,* she found her way to romance novels in middle school and never looked back. She started writing her own books in 2007, finaled in the Romance Writers of America® Golden Heart® contest in 2012, and signed her first publishing contract with Montlake Romance later that year. A former disc jockey turned cubicle dweller turned writer, Terri lives with her teenage daughter, a high-maintenance Yorkiepoo, and two fat and happy tabbies on the coast of Virginia.